The Tainted Prize

Under Admiralty Orders – The Oliver Quintrell Series

The Tainted Prize

Under Admiralty Orders – The Oliver Quintrell Series

M. C. MUIR

GRINDELWALD

For Jacob

ACKNOWLEDGEMENT

My special thanks go to Judith Binder, Ian Broadbent, Robert W. Barnett, Rose Frankcombe, Roger Marsh and Roger Moore for their invaluable comments, input and advice.

Garamond

Chapter 1

Patriotism - October 28, 1803

Oliver Quintrell rapped his knuckles on the carriage roof. 'Why are we not moving, driver? I have a pressing engagement and I have no desire to be late.'

'Ain't my fault, Capt'n,' the driver replied. 'And I can tell you, you'll not be going nowhere in an 'urry.'

Oliver took out his pocket watch, glanced at the hands, huffed and snapped the case shut. After cogitating for another minute, he opened the cab door and stepped down to the road where the problem was immediately evident.

'It ain't the driver's fault, Capt'n,' Casson called, from the box-seat.

Oliver shook his head. He didn't need his steward to advise him what was blatantly obvious. Whichever way he looked along the street, his view was met by vehicles of every description – small and large, some drawn by a single horse, others by four, and all had ground to a complete standstill. To further confound the situation, every carriage and cart, apart from the one in which he was travelling, was heading in the same direction. And from the cries and curses issuing from within them, it was obvious, he was not the only passenger becoming increasingly irritated by the delay. The drivers too were exasperated, and even the horses were displaying signs of agitation.

'The cabbie says he ain't never seen nothing like it before this week. He blames it on the gathering in Hyde Park.'

'To honour the volunteers,' the driver added. 'The King'll be there to inspect 'em. There were five-hundred-thousand at the meeting just two days ago and probably the same number heading there today.'

'Five-hundred-thousand!' Oliver retorted. 'Ridiculous! That is half the population of London.'

'It's true, Capt'n,' the driver called. 'It were printed in the newspaper. Folk have come from half-way across the country to show their support. It's not just Londoners that's 'ere.'

Clenching his teeth, Oliver paced back and forth in the limited space available. There was little else he could do. Unfortunately, by attempting to travel in the opposite direction to the rest of the traffic, his sister's carriage had become completely blocked. It could go neither forward nor back, nor turn around, and whipping the horse in an attempt to force it to walk on was to no avail. The bay mare reared to the crack of leather, kicking its hooves at a pair of black Shire horses vying for right of passageway directly ahead of it. The suspension creaked, as the carriage jolted violently on the cobblestones almost throwing Casson from his seat.

'This ain't no bleedin' good,' the driver cursed. 'It'll be a lame nag or a broken wheel, if I don't get out of 'ere afore long.'

'I'll walk,' the captain announced to his manservant. 'Stay with the carriage. The driver may need your assistance. Return to Grosvenor Square and inform my sister what has happened, then make your way to Admiralty House on foot and, if you are able, secure some alternate mode of transport and wait for me on Whitehall.'

'Aye aye, Captain. Good luck, sir.'

Luck, thought Oliver cynically, as he strode away, was not an entity which would have any bearing on the outcome of the day's events. Either he would be granted a commission or he would not. And that decision would have been arrived at long before the Admiralty's dispatch was delivered to his home on the Isle of Wight.

Weaving between pedestrians and staying clear of the high-spirited horses, the captain reached the corner of the street, only to find the junction was also congested. He cursed under his breath for allowing himself to arrive in such a predicament. It was inexcusable. He should have made provision for such contingencies, but when his sister had insisted he would have ample time to reach the Admiralty from her house, he had listened but not questioned. And now he was late. But he should not blame her.

Elbowing through the milling throng who were heading to Hyde Park, he continued to berate himself. Ignorance was no excuse. Notices detailing the event had appeared in the *Portsmouth Telegraph*, more than a week earlier. He had even read the broadsheets pasted on shop walls with the heading: *An Insurrection of Loyalty*. Those were the words Henry Addington had used in Parliament when describing the volunteer movement that had attracted over 350,000 civilians. Even the *Naval Chronicle* had announced details of the forthcoming royal inspections as an addendum to its extensive article about the Sea Fencibles.

But in the euphoria of receiving that long-awaited letter requiring him to attend the Admiralty, any mention of the public gatherings had completely slipped his mind. Preparations for travel to London had further distracted him and on arriving at his sister's house in the early hours of the morning, dusty, weary and hungry after a tedious overnight coach journey from Portsmouth, the opportunity for a bath, a satisfying meal and a brief period of pleasant relaxation had been the only things of concern to him at that time.

Damnation. He would never tolerate such a lapse of mental alertness at sea. He could not afford to. Men's lives depended on his acute observations and the decisions he made as a consequence of them. He cursed the miasma which had infiltrated his brain and dulled his thinking, and recognized it as a recurrent malady he manifested whenever he spent long periods ashore. Hopefully, it was not a repeat of the malaise which, two years ago, had resulted in a spell in the Greenwich Hospital. Hopefully, once at sea, the first fresh breeze would divest him of it.

Quickening his pace, Oliver Quintrell left the busy street and headed towards St James's Park. It was not the shortest route but, by going that way, he considered he would meet with less obstruction. With a little over a mile to travel, he estimated it would take him fifteen minutes providing he extended his stride. As if privy to his thoughts, bells from several church spires rang out announcing the hour which coincided with the much anticipated arrival of King George in Hyde Park.

Though most of the general public seemed not to be constrained by clocks and their demanding chimes, his life, since entering the service, had been controlled by them. For seamen of any rank, the ship's bell was the pulse they lived by. The number of chimes determined the time to rise, to eat, the time for duties and the time to retire. Failing to abide by the ringing of the ship's bell was construed as disobedience and sufficient reason for a man to be seized up to a grating to receive a dozen lashes.

Striding out briskly, Captain Quintrell was surprised at the number of people in the park. Unlike the usual smattering of nannies with their charges, uniformed soldiers and fashionable young ladies strolling arm in arm, today's mob were a motley crew representing almost every station in life. Many seemed quite misplaced on the lush green parkland in this particular area of London. Though they ranged from youths to old men, farmhands to labourers, mechanics to clerks, and businessmen to beggars, for the present, status appeared to be of little account. With a united resolve, some carried pikes or pitchforks, poles or crooks, others swords or spades – anything that could be displayed as a defensive weapon to be used against the threatened French invasion force. It was obvious to the captain that from the direction the crowds were heading, the gathering in Hyde Park was their intended destination.

While a hazy sun was attempting to break through the clouds, beneath his feet, the ground was spongy from recent rain and a veil of mist hung over the lake. Already the autumn days were growing short and winter was looming on the horizon. It was a good time of the year to be sailing south.

It had been early spring when Oliver had returned from sea, over half a year earlier. At the time, the Treaty of Amiens had still been intact but shortly after, Henry Addington had determined the country's finances were sufficiently recovered to support another conflict and England had declared war on France. The peace, which had lasted only twelve months, had ended. By mid-June, every able-bodied seaman, foremast Jack and one-legged sailor was back at sea. Even the ageing Admirals, who had grown fat and idle during the peace, had been re-commissioned. By mid-summer, every ship of the line and sloop-of-war was at sea. Even the discarded victualler's barges, which had been stuck in the Gosford mud for over a year, had been refloated, re-caulked and refurbished, and called back into service. Sailors had been quick to sign on any ship afloat, emerging from their hovels and haunts, eager to bring an end to their enforced period of poverty. They knew full-well the dangers that lay ahead but they also knew that with sea war comes the prospect of prize money, which for them was an added incentive.

Since the resumption of war with France, ships of the line had sailed from every English port heading for the Channel or Mediterranean Sea. And where any berths had remained vacant, unfortunate landsmen found wandering the wharves, had been pressed into service. After being hurried aboard and secured in the hold until the vessel was out of sight of land, the rules contained in the *Articles of War* would have been read to them. Then the words *compulsorily enlisted* would have been entered against their names in the muster book. For many of the pressed men, it would be more than a year before they set foot on English soil, but for many unfortunate souls, they would never ever see England or their wives or sweethearts again.

Details of recent naval commissions had been gazetted, so Oliver was aware Admiral Cornwallis, Rear Admiral of the United Kingdom was blockading Brest, while the Commander-in-Chief of the North Sea, Admiral Keith was commanding a fleet between the Downs and Selsey Bill. It was Keith's job to prevent Napoleon's ships ever reaching the beaches of southern England, while in the Mediterranean, Admiral Lord Nelson had raised his flag on *Victory*. His fleet, patrolling off Toulon, was ready to encounter any new ships slipped from the French dockyards to be added to Napoleon's rapidly enlarging fleet. The man who would be Emperor had stated quite emphatically – *I want only a favourable wind to plant the Imperial Eagle on the Tower of London*. The British blockades were intent on preventing that.

Why was it, Oliver asked himself, in this frenzy of patriotic unanimity against a threatened French invasion, he alone had been left on the beach, when it appeared that every other post captain on the list had received a commission? This unanswered question vexed him and he fully intended to express his dissatisfaction to the First Lord if the opportunity presented itself.

His thoughts were momentarily distracted by a gaggle of geese that emerged from the reeds beside the lake. Waddling directly across his path and honking noisily, the mob of two-dozen or more showed no signs of halting or changing course. Likewise, Oliver had no intention of stopping and strode on. In a desperate effort to escape the invader's legs, wings flapped as the geese paddled along the grass in an effort to take to the air. To the captain, the sound was reminiscent of a badly set, salt-hardened headsail. It served to remind him of his purpose.

His pocket watch showed ten minutes past the hour. *Double damnation*. But to run would be undignified. That was something he reprimanded his junior officers for, even at the height of battle.

As he passed beneath a row of young plane trees, the sun broke through the remnants of dying foliage. Despite the changing colours of autumn being painted across the park, he was in no mood to stop and consider the scene. Even the crunch of footsteps on freshly fallen leaves, did not induce him to slow or look around. A glancing knock on the elbow, however, alerted him to the offender – a boy of perhaps little more than a dozen years.

'Sorry, Mister,' the lad called, his legs slowing to a trot till his pace was equal to that of the captain's.

'Watch where you are heading!' Quintrell complained.

'Are you a sailor?' the boy asked, dropping back half-a-yard, then speeding up to accommodate the captain's longer strides.

Oliver ignored the question, treating it with the contempt it deserved. In full dress uniform, trimmed with braid and laced buttons, and complemented with a pair of gold epaulettes, it was blatantly obvious he was at least a post captain with a minimum of three years service in His Majesty's Royal Navy.

Oblivious, the boy continued, 'I'm looking for a ship, Mister. Can you tell me where to find one?'

With the tall chimneys and weather vane of Admiralty House now in view, Oliver had neither the time nor the inclination to answer a question to which any blind beggar in London would know the answer. 'Be off with you!' he scolded.

Undeterred, the lad continued trotting alongside, eager for information. Measuring little over four-foot six-inches from head to toe, he was gaunt in the face and spindly as a broom handle. The collar of his woollen jacket was frayed, the elbows patched, and from the length of the sleeves, it was obvious, it had been handed down from an older brother. His only apparent possession was a blanket, rolled into a bundle and secured with a piece of cord which was tucked tightly under his arm.

'Are you off to join a ship, Mister?' he repeated, 'Because, if you are, I beg you to take me with you.'

Oliver flicked his wrist indicating for the boy to go away. These inconsequential questions were beginning to inflame his usual reasonable temperament.

'Mister—?'

Stopping dead in his tracks and turning to face his assailant, the captain took a deep breath, 'You are an infernal nuisance, boy. Go home this instant.'

'I can't do that. I came from up north. I came to London to find a ship.'

Quintrell resumed his stride. 'Then I suggest you either return to the north or go directly to the West India Docks.'

'I don't know where them docks is,' the boy said, puffing a little and taking four steps to every three of the captain's. 'A fellow pointed me to come this way. Said I should ask at the Admiralty. He said they would know. Is that where you are going, Mister?'

Oliver sighed. 'Indeed I am,' he said, 'and I will travel there with more speed, and arrive in a far better humour if you were not disturbing my passage.'

'Sorry, Mister,' the boy said, swinging his bundle at a dog who was snapping at his heels. 'But I can't go back up north, not least till I've been on a ship.'

Oliver walked on. The Horse Guards' parade ground was ahead of them with the Admiralty building beyond, its courtyard and entrance facing Whitehall. But as the pair left the green, a troop of mounted guards rode across their path, leaving them no option but to wait until the procession had passed.

Gazing in awe at the brightly uniformed soldiers, their breast-plates glinting, the boy continued chattering non-stop though his voice was drowned by the clatter of hooves, and clink of spurs and swords. Waiting impatiently, Oliver breathed deeply as he unfastened the three lowest buttons of his waistcoat. The enforced rest had been unkind to his waistline.

'I saw them soldiers two days ago in Hyde Park,' the boy announced. 'I even saw the King's coach as it drove by.' He received no answer. 'Honest, I did. I never seen so many people in all my life.'

Oliver studied the pimple-faced, wide-eyed urchin. Though only the height of a powder monkey, he boasted a sparse fuzz of fine pale whiskers on his chin, the same colour as the unruly mop of yellow curls on his head. He was probably older than he had initially estimated.

'I can assure you, London is not always so congested,' Oliver said, relieved to see the last of the column of foot soldiers that brought up the rear.

'For your information,' he said, gesturing with his hand, 'the Thames is that way. There you will find all manner of boats working the waterway – lighters, barges and wherries. If you are in luck, one of the masters may be looking for a boy.'

Having reached the Admiralty, a pair of marines standing on guard duty at the Whitehall entrance acknowledged the captain but challenged the lad preventing him from going into the courtyard.

'That's not what I came to London for,' he yelled, as the captain strode across the yard. 'I want a ship.'

Oliver shook his head. Such blatant insolence was tantamount to insubordination and would merit a dozen lashes for any seaman under his command. Then he reflected on the boy's words and realized his trip to London was for the self-same purpose. *I want a ship too*, he mused.

On entering the building, Captain Quintrell was directed into a large reception vestibule. It was sparsely, but elegantly furnished and the imported silk carpet added a lubberly gentility to it. The walls adorned with paintings, depicting ships at sea or engaged in battle, added atmosphere to an otherwise staid environment. An item of particular interest that attracted his attention was a *papier mâché* model of a port. Displayed on a large oval rosewood table, the contoured hills, coast, an extensive bay and winding river were all carefully painted in appropriate shades of blue and green, while black ink indicated the position of several fortifications. Without reading the name on the plaque, Oliver recognized Valdivia, a port situated on the west coast of South America. He had entered that bay and sailed beneath those batteries on more than one occasion.

With footsteps approaching from the corridor, Oliver fastened his waistcoat, adjusted his sword-belt then, glancing down, noted with a frown that his woollen stockings were double-reefed around his ankles.

'Captain Quintrell,' the clerk called.

Oliver nodded.

'Kindly follow me.' Not waiting for an answer, the clerk sailed out of the room and headed for the staircase leading to the first floor. From the landing, a corridor ran the length of the building. It lacked windows and, with only one lamp burning, was dismal. When the pair reached the door at the far end, the clerk stopped, knocked, entered, and instructed the captain to wait.

After pushing a recalcitrant length of hair behind his ear, Oliver attended to his stockings, successfully easing them up and smoothing them around his calves before the door re-opened. Stepping aside, the clerk ushered him into the Admiralty's Board Room.

Never having been admitted to the inner sanctum before, the captain discovered it to be refreshingly bright with light streaming in from the tall windows along one side. Seated at a large walnut table which occupied half of the far end of the room, were several high ranking officers bearing stars of various Orders on their chests – Lords Commissioners, ageing admirals, plus two other elderly gentlemen, presumably representatives of the government.

The First Lord of the Admiralty, John Jervis, Earl of St Vincent was not a man to mince words. 'You are late, Captain! Kindly be seated.'

Oliver took the chair obviously designated for him facing the dignitaries.

'Time is precious and, as there are several matters to attend to, plus the gentlemen gathered here today have little time to squander, I will not waste my breath on preliminaries.' St Vincent paused, directing his gaze at Oliver.

'Captain Quintrell, you come here in the hope you will receive a commission. When you leave, you will not be disappointed. As to what this entails, I will not keep you anguishing any longer, though the information I am at liberty to divulge is limited, for obvious reasons. Your mission carries a degree of secrecy, as did your previous, but we are unanimously agreed that we can depend on you to discharge your duties judiciously and with expediency.' He paused. 'The delay of some months has been unavoidable, as it rested on certain eventualities over which the Admiralty had no control. However, I trust you have made the best of your enforced rest and it has provided time for you to support your wife through her recuperation.'

Surprised by reference to his wife's health, Oliver was unconvinced of any sentimental reasons for his beaching. 'Thank you, my Lord. My wife has regained much of her strength and vigour of late.'

'I am pleased to hear it. Let us proceed.' Momentarily taking his eyes from the captain, he addressed the dignitaries seated at the table.

'Gentlemen, we are all acutely aware that the war which is now upon us will make the events of the past ten years feel like a mere dress-rehearsal. As we all know, Napoleon is intent on invading Europe and taking England as his prize. For the present, the Spanish Crown has an alliance with France but, so far, has been disinclined to commit to conflict. However, as Napoleon has Spain dangling on a financial leash, it will be only a matter of time before he reels it in. Alone, Spain is not the mighty maritime force it once was, but as a combined enemy, the French and Spanish fleets would constitute a formidable naval adversary which Britain will be unable to equal.'

There were a few raised eyebrows, but no one disputed the statement.

Turning his attention to the captain, 'The resumption of war has presented the Admiralty, the Navy Board and the British Government with many problems – some expected, others unexpected. Finding men and officers to man our ships was not difficult. Initially the problem was selecting which officers to turn away. As to the situation we presently find ourselves in, with every able-bodied man volunteering to serve his country, I must question how long this wave of enthusiasm will last.' The First Lord paused, and glanced through the window. 'However, it is donations of pennies and pounds rather than displays of pitchforks and palings that we require to combat this threat. This could be a long war, and even though Addington has doubled the efficiency of the income tax, it will surely affect us all.'

He turned his attention to the two gentlemen at the end of the table. 'Conflict can prove disastrous to Britain's economy, and while some argue that maintaining the slave trade is the only way to support an on-going war, it is my belief, even the Parliament may be swayed towards abolition before very long. However, that is a matter of conjecture and a problem for the Government and Treasury to address, not the Sea Lords or the Navy Board.

'Finding sufficient ships to defend England against this threatened invasion is our immediate concern. Over the past year, while Napoleon's yards have been busy building ships, Britain has been dispatching her old vessels to the bone-yard or stripping them naked and converting them to prison hulks. Portsmouth, Chatham, and Deptford can boast some of the finest fighting ships Britain ever built – proud men-of-war dismembered, disassembled, disrespected and now used as repositories for French spies or convicted criminals. Such an ignominious end is a travesty. After bearing England's finest into battle, the Navy has turned its back on them, and like the murderers, rapists, thieves and cut-throats they house, they are sentenced to rot, chained to a bed of river silt.'

Oliver had heard this address of condemnation once before. Obviously it was one of the First Lord's on-going concerns.

'However,' the aged Admiral continued, 'that is not your problem, Captain. You will be relieved to know we do not intend to station you on one of these floating prisons.'

'Thank you, my Lord.'

St Vincent sighed. 'As you are well aware, politics, patronage and promotion within the service are constant bedfellows. They are a bane in the navy's side and in mine too. Politicians seek support with handsome bribes, while wealthy naval officers extend favours between friends granting family members rapid promotion within the flag ranks. And here we have little control over these promotions.' He sighed. 'During the twelve-month's peace, few admirals or seamen died, and because the number of positions we have available to allocate within each level of the service is limited, captains and admirals must wait their turn on the ladder for promotion.'

His address was interrupted, when the door creaked and the clerk, who had ushered Oliver into the room, attempted to re-enter without being noticed. However, before he had taken two paces, the First Lord directed his gaze at him. 'Kindly remain outside. I will call you when I am ready.'

When the door closed, St Vincent continued. 'The problems of promotion through privilege and patronage are exacerbated where mutual interest and advancement are the determining factors. It occurs where naval honour must be seen to be upheld and loyalty between officers demonstrated.'

Oliver Quintrell was blatantly aware that any chance of his promotion within the ranks was far from imminent. Though his name was well advanced on the post captains' list and he was thirty-three years of age, he was lacking in years of naval service. Having entered the Royal Navy at the relatively old age of nineteen, his time fell far short of those officers, (privileged sons, nephews and grandsons of titled nobility) whose names had been entered in ships' books from the tender age of eight or nine years – some even younger, despite them never having stepped aboard a vessel until they embarked as a midshipman.

'Captain, this discussion may seem irrelevant to you, but these matters must be considered when important decisions are made. We value your experience and would not offer you a position as flag captain on a ship of the line, even if we were at liberty to do so, as this would not allow you to utilize your ability, which, I might add, is well regarded, as you will discover.'

Conscious all eyes were on him, Oliver showed no response.

'Enough said. Here are your interim orders. The frigate, *Isle of Lewis*, Captain Slater will be sailing from Deptford tomorrow. Seven days hence, you will join this vessel at Spithead and take passage to Gibraltar. Captain Slater will be expecting you. As to your commission – His Majesty's Frigate, *Perpetual* awaits you in Gibraltar. She sustained some damage in a fracas off the coast of Minorca and is presently undergoing repairs which, I am assured, will be completed by the time of your arrival. You will collect your further orders from the Port Admiral on The Rock. He will provide you with any assistance you require. Acquiring a crew should not prove difficult, as ships of the Mediterranean fleet are continually putting into that port for repair. I wish you well.'

Oliver was anxious for more information, not least his destination and the purpose of his mission.

'One other item,' the First Lord added, 'We have appointed Mr Parry to serve as your first lieutenant. I understand he served with you on *Elusive*. His transfer has been arranged and he will be awaiting your arrival in Gibraltar.'

Oliver was delighted. He could wish for no better officer than Simon Parry to sail with him. 'Thank you, my Lord.'

With no other intelligence forthcoming and Earl St Vincent engaging in muffled conversation with the aged Admiral sitting to his right, Oliver presumed the interview had come to an end.

'One final question,' St Vincent said, glancing over his shoulder. 'What do you know of Captain Crabthorne?'

'Very little, my Lord. Only what I have read in the *Gazette*.'

'Indeed.'

With that, Oliver rose to his feet and stepped forward to retrieve the pouch containing his immediate orders.

'Remain seated,' the First Lord ordered. Reaching for a small brass bell on the table, he gave it two brisk rings, summoning the clerk who had been waiting without.

'Kindly usher our guests in.' the First Lord said.

Chapter 2

The Lloyd's Registry Fund

When almost two dozen civilians shuffled into the Board Room, Oliver felt slightly bewildered. The Admiralty was the domain of naval officers – all uniformly dressed in various shades of blue. And while white trimmings adorned some collars and lapels, gold lace predominated. The sight of an occasional drably dressed civilian did not raise eyebrows, but the arrival of a convoy of them was most surprising.

In deference to the age of the new arrivals, and to the scarlet sashes sweeping diagonally across two of the gentlemen's chests, Oliver rose to his feet. The group was followed into the room by a young lieutenant cradling a polished mahogany case in his arms. Taking directions from the First Lord, he deposited it gently on the table then returned to the back of the throng. Though the company behind him was obliged to remain standing, the captain resumed his seat.

Earl St Vincent rose. 'My Lords, Gentlemen, I am aware of the inconvenience many of you have encountered in presenting yourselves here today, and I thank you for your attendance. It is well that this sort of display of patriotism in a public park does not occur too frequently.'

With nods and muffled responses, the First Lord walked around the table and released the brass hasps on the box, lifted the lid, then carefully slid both hands inside and lifted out a finely honed sword, its gold hilt elaborately decorated. The blade was also engraved, and the scabbard and belt were equally ornate. The metal gleamed as it sliced the sun's rays evoking a spontaneous hiss from the assembled group.

In his mind, Oliver questioned if it was awe or envy, admiration or extravagance that ushered such a response.

'Captain Quintrell, please step forward.'

Facing the captain, but addressing the gathered assembly, the First Lord began, 'Gentlemen, you are all aware that the Lloyd's Registry Fund has collected donations from members of the business community, such as yourselves, and allocated those funds specifically for a number of awards to be made in recognition of courage, leadership and performance of duty in the Royal Navy for which no other recognition has been received. These awards vary from medals to swords of twenty-five, fifty, and one hundred guineas. As you can see from the item I hold in my hand, today's award is one of the most prestigious and I acknowledge the Dress Sword Makers to the Patriotic Fund of the Strand for their fine craftsmanship.'

He continued. 'My Lords, Sea Lords, Lords Commissioners of the Admiralty, Members of the Navy Board, representative of both Houses of Parliament, Gentlemen – you are probably unaware of Captain Quintrell's service to his country, and that will remain as is for the present. But in case any one of you would question the value of this gift at a time when the country is struggling financially, I must remind you that it has not been funded by the Admiralty or the Government but through public subscription. Britain is a trading nation and it is her ship owners and businessmen who have donated the money in recognition of their faith in this great institution and the men who defend our seas and insure mercantile trade is allowed to continue despite the best efforts of the enemy to halt it.'

Earl St Vincent stepped forward. 'Captain Quintrell, I present this to you on behalf of the Lloyd's Registry Fund. It carries with it the thanks and goodwill of the people. And I might add that His Majesty the King was disappointed that this presentation could not be made at the palace.'

Receiving the elegant sword into his open palms, in the presence of such auspicious company, was overwhelming. Oliver responded with a muffled, 'Thank you,' the words sounding hollow and totally inadequate.

'My Lords,' the First Lord announced, 'All that remains is for a round of applause for Captain Quintrell.'

Instantly, feet stamped on the timber floor, hands clapped and the sound of huzzahs echoed in the Board Room. 'Gentlemen, I thank you for your presence here today. I am aware many of you have important business to attend to but, for those not pressed for time, refreshment will be served in the dining room. Kindly follow the usher.'

Still holding the sword in his hands, Oliver gazed down at it, his mind in a spin. He had his commission, which was what he wanted. And now he had this award which was overwhelming, but was something he could well do without.

'May I?' said the Sea Lord, retrieving it from the captain's hands and returning it to the velvet-lined case. 'I trust your good wife will encourage you to stand for a portrait. It would be an appropriate response to Lloyds' generous gesture.'

The idea appalled Oliver, but St Vincent was right – his wife would certainly encourage that response. Furthermore, she would insist on a full-length portrait and have it displayed on the most visible wall in the house. And no doubt she would wish for the sword to be mounted above the fireplace. Both items would then be the subject of conversation when entertaining. For Oliver, however, it would be a constant source of embarrassment that would result in him spending more time in his study in order to avoid his wife's invited guests. A glance at the Sea Lord, told him St Vincent was privy to his thoughts.

'I trust, Captain, that this honour bestowed on you by Lloyd's, and through the generosity of the people whose donations contributed to it, is received in the gracious manner in which it is given.'

'My Lord, this is indeed an unexpected honour and one I feel I am not deserving of.' Oliver paused. He was endeavouring to sound sincere but was aware his old vein of cynicism was bleeding again. The sword was magnificent, there was no doubting that and being a recipient of it was indeed a great honour. The First Lord himself and Horatio Nelson had both received ceremonial swords in recognition of the parts they had played in the Battle of Cape St Vincent.

But, for Oliver, the sword carried something he personally could do without. It was a reminder that the two-hundred men, who served him on his previous mission, had received not a penny-piece for their efforts. He considered they were more deserving of a reward from the Lloyd's Registry Fund than himself. Or even better, the money expended in producing a gold sword could have been directed to the seamen's fund for widows and orphans.

Oliver chose his words carefully. 'My mission was successful only thanks to the loyalty of my officers and the steadfastness of the men.'

St Vincent returned to his seat. 'Let me remind you, Captain, of two things I have learned during my fifty years at sea. Firstly, sentimentality, while an honourable characteristic, has no role on the quarterdeck. Furthermore, Britain is again at war and there will be ample opportunity for many rich prizes to be shared amongst officers and men of all ranks. Let me suggest you relish this moment for tomorrow we may find ourselves shoeless paupers trampled beneath the boots of a French dictator. England depends on its navy for protection. We are Britain's only hope for if that line of defence is penetrated a mob of pitchfork wielding peasants will be no barrier to a well-armed foreign invasion force.'

As the portly earl returned to his seat, Oliver glanced around the room. The invited guests had all departed. For a moment the room was silent but for the regular *tick tick* from the long case clock standing beside the door. The hearth in the fireplace was cold, while above the mantelpiece, the hands of the great circular wind vane showed no inclination to move.

With apparently nothing more to be said, Oliver shuffled uncomfortably for a moment, expressed his thanks once again and, after bowing his head to the dignitaries, left the Board Room. The mahogany case housing the ceremonial sword was conveyed behind him, cradled in the arms of the young naval officer.

Stepping outside to bright sunlight, Oliver inhaled deeply. The late October air had a briskness about it which was refreshing. Scanning the courtyard, he had hoped to see his steward waiting with some form of transport but the yard was empty. After a moment, a carriage rumbled to a halt and an Admiral, he did not know, alighted. Not wishing to remain on the steps, Oliver instructed the young man who was shadowing him, to return to the reception vestibule and wait there for his instructions.

How ironical it was, he thought, that his deepest desires had turned a full circle. Over the past months he had spent sleepless nights and long daylight hours wishing for a letter requiring him to attend the Admiralty. Now all he desired was to vacate the building and move from the courtyard and onto the street. He had a ship – *Perpetual* – waiting for him in Gibraltar. But as yet he had no idea of his orders. The presentation sword, while an honour, was likely to be a source of aggravation, but that was something he would have to contend with when the time arose. He chided himself that most officers would be overwhelmed and reminded himself that there were many deserving officers who had never received any recognition whatsoever. Many died in battle and were quickly forgotten – not even a tombstone acknowledged they ever lived or held a command.

Striding across the yard to Whitehall, Oliver scanned the street for any sign of his steward. But the usually busy thoroughfare was remarkably quiet. The line of carriages, that regularly operated from the opposite side, was absent. Only an empty nosebag left on the pavement, the stone water-trough and several heaps of cold horse-droppings indicated their place of trade.

Paying no heed to the apparent beggar huddled on the pavement, the captain was surprised when the figure stirred and spoke.

'Hey, Mister, are you going to your ship now?'

Oliver recognized the boy who had accosted him in the park but didn't respond.

Stretching his legs and rubbing the crusted dust from the corners of his eyes, the boy tilted his head and peered up at the captain, in the manner of a hungry dog hoping for a morsel of food. 'I walked a long way to get here,' he said.

Oliver sighed.

'Do you have a ship, Mister? Do you have a ship?'

Unable to remain silent, the captain conceded, with a flickering smile, 'It would appear that I do. But for your information it is not in England.'

Sitting upright on the paving slabs, his bundle wrapped in his arms, the boy's gaunt face spoke of disappointment. But the rhythmic movement of the naval officer tapping his index finger impatiently on his leg quickly distracted him. Screwing up his nose, the lad pointed, 'What happened to your hand, Mister?'

Oliver grinned. No one had ever been so forthright in asking such an impertinent question and in such an off-handed imprudent manner before.

'An unfortunate accident with a cannon ball,' he replied.

'I bet that hurt! Does it still work?'

Oliver was stumped for an answer. The brain fever, he had suffered in consequence of the injury and the months he had subsequently spent in Greenwich Seamen's Hospital, had robbed him of any memory of the pain. But even though he had lost three fingers and some knuckles from his right hand, his claw-like grip with the remaining thumb and forefinger was strong, as was his reasoning and determination. He had justified his physical and mental capabilities to the Sea Lords over a year ago – and he had no intention of justifying his ability to the urchin who was presently interrogating him.

Then he bethought himself and considered the boy's tenacity – the spirit of dogged determination that had brought him all the way from the North Country to find a ship. He respected courage and determination, and considered how many grown Englishmen were fearful of the Impress Gangs, the sea, Napoleon and the French. But it was obvious they loved their country, hence the reason hundreds of thousands of working folk had converged on Hyde Park to show their support for those who had volunteered to protect Britain's shores. Yet not one of those men would choose to sign on and serve in a navy ship, or face a broadside from a French man-of-war. Was the boy brave or just ignorant of what life at sea was like? He wondered.

His thoughts were interrupted by the rumble of wheels, when a carriage rolled to a stop. Hauling the reins, the driver stamped his foot on the brake, as the horses appeared intent on walking on. Casson appeared from within the cab looking slightly guilty and jumped down.

'Sorry to delay you, Captain, but I had the Devil's own job finding a cab,' he said. Leaning back inside, he brushed the seat with his hand. 'Ready, Captain?'

Oliver was about to place his foot on the step, when he remembered his award. 'Wait a moment,' he called to the driver, before instructing Casson to return to the building and collect the presentation case for him.

'If you have a ship, Mister, will you take me with you?' The boy's pleading voice had grown weary. The only possession he had to cling to was the grey blanket.

'You have much to learn, lad,' Oliver said, 'not least respect for your elders and people in positions of authority.'

The boy hopped to his feet, gripping the rolled bundle to his chest. 'Ma always taught me to be polite.'

'I don't doubt she did,' Oliver said. 'What is your name?'

'Tommy, sir, Tommy Wainwright.'

'And how old are you Master Wainwright?'

'Fourteen, sir, though most folk say I don't look it.'

'And how did you arrive in London?'

'I walked.'

'All the way from the north?'

'Not all the way. I got to ride on the back of a cart part-way, 'cause I'd worn a hole in me boot. I stuffed it with grass and leaves but that didn't hold for long. But I heard tell that on a ship you don't need shoes, so I'll be all right, won't I?'

'Hear me, Master Tom,' Oliver said, 'for this is probably the first and last conversation that you and I will ever engage in. Let me advise you that if you ever wish to speak to me again, you will address me as captain.'

'Yes, Mister – Captain.'

'Captain alone, will suffice,' Oliver replied.

By this time, the captain's steward was leaving the building and heading towards them. A young midshipman was following a few paces behind, obviously unwilling to part with the wooden case under his arm. Casson, meanwhile, was making every effort to hurry him along.

Climbing into the carriage, Oliver glanced down at the forlorn expression on the boy's face. 'Listen to me, Master Wainwright and follow my instructions carefully. From here, head to the Thames and follow it downstream until you come to the bridge. Cross the bridge and continue in the same direction until you reach the dockyard at Deptford. Enquire there and you will find a ship with the name *Isle of Lewis* preparing to sail. Ask for the officer-of-the-watch and tell him that you have spoken with Captain Quintrell. Remember – Deptford Dockyard, *Isle of Lewis*, and Captain Quintrell.'

'Your sword, Captain,' the midshipman said, as he leaned into the carriage and placed the polished case on the empty seat.

Oliver thanked him and turned to the window, but the boy had gone.

Before climbing to the box-seat, Casson could not resist one question. 'Do you have a ship, Captain?'

'Not you too!' Oliver retorted, confusing his steward as to the meaning behind the remark.

'At Gibraltar,' he explained, allowing himself a slight grin. 'We sail from Spithead, one week from today.'

'Praise be!' Casson hissed, closing the carriage door, his smile stretching from ear to ear.

'Indeed, and much to do in that time.'

'If you'll pardon me for saying, the mistress will miss your company.'

Oliver wondered. Since the arrival of her sisters and their children, his wife's time had been fully occupied, to the extent that he considered his absence would hardly be noticed.

'My wife looks forward to the possibility of the three *p*s,' he said.

'Three *p*s, sir?'

'Aye, *prestige*, *promotion* and *prize money* – in no particular order.'

'And you, Capt'n, would you agree with that adage?'

Oliver Quintrell thought for a moment. 'I think I would rather opt for three *s*s – *seas*, *sails* and—' He mused, pondering over the final *s* – sailors, southerlies, sea-shores? *Ships*, of course,' he said emphatically. 'And let us pray for a sound vessel, a safe passage and favourable winds. What say you, Casson?'

'I say amen to that, sir.'

On releasing the brake and grazing the tip of his whip on the horse's flank, the driver wore his cab around in Whitehall and headed for Grosvenor Square. The sound of creaking timber and the swaying motion of the carriage were reassuring movements to the naval officer as he gazed from the window. In the distance, near the end of a narrow alley, he glimpsed a boy running, head down, grey bundle tucked under his arm, haring along as though the Hobs of Hell were chomping at his heels. To Oliver Quintrell, it was obvious where the lad was heading – first to the Thames, then to the dock at the Deptford naval yard and finally to a ship by the name: *Isle of Lewis*.

Leaning back against the threadbare upholstery, Oliver recollected a time when his own enthusiasm for the sea was just as keen. A time when his mind was oblivious to danger and his thoughts and responsibilities were for no one but himself. That was a time long ago, when a good haul of herring on his grandfather's boat was reason enough for a celebration and a pebble skimming across a lake was the only projectile of significance.

The innocence of youth is to be envied, he thought.

Chapter 3

Isle of Lewis

It was a bleak morning when Captain Quintrell crossed the pebbled beach near the Sally Port and stepped aboard the boat waiting to convey him to His Majesty's Frigate, *Isle of Lewis*. With favourable winds, it had sailed from the dockyard near London and entered The Solent three days earlier. It was now anchored amongst an assortment of other vessels in Spithead.

With his dunnage shipped the previous day, the captain was confident his steward would have attended to everything satisfactorily and, that by the time he embarked, all his personal items and special stores would have been stowed aboard the frigate.

Following his return from London, the intervening days had flown by. His precious hours had been consumed by various obligatory engagements and social gatherings at home – two dinner parties and attendance at a ball in Ryde on the presentation of one of his nieces. Surprisingly, he had enjoyed participating in those events and wondered if that was due to the fact that his remaining days at home were limited? Or was it that within a week he would be in Gibraltar where he would take up his commission and learn the details of his forthcoming mission? If those orders entailed a voyage across the Atlantic then Madeira would be his first port of call and the possibility of seeing Susanna had certainly crossed his mind.

Being conveyed as a passenger aboard Captain Slater's frigate meant he would have no ship-board responsibilities. That, in itself, would be a novel experience he had only previously sampled when injured and incapable of performing his duties. However, if he eventually rose to the rank of Admiral, his responsibilities would again change but, as the war with France was considered likely to run out of steam before he was stepped up, it was of little concern.

Because of the lack of wind on the roadstead, the boat's mast had not been raised, therefore Captain Quintrell sat in the sternsheets which offered the best view – not of the eight uniformed sailors pulling on the oars, but of the convoy of ships anchored in Spithead. All thoughts of what he was leaving behind were quickly dispelled by the rhythmic creak of the oars in the rowlocks. His only concern now was for what lay ahead, yet his expressionless face revealed nothing of the eager anticipation burning within him.

At eight bells and the beginning of the afternoon watch, *Isle of Lewis* weighed anchor and drifted slowly from the roadstead. With a light drizzle falling and a haze of mist hanging over the water, the glims in the stern lanterns had already been lit. Being in the lee of the Isle of Wight meant there was little wind, but The Solent's out-flowing double-tide, offered some assistance to the frigate in making way. Hopefully, once around the lee of the island and into the English Channel, they would be afforded an adequate breeze.

With an ample crew of two-hundred-and-fifty men, the naval vessel headed a small convoy of four supply ships. With thirty-two guns aboard *Isle of Lewis*, the frigate's role was to protect the heavily laden cargo vessels against attack from pirates, privateers or French ships of the line.

With the anchor cable hauled aboard and flaked out on the deck to allow some water to seep from it, additional sail was made in anticipation of a wind. Having being invited to the quarterdeck, but being a passenger, Oliver maintained a respectable distance from Captain Slater and his senior officers as the frigate and convoy of cargo vessels proceeded to sea.

The gun salute to the fortifications reverberated along the ship's timbers delivering a slight judder through the soles of Oliver's shoes. It was the first such feeling he had experienced for some time and it reminded him how good it was to be back at sea. The responding salvo from the saluting platform was dulled by the mist and distance, and raised not the slightest response from the sailors casting the gaskets from the canvas on the topgallant yards.

With only a light breeze, Spithead and St Helens Road were unruffled, unlike the crew. *Isle of Lewis* had made an easy passage from the Thames but since arrival in the road had stood off Portsmouth Harbour for three days during which time no one had been permitted to go ashore, and no visitors – in particular women – had been allowed aboard.

While wandering the deck, Oliver caught snippets of conversations and heard whispered mumblings, though most voices clammed shut when he ambled by, but it was not hard for a seasoned officer to sense the sailors' disappointment at being deprived of female company. However, apart from that minor observation, *Isle of Lewis* appeared to be a well-maintained ship and he could only wish it was his command. But, for the present, he was satisfied and wished for nothing more. He was heading south to take up his own commission.

While the frigate drifted slowly down the east coast of the Isle of Wight, Oliver observed the sights familiar to him – a sheen of grey silt at the mouth of the Bembridge River where he took his regular morning dip. The winding cart-track leading up to his house on the hill overlooking The Solent, and the line of tall poplars behind it, which in spring and summer offered protection from the westerlies. Despite their age, the trees grew taller every year, but now, almost stripped of their autumn leaves, the branches appeared like bony fingers etched against the November sky. Soon they would offer no shelter from the westerly gales of winter.

As always, Oliver wondered if his wife was observing from one of the house windows. He had informed her of the day and tide of his departure, but he doubted she would be inclined to watch.

After heading south, the ships commenced their slow sweep into the English Channel where the remnant thrust of the Atlantic swell reminded everyone on board of the direction they were heading.

The involuntary smile, hovering on Captain Quintrell's lips, was one of satisfaction – the type of unconscious smile, usually accompanied by a deep sigh, when relaxing in an armchair, while warming a glass of French brandy in his cupped hands. The fine liquor was one thing the French deserved to be complimented on and Oliver hoped that this war, and Napoleon's demand for men, would not prevent the growers from harvesting their annual crops. His thoughts were interrupted by the approach of a young midshipman who dutifully touched his hat.

'Begging your pardon, Capt'n. Captain Slater asked if you would care to join him for a stroll.'

'Thank you,' Oliver said, striding across the quarterdeck, his gait easily accommodating the gentle heel of the ship.

Captain Slater's mood, however, was glum. 'At this rate, unless we find a decent wind, it will take three days for us to arrive off Ushant.'

'Are all the ships proceeding to Gibraltar?' Oliver asked.

'Not so. Two are for Cornwallis off Brest. Once I have delivered them to the fleet, we will part company and proceed south. When those vessels have discharged their cargo, they will return to Portsmouth unescorted.'

'That would make them vulnerable to attack from pirates or privateers, would it not?'

'Quite possibly,' Captain Slater replied, sounding unconcerned. 'But at least their holds will be empty. The other two, however, will continue with me to Gibraltar. It is imperative these supplies arrive safely for, without them, England would be hard-pressed to maintain a fleet in the Mediterranean.'

'May I ask what cargo the supply vessels are carrying?'

'The largest has a live cargo – pigs, chickens and sheep, calves and a few horses – a veritable menagerie stored below deck. The others are laden with the unusual stores, plus spars, sails, blocks and new cordage. Far better for ships to repair at Gibraltar than attempt to limp back to Falmouth reeling like lame ducks on the Bay of Biscay. But I agree with you, pirates and privateers are a problem. They have the nostrils of hungry foxes. I am convinced they can smell a damaged ship before it rises on the horizon.'

'Let us pray the blockades hold,' Oliver said, 'and not a single French ship slips through the net.'

'Let us hope so, indeed.'

'And what of Gibraltar, sir? It is many years since I visited that port.'

'Busy and demanding as always, and more so since the resumption of war. The Port Admiral has an unenviable task coping with the contingencies of battle with the constant demands for refitting and repair work, along with the day-to-day necessities related to docking, watering, stevedoring and victualling. Fortunately the garrison, which is responsible for defending the area, is very well manned. With Spain only a stone's throw away across its narrow border, Britain's hold on Gibraltar is extremely tenuous. Imagine how disastrous it would be if that strategic position were lost.'

'And what of the French in the Mediterranean? Will Admiral Lord Nelson's fleet be able to maintain his blockade of Toulon?'

'A good question. The French wrights build faster ships than those slipped from our naval yards, and during the peace, while we were converting our men-of-war to coal hulks, the French yards were busy building a bigger and better fleet.'

'They may have fine fast ships,' Oliver added, 'but they will never produce the disciplined seamen the Royal Navy boasts'.

'Despite that, I fear afore long, we will face a formidable armada. As Spain already has an alliance with Napoleon, the next step will be for them to join forces and declare war on England.'

'And if the fleets of France and Spain unite, will we have the naval power to stop them?'

Captain Slater shrugged off the question. 'Tell me, Captain Quintrell, are you at liberty to divulge your orders? Will you be staying in the Mediterranean or heading across the Atlantic?'

'My interim orders are to attend the Port Admiral in Gibraltar. That is the extent of my knowledge. I will speak with him as soon as I go ashore. No one is more anxious than I to know what is required of me.'

'Then I wish you well, Captain. And, tomorrow evening you will join me and my officers for a meal, so we can talk at length. But, for now, you must excuse me. I must go below. There are matters I must attend to.'

Oliver nodded and strode back across the quarterdeck. The much anticipated wind was teasing the hem of his boat cloak, ruffling the face of the square sails but failing to fill them. From the starboard rail, he regarded the Needles of the Isle of Wight. Hopefully, if they were blessed with a blow, by morning England's southern coastline would have disappeared from view.

As always, Oliver's feelings were mixed. Guilt was spawned by his elation at leaving England and home, though he had no reason to feel guilty. His wife, Victoria, was well. Her health had returned to a greater degree, though it ebbed and flowed with the inconsistencies of the Portsmouth harbour tides. Recently, with the arrival of her devoted sisters and their children, she had become the centre of attraction, which in turn had improved her spirits further.

For Oliver, however, the mere thought of entertaining a house filled with guests was as disenchanting as being offered a post as commander of a prison hulk. He valued his privacy – a legacy of being a ship's captain – yet, at home, there were constant demands for his attention. His participation in board games, card games and charades was deemed obligatory, as were the tedious hours spent listening to poetry readings and musical recitals, often poorly performed, which he had to endure with stoicism. Worst of all, his guests pressed him for anecdotes about his career at sea (politely side-stepping any reference to his disfigured hand). Though, thankfully, he soon discovered that their interest in his seafaring pursuits was superficial and easily satisfied. Society gossip and the latest London and Paris fashions were the major subjects of interest but, as he had little time to indulge in such matters, his contributions were limited. It was just as well that news pertaining to his missions was of little interest to the ladies, so it was not necessary for him to appear rude or evasive by remaining silent.

On this latest occasion, his time ashore had been far longer than he would have wished, however, he was satisfied that during that time he had done his lubberly duty to the best of his ability. Furthermore, with her siblings milling around her, it appeared Victoria, no longer had need for his attention, which allowed him to depart with a clear conscience.

'Begging your pardon, Captain,' the lieutenant said, lifting his hat. 'It is you!'

Oliver turned his eyes from the fading coast.

'Good to see you, sir,' the officer said. I'd heard we were carrying another captain aboard but I didn't know it was you, till just now. Do you remember me, sir?'

'Mr Hazzlewood, but of course I do. How could I forget? And I see from your new uniform that congratulations are in order.'

'Thank you, sir. Passed my exam for lieutenant soon after I left *Elusive*. It only took me sixteen years serving as a middie,' he said, smiling. 'I was the oldest candidate presenting for examination but I was able to answer every question the Board put to me – and they asked me plenty.'

'Well done, Mr H, your promotion is well deserved.'

'Commissioned third lieutenant, I am, but I would never have made it were it not for you – and Mr Smith,' he added.

'Ah, the Honourable Algernon Biggleswade-Smythe,' said Quintrell with a wry smile.

'Aye, that's his handle!' then he corrected himself, looking around to see if anyone was listening. 'I mean, that's his full title. But, I call him Algy when we're on us own. Good mates we are, though, as you no doubt remember, we're as different as chalk and cheese, him being from landed gentry and only a lad, and me being what I am, and nearly old enough to be his father.'

Oliver nodded, his thoughts flashing back to his previous command.

'He was granted special permission to attend the exam at the same time as me, though he didn't meet with all the navy's requirements. I think some relative must have put in a good word for him. Even so, they couldn't grant him the promotion so he's still serving as a middie. Problem is, he's not old enough to make lieutenant and not done enough shipboard service. He's only served aboard *Elusive* with you, Captain, though his papers show him serving since he was eight years old.'

'And what ship is Mr Smith serving on now?'

'He's right here, sailing with us on *Isle of Lewis*. Captain Slater sent him over to one of the supply ships with a message, but he'll be back afore long.'

'Then I will look forward to meeting him later.'

'I reckon if this war runs on a few years, Mr Smith'll be stepped up. I wager he'll see his first command before he reaches his nineteenth year.'

'I am sure you are right, Mr H. He has the makings of an excellent lieutenant. But if this war continues, you may well find yourself with your own command.'

'I don't know as I'm ready for that, sir,' Hazzlewood said apologetically.

'You will be surprised, and you will soon discover that men respect a commander who knows the ship's rigging better than the back of his hand.'

Bert Hazzlewood's cheeks flushed a little. 'Might I ask as to your commission, Captain?'

'A frigate. I will learn more when we arrive in Gibraltar.'

'And what of crew?'

'Hands transferred from ships brought in for repair. I am advised there will be no difficulty in filling the berths.'

'That's good,' the new lieutenant said sagely. 'Most men in the Mediterranean fleet are Portsmouth and Plymouth men and if not, at least they're all seasoned sailors. Better than the dregs the Press Gang drags in to the London Docks.'

'It's still possible there will be a few aboard who were only pressed during the last few months.'

'That's no matter. I reckon a couple of months is long enough for 'em to get a taste of salt air, find their legs, and learn the pins and lines. And there's no point them trying to run from The Rock. Nowhere to run to unless you want the Moors, Spaniards or Froggies snapping at your heels. I don't know which would be worse.'

From the ship's belfry, the bell rang twice.

'If you'll excuse me, Captain. I best get a move on.'

'Of course, but first tell me, are there any familiar faces amongst the warrant officers on board?'

I don't think so, sir, but there are a few *Elusives* amongst the crew. That were quite a cruise weren't it?' the lieutenant said. 'If you'll pardon me for saying.'

'It was indeed, Mr H. But I think the less said about that the better.'

'Aye, sir, but you can't stop the memories flooding back.'

'Indeed.'

As the lieutenant touched his hat and hurried forward, Oliver cast his mind back. It had been a remarkable mission fraught with near insurmountable dangers, but his ship and his men had survived. He could but pray that this forthcoming cruise would not push him, his ship or his men to such extreme limits, but that the outcome would be equally successful.

The following evening, Oliver was pleased to join Captain Slater for dinner. With ten officers seated around the table, the cabin was crowded.

'Gentlemen, let me cordially introduce Captain Quintrell who, as you are aware, is sailing with us to Gibraltar.'

As each man was introduced by name, Oliver nodded, or offered an appropriate greeting in acknowledgement. The fact he was not partial to his wife's dinner parties did not make him adverse to shipboard dinners in either the captain's cabin or the wardroom.

'Mr Smith,' Oliver said, when reacquainted with the Honourable Algernon Biggleswade-Smythe. 'I must congratulate you on sitting the examination for lieutenant after such a short time in the service.'

'My sentiment entirely,' Captain Slater interrupted, not giving the midshipman the chance to answer for himself. 'Seems his father had him listed on an Arctic expedition as soon as he was taken off the teat.'

With his fine upbringing, the young man sat upright in his chair displaying no sign of embarrassment by the titter which ran around the table.

'And he is able, on paper, to claim that he sailed in the same fleet as Horatio Nelson. Is that not so?' Captain Slater added.

'A claim the first lieutenant on my previous mission was also able to make, though both he and Lord Nelson were but fresh-faced midshipmen at the time.'

Mr Smith said nothing, though he was obviously interested in that piece of information.

'I read in *The Times* that your father has been quite vociferous in Parliament recently regarding the slave trade.'

'I believe so, sir,' the midshipman replied, looking to Captain Slater for liberty to voice his opinion.

'Speak up, man,' the captain ordered. 'We are all waiting.'

'My father vigorously opposes the latest Bill presented by Mr Wilberforce for the abolition of the slave trade.'

'And are you of the same mind?' Oliver asked.

All eyes looked to the young man for his answer.

'My father is of the opinion that it would be unwise to end it. Without Britain's trade with the islands of the Caribbean, there would be a marked reduction in income associated with that trade and that is valuable income which helps fund the war with France.'

Oliver put the question: 'Is there any reason why there cannot be a direct trade with the West Indies without using the triangular route sourcing slaves from West Africa? Are there not already sufficient slaves in the colonies without importing more?'

The Doctor, who had been listening to the conversation, joined in the discussion. 'But the more slaves that are transported to the colonies means more chances of major uprisings. Before long, there will be so many of them it will be impossible to quash a major rebellion.'

'And I would remind you,' Oliver retorted, 'that the Bills being brought before Parliament are to bring an end to the trade in slaves – not to end the practice of slavery itself. And the threat of rebellion will not end with the passing of a Bill. This is an important factor which is being overlooked.'

'But isn't it the money from the sale of slaves that buys the goods which the English now demand, such as sugar, rum, chocolate and tobacco?'

'You must realize,' Oliver said, 'slaves are not acquired freely. The British traders pay the African dealers with guns and metal goods made in our factories. So, why not bring an end to this diabolical trade and send the money directly to the Indies to purchase sugar and rum etcetera?'

'But to sail with empty ships would be uneconomical,' Captain Slater argued. 'And it would provide a damned uncomfortable passage. Imagine crossing the Atlantic on a ship bobbing like a piece of cork!' He laughed, 'I, for one, see no harm in filling the holds with slaves. It saves the effort of loading tons of pig-iron for ballast.'

One of the junior officers giggled and whispered to the midshipman beside him, 'This ballast has got legs.'

Oliver cast the pair a disparaging glance, as the steward arrived to refill the glasses.

'What say you, Doctor?' Oliver enquired, after a lull in the conversation.

'Well, I would not choose to travel on such a ship. African slaves constitute an unhealthy and unwholesome cargo and the ships engaged in the trade are generally old and dilapidated merchantmen reputed to be disease-ridden, vermin-infested death traps.'

'But with your interest in tropical diseases, such conditions could afford you a constant supply of patients,' Captain Slater quipped. 'Although from what I have heard, most slave ships do not even carry an apothecary and certainly not a surgeon or physician.' Captain Slater leaned back in his chair. 'The ships' masters have their own answer to sickness and any slave who shows signs of disease is quickly disposed of.'

'To a sick berth?' a young midshipman asked.

'No, to the sharks,' the sailing master quipped.

'That is why there are so many well-fed sharks in tropical waters,' Slater mused. 'I heard of one caught on a line that was nineteen feet in length and was found to have a dozen young inside it.'

'Young sharks?' one of his midshipmen asked.

'No, young slaves!'

The company stamped their feet and applauded but neither Lieutenant Hazzlewood nor Midshipman Smith nor Captain Quintrell joined in the laughter.

When the frivolity subsided, Captain Slater turned to his guest and asked Oliver his opinion on the abolition of the slave trade.

'I gather it is a subject of much talk in the coffee shops in London, and is creating heated arguments in the Lower House. Questions are even being raised at the Admiralty.'

'A storm in a teacup,' Slater stated. 'Created by eccentric abolitionists like William Wilberforce who stir the populace with prefabricated lies. These politicians even solicit blacks to tell tales to attract sympathy. One was even reputed to have written a book about his life.'

'*An Interesting Narrative*,' Oliver added.

'I have no time for such publications,' the purser commented. 'You cannot expect an educated man to honestly believe that a slave, taken from the jungles of Africa, would have the intelligence to write such an account. Most do not know one end of a pen from the other and struggle to make their mark when they sign on.'

'Have you read Equiano's story?' Oliver asked.

'I would not waste my time on such rubbish.'

'I found it intriguing,' he said. 'And in London the Abolitionist Movement is gaining support at all levels.'

Slater sighed. 'England will rue the day if that Bill is ever passed. Mark my words, the major mercantile businesses in all major cities will be bankrupt within a year. The slave trade has been operating successfully for at least one-hundred-and-fifty years. And England is not alone. The Portuguese, Spanish, French and Dutch are all doing it to their advantage, so why change it now?'

'Why not?' Oliver asked. 'Why not encourage the merchants to ply their trade elsewhere, even if it derives England of rum and tobacco, which my wife attributes to being the root of all evil?'

Captain Slater laughed. 'No disrespect to your wife, sir, but what are women to know of trade, or the economy, or black slaves for that matter?'

Oliver conceded. 'Very little, I admit, though despite her incapacity, my wife insisted on being conducted to a talk by the abolitionist, Clarkson, held in Ryde some months ago. She said it was very engaging.'

'But women are easily influenced by a sorry tale. They take pity on the destitute, the aged and suffer infantile minds. They are gullible targets which are easily swayed by emotional causes.' Captain Slater scoffed, 'This Wilberforce fellow is aiming to set up a society against harmful treatment to animals. Afore long, a carriage driver will not be permitted to crack a whip. Imagine how long it will take to travel from London to Portsmouth, if that happens.' The captain had his men's full attention. 'Good God, what will he think of next? Well, I for one am pleased the navy does not take heed of women's views. And I am against warrant officers hoisting their wives on board with them. I am a God-fearing man and I tolerate no misbehaviour on my ship.'

'I agree with you on that score, Captain,' Oliver said. 'Members of the fair sex are a distraction that men can well do without at sea. If we officers choose not to be accompanied by our wives, then I see no reason why such concessions should be made to the lower ratings.'

'Eat up gentlemen,' Captain Slater reminded his guests. 'This is the last of the duck and hare until we reach Gibraltar where I hope my steward will be able to purchase some local birds and perhaps a hog or two.'

'I noticed you have some black Jacks aboard *Isle of Lewis*?' Oliver said. 'How do you rate their performance?'

'I have half a dozen of them. They were picked up a month ago from a fishing boat adrift off the Portuguese coast, probably trying to escape their masters on the Canary Islands or Madeira. I could have left them to drown but I find, once they are taught manners, they perform their duties with blind obedience. Besides, they are extraordinarily strong. I witnessed two black tars haul the main course around in a stiff breeze that would have taken near a dozen landsmen to achieve. Brawn but no brain is their chief attribute. Yet brazen! I overheard one the other day clicking his tongue in a foolish fashion at one of my officers. I always double the punishment for those men. Their skin is as tough as rhinoceros hide, so I doubt they feel the pain.'

'They bleed the same, however.'

'So it would seem, which reminds me – I had one flogged yesterday. Mr Oldfield, make sure the gratings are lowered overboard and towed during the night. The men complain that it's a Devil of a job to scrape the blood off once it has set hard.'

Captain Quintrell passed no comment, allowing Captain Slater to continue.

'I heard tell of a slave ship bound for Santo Domingo,' he said. 'Having lost all its anchors, it was in danger of drifting onto a reef. Afraid of losing his vessel, the master chained twenty slaves in line and cast them overboard.'

The surgeon frowned. 'Surely they would have floated?'

'Not with iron shackles around their necks, wrists and ankles. They dropped like lumps of lead.'

'Did it hold – this black anchor?' the purser asked.

'It did indeed. It dragged for a while then caught and prevented the ship being carried onto the rocks. When the wind changed the master was able to cut the cable and sail clear.' Captain Slater perused the mixed expressions around his table. 'Surely it is better to forfeit a few head of livestock and a length of line, in order to save his ship and the rest of his cargo. One must balance risk with cost and outcome. A simple equation, is it not? Personally, I think the ship's master should be commended on his ingenuity.'

Oliver Quintrell had heard enough. Emptying his glass, he dabbed his mouth and pushed his chair back. 'If you will excuse me, gentlemen,' he said, lowering his head to the deck beams – a gesture interpreted as a bow by the company at the table. 'There are letters I must write before we reach Gibraltar. And I will be sure to inform my wife of your views on the triangular trade. I am sure she will find it interesting. Gentlemen, I bid you good evening.'

Chapter 4

Boris the Florist

Arriving off Ushant a day later than anticipated, no time was wasted in consigning the two supply ships to the care of one of Admiral Cornwallis's frigates. With the responsibility transferred, the *Isle of Lewis* and the two remaining supply vessels headed south across the Bay of Biscay towards the coast of the Iberian Peninsula. This placed them in the major lane for ships heading to the Mediterranean or south to the Cape of Good Hope and beyond.

However, with the British fleet blockading Brest, the number of French ships in the Bay was far less than in peacetime. As France had the distinct advantage of having coasts and seaports on both the Mediterranean Sea and the English Channel, there was little necessity for Napoleon to ship supplies around the Iberian Peninsula.

The following morning, while making an entry in his personal log, Oliver was alerted in his cabin by the sound of drums and running feet. It was a familiar, rousing, but often unnerving sound. Within an instant, sailors appeared and, without so much as a *pardon me* or *by-your-leave*, began dismantling the bulkhead that formed the wall of his cabin. Fastening the buckle on his sword belt, Oliver quickly slipped on his shoes and accepted his hat from his steward, who was waiting for him at the bottom of the companionway.

'What is the hour?' Oliver enquired.

'A little after 9 o'clock, sir. Fine weather. Fair winds.'

'And the reason for the call?'

'Don't know, Capt'n.'

'I presume Captain Slater is on deck?'

Casson nodded. 'Shall I bring up some coffee to you?'

'I think that must wait for the present. Thank you, Casson.'

Oliver wondered if he should stay below and wait for an invitation to the quarterdeck, after all *Isle of Lewis* was not his ship, and if a fight was about to explode around him, it was not his battle. But he wanted to know what had prompted the drum-roll sending the men scurrying about like frightened rats. The necessity to clear the deck for action was more of a concern. With the rumble of trucks on the gun deck and the calls for powder, it was likely the enemy was close at hand.

'Good morning,' Oliver said, glancing across the ocean as he stepped up to the quarterdeck. 'I trust you will not object to my presence?'

'Of course not,' Captain Slater replied. 'Gun practice, Captain. I had a sudden urge to take advantage of the sea room, and it does the men good to be stirred into action when they least expect it.'

'Then, if you will permit, I would welcome the opportunity to observe.'

'Please feel free. It may encourage the crews to make a little more effort if they find themselves under scrutiny.'

After two rounds of firing from the larboard and starboard guns, the order rang out to make more sail. Immediately, sailors left their posts on the guns and climbed aloft to shake out the reefings. Four, sometimes five men departed a station, leaving insufficient hands to handle the subsequent order to fire.

'You have guns standing idle,' Oliver commented, to one of the midshipmen.'

'Yes, sir.'

The guns rang out again and a dozen shots flew across the water slicing the wave crests like flying fish but, with no order to reload, the men stood about idly.

'Ware ship!' the Captain ordered.

'Clew up the mains'l,' the lieutenant called. 'Look lively there.'

The manoeuvre, of turning the ship through a great circle of sea, was tediously slow and, had it been attempted during a battle, it would have provided the enemy with ample opportunity to escape or prepare for further action. Oliver considered it fortunate this was merely a practice. He noted the disorganization caused to the gun crews when sailors were torn from their stations and ordered to the lines or sent aloft to take a reef in the topgallants. He was aware it was a problem on all ships in action when sudden changes of wind or course meant sail handling was called for. But any man was capable of hauling on a halyard and securing it to the pin rail, or sponging out a flaming barrel. Those jobs took little expertise. But working in the tops was different. Topmen were not made from lubbers pressed from the ports or city streets of England, they were seasoned seamen who had been climbing aloft since they were lads. Topmen were respected as the elite of the sailing crew and to use the best sailors on the guns was, in Oliver's opinion, a foolhardy choice. It was something he intended to discuss with his first lieutenant, to ensure it didn't happen on his new command.

Late in the afternoon, prior to their arrival at Gibraltar, all the officers gathered on the larboard deck as the ship raised Cape Trafalgar. Some miles away along that coast was the Bay of Cadiz with its Moorish buildings reflecting the days when the invaders from the south had an overwhelming presence in the region. But Oliver was directing all his thoughts to the next morning when *Isle of Lewis* would enter the Strait of Gibraltar, slide into Algiceras Bay and drop anchor in the shelter of The Rock.

At dinner, being the final evening on board, Oliver was again invited to dine with Captain Slater and his men. Once again the cabin was filled to capacity and the table laden with a variety of tempting dishes.

There were questions Oliver wanted to pose regarding the *Isle of Lewis*'s gun crews, but this was neither the appropriate time nor place. Instead, having learned that Captain Slater had made three trips to Gibraltar in the last two months, he confined his conversation to enquiries about their destination and its vulnerable position on the Iberian Peninsula. The Rock itself was indeed significant, its near perpendicular face acknowledged as one of the legendary Pillars of Hercules marking the western end of the Mediterranean.

As the evening's meal proceeded and conversation dropped, Oliver picked an appropriate moment to speak with Captain Slater. 'A fine table, if I may say, sir.'

'It is something I pride myself on whenever I have the opportunity. And,' he added, with a wry smile, 'because I am never more than a couple of day's sailing from a port, it is a regular indulgence.'

'One question, Captain, are you familiar with a Captain Crabthorne?'

'Boris Crabthorne? *Compendium?* I have heard of his reputation, but never met him. Might I ask what your interest is in the name?'

'No specific interest, sir, I merely heard mention of him when I was in London. I am afraid one reads so many names in the *Gazette* these days, it is hard to keep pace with the recent commissions.'

'*Boris the Florist,*' Captain Slater said, smiling. 'Rumoured to be of Russian descent. Distantly related to the royal family on his grandmother's side – or so the story goes.'

'And the unusual nickname?'

'Dubbed, *the Florist,* because his cabin resembles a flower shop. I understand his window boxes would not be out of place in the Royal Botanical Gardens of Kew. It is said that even Sir Joseph Banks commended him on the quality of his blooms.'

One of the midshipmen looked puzzled and elbowed his mate. 'Where do his flowers come from when he's on long cruises?'

'He grows them in clay pots from bulbs and seeds,' Captain Slater interjected, addressing his junior officer. 'I understand when they are brought aboard, the men are told to handle the clay pots as though they were moulded from Venetian glass. In spring his cabin is said to be perfumed with crocuses, jonquils and hyacinths, and he manages to have roses blooming for many months of the year.'

The company found the image highly amusing.

'Sounds quite odd to me,' the surgeon said, 'but then some captains find tapestry work or knitting relaxing.'

'Which is acceptable if it involves no one else's services,' the sailing master argued. 'But I heard he employs the ship's boys for pruning, watering and repotting duties. I've also heard that when his ship is short of water, he allocates one man's water rations for his plants. I believe he is quite eccentric.'

'Perhaps it has a beneficial effect on his state of mind,' the doctor added.

The sailing master frowned. 'I could make allowance for a cottage garden, Doctor, to grow fresh vegetables for the table, but a floating flower nursery has to be questioned.'

'And of course,' Captain Slater added, 'bringing flowers aboard a ship is regarded by the men as bringing back luck aboard.

Perpetual's third lieutenant cleared his throat. 'Might I be permitted to say a word in Captain Crabthorne's defence?'

'Go ahead, Mr Hazzlewood.' It was obvious from the glow on Captain Slater face that his spirits were rising to the evening's discourse.

'I sailed with him as a middie five years ago and I discovered that his keen interest in potted plants is something he's always had. He's written articles about his botanical collections and been published in the Royal Society's papers. In fact, he's well respected in those circles. But I can assure you, sir, he doesn't squander or misuse the ship's water rations and he always insists on tending to his plants himself. Perhaps it is Captain Bligh you are confusing him with.'

The sailing master didn't appreciate his story being questioned but before he had the opportunity to respond, Oliver turned to his host.

'Would you know where Captain Crabthorne is presently?'

'According to the *Gazette*, he sailed for South America some months ago.'

'No doubt taking every opportunity to go ashore with a shovel,' the sailing master added, much to the amusement of the midshipmen.

Oliver interrupted their jokes. 'Gentlemen, we should not jest about a captain in His Majesty's service. Might I remind you that we sail on a ship made from wood with rigging and sails made from plant fibres.'

One of the midshipmen laughed out loud at Oliver's remark.

'Think about it, young man. Our sails are made from canvas woven from the fibrous stems of flax plants. And was not Captain Bligh's unfortunate expedition to the South Seas for a purely botanical purpose?'

The young officer looked puzzled.

Captain Slater shook his head. 'You should be aware of what is going on in the world, young man. That mission ended in mutiny and court martial and the facts of that voyage will long be remembered. Tell him, Mr Smith.'

'I believe the reason behind Bligh's voyage on *Bounty* was to collect and transport breadfruit plants.'

'For what purpose?'

'To provide a fast growing staple food for the slaves in Jamaica.'

'Thank you, Mr Smith,' Captain Slater said. 'It is good to see that at least one of my junior officers is familiar with the bitter-sweet happenings in the world.'

The other young midshipmen did not lift their eyes from their empty plates.

'Then perhaps I should applaud the seagoing activities of the good captain.' Captain Slater drawled. 'Gentlemen, I charge you to raise your glasses. A toast to Captain Boris Crabthorne. May his flowers continue to bloom that he may scatter petals on the ocean in memory of our glorious dead.'

Be it full or empty, every man lifted his glass and echoed the toast to Captain Crabthorne.

As the voices subsided, the captain's steward entered with two large plates of mouth-watering deserts and assorted continental cheeses from Captain Slater's private larder. The conversation abated for a time, while the men indulged their seemingly insatiable appetites. By the time the brandy arrived, Oliver was feeling agreeably relaxed and embarked on a conversation with the surgeon.

'My wife has an interest in botany,' he said. 'In particular the cultivation of exotic herbs and spices. She is convinced of their natural medicinal and therapeutic qualities.'

'I trust she benefits from her interest.'

'To some degree, Doctor. The time she spends tending her seedlings appears to distract her from her other discomforts so, to that extent, the effect is positive?'

'An interesting observation, Captain Quintrell. All I can add is that there are many mysteries hidden in nature which are yet to be discovered. Did you know the South American Indians crush the roots of a vine and use it as a deadly poison on their arrows? Yet when they administer it as a potion to their old folk, not one of them suffers from the stiffness of joints that we do. It is known as curaré. And in China, men inhale the smoke of the opium poppy to relax the mind while in my profession we use laudanum, also derived from the poppy, to dull the brain and combat pain during surgery.'

'Very true,' Oliver added. 'Yet it is interesting that when Captain Slater mentioned the presence of a pot of crocuses onboard a ship, the whole company found that amusing. Do you know that the cost of saffron, collected from the crocus flower, is far higher than every other spice on the market? And tell me,' he continued, addressing the whole table, 'what is the major cargo of all the ships of the Dutch, French and British East India Companies?'

'Spices,' Mr Hazzlewood replied.

'Indeed – spices. The seeds from tropical plants make up the major cargoes. And they are worth millions of pounds. Consider the voyage Columbus embarked upon across the Atlantic, it was not to discover the continents of the Americas but to find a quicker and more direct route to the East – to shorten the passage for shipping engaged in the spice trade. I ask you, Gentlemen, who are we to decry a man the right to grow a few flowers in his cabin?'

'Well said, Captain. Perhaps it is a pastime which should be encouraged.'

'Well I for one would never condone it,' the sailing master argued. 'I have no wish to sail with a man who is more concerned about a bowl of daffodils than a broadside. If you want my opinion, flowers, like women bring bad luck and are best left ashore. I tell you, no good can come from carrying either of them aboard one of His Majesty's ships.'

Chapter 5

Gibraltar

As the sun rose from behind The Rock, it cast a cloak over Gibraltar's moles and yards, whilst less than five miles away, directly across the bay, it glinted on the white buildings of Algiceras. Once a stronghold for Phoenician sailors and Romans and Moorish invaders, the Spanish port was a constant reminder to the tiny British territory of how vulnerable it would be if Spain declared war on England.

In the still morning air, the *Isle of Lewis*'s jollyboat swam smoothly alongside a seventy-four. The slap of oars and squeal of timber in the rowlocks were the only sounds from the clinker-built boat as it slid beneath the bow of the Royal Navy ship of the line. Sticking his head through one of the gun ports, a sailor failed to glance down, before tipping the contents of a bucket into the sea. The smells of men, meat fat, heated pitch and vinegar exuding from the open ports settled across the water like morning mist over a marsh.

'Sorry, sir,' one of the boat crew murmured, when he shipped his oar, dousing a stream of water over the passengers.

Unperturbed, Oliver removed his cocked hat, allowed a trickle of water to spill from it then seated it back on his head. The doctor, sitting beside him, brushed the beads of moisture from his shoulder with a disparaging *tut-tutting* noise.

Ahead, a dozen stairs carved into solid rock, led up to the quay. Creating barely a ripple or a sound, the boat swam forward till it nudged alongside the rock face.

'Take care, Captain,' the coxswain advised, securing a line to a rusted iron ring in the rock wall.

Whether he was alluding to the green weed covering the stone steps, or the new leather-soled shoes the captain was wearing that were totally unsuited to such surfaces, Oliver was uncertain, however, he acknowledged the warning and climbed carefully.

Waiting on the wharf was an immaculately dressed officer – of pleasing features, tall, with a straight back and prematurely grey hair which curled from beneath his hat.

'Captain Quintrell,' the lieutenant said, lifting his hat.

'Simon,' Oliver smiled, offering his hand. 'I am delighted to see you.'

'Welcome to Gibraltar, Captain. I trust you had a reasonable voyage.'

'Tolerable passage,' Oliver replied, but before more could be said, the pair was joined by the Doctor wearing a preoccupied expression on his face.

Oliver made the necessary introductions. 'Mr Parry served as first lieutenant on my last cruise.'

'Parry? I recollect something familiar about that name. I remember mention of Vice Admiral Francis Parry a few years back, and another captain of the same name. Could that be your father or a brother perhaps?'

'No sir, I doubt it,' the lieutenant replied. 'My father never served in the navy and died many years ago. And I am an only son.'

'Then it would appear I am mistaken. I am pleased to make your acquaintance, but if you will excuse me, Gentlemen, I must away to make some special purchases for I understand *Isle of Lewis* will not be remaining in port very long. Will you be sleeping aboard this evening, Captain?'

'I think not,' Oliver said. 'I prefer to take lodgings in the town until I am able to take up my commission.'

'Then I suggest you select your lodgings with care.'

'Indeed, I will. I wish you God speed, for your safe return to England.'

'And to you too, Captain Quintrell. Good-bye, Mr Parry.'

The pair stepped aside, as a well-worn leather bag was handed up to the doctor who collected it and scuttled off, in the direction of the town.

'So, Simon, tell me how you are.'

'I am well, and all the better for seeing you.'

Oliver wished there was occasion to congratulate his friend on a promotion, but the lack of an epaulette indicated he had not been granted the promotion to the rank of captain which had once been stripped from him. The only consolation was that if Simon Parry had been stepped up, he would not have been commissioned to sail with *Perpetual*. 'Have you been in Gibraltar long?'

'I arrived a little over a week ago, having been serving as second lieutenant on a sixty-four. We had been patrolling off the French coast for a month and came back in to re-supply. The message about your expected arrival was waiting for me but confirmation of my commission only arrived two days ago.'

Oliver was delighted and saw no reason to hide the satisfaction he was feeling. It was a splendid start to the day. 'Let us walk. Perhaps you would accompany me to the Port Admiral's office where I will collect my orders.'

The cobbled wharf was milling with sailors, victuallers, street vendors, naval officers and stray dogs. A stream of carts and dray wagons stood in line waiting to load or unload cargo from the lighters ferrying supplies back and forth to the ships in the roadstead.

Oliver lifted his head and sniffed. 'What on earth is that smell?'

'It depends on the direction of the wind,' Simon Parry replied with a curious grin. 'If it blows from the north, it carries the smell from the swampy area near the neutral zone abutting the Spanish mainland. That is where the cattle are unloaded and left to graze. After a week spent fouling the already vile-smelling wetland, the beasts contribute to this obnoxious miasma which hangs over the town for days. We are fortunate it is only November. I am told it is particularly offensive in mid-summer.'

'And if the smell comes from the other direction?'

'It is from the cemetery, which can be equally as bad, if not worse. Surprisingly one gets used to it after a while.'

'Like a hold filled with ambergris,' Oliver suggested with a smile.

'Indeed, though that is a more tolerable odour.'

'Then, I suggest, the less time we stay here, the better.'

Simon nodded. 'Might I enquire as to your commission?'

'A 32-gun frigate by the name – *Perpetual*. Because she was in need of repair, I understand the crew was paid off. Naturally, as my first officer, I will leave the signing of new crew in your hands. As to the other officers, I was pleased to invite Mr Hazzlewood and Mr Smith to sail with me. They intend to request a transfer from *Isle of Lewis* and by tomorrow will be available to assist you.'

'The Right Honourable—?'

'The very same. Young Mr Smith is still a midshipman, but Mr Hazzlewood passed for lieutenant.'

'That is good,' Mr Parry said, as they strode along past ship's chandlers, victuallers stores, and naval workshops.

'Do you remember James Tinker, Captain?'

'Tinker?' Oliver queried.

'You may know him better as Bungs – the cooper.'

'Indeed. How could I forget him?'

'I encountered him yesterday right here on the quay. He is working in the yard over yonder. Perhaps he would care to sail with you again.'

'And escape from this place.' Oliver thought for a moment, 'He would need to apply to the Port Admiral for a warrant, but I foresee no problem in that. Let us speak with him.'

The red-brick building across the street looked out of place in a region where the walls of most houses had either been washed with white lime, or built from rock hewn from the promontory. With bricks shipped from England, the building's appearance would have more befitted a London wharf. But the sounds emitting from it were the same as those from any dockyard from Chatham to Calcutta. Though a pair of large wooden doors was propped open, the workshop was dark inside. The faint glimmer of several lanterns competed only with the red glow of burning braziers to provide sufficient light for the coopers to work by. Suspended from the overhead beams, strips of metal hung from huge hooks. Heavy rectangular blocks of pig iron were stacked four or five high in places, whilst damaged barrels and rotten staves were heaped against the wall to be used as kindling for the fires. The rank smell in the air was not from the nearby swamp or the cemetery, but from the empty barrels saturated with congealed fat, vinegar and rotten meat. The clanging of several hammers was the only indications of the number of men working within.

'Mr Tinker,' the lieutenant called, as they stepped through the doorway.

The cooper nearest the entrance looked up, tossed his hammer onto the bench, rubbed his hands down his blackened leather apron, then knuckled his forehead.

'Mr Tinker,' Oliver said. 'Or shall I call you Bungs?'

'Bungs will do, Capt'n,' he replied, a hint of a smile curling his lips. 'Mighty fine to see you, sir. If I might be so bold as to say, you're looking well.'

Oliver was conscious the cooper was probably referring to the additional inches he had gained during his long spell ashore. Dining daily with Captain Slater had not helped. It was something he preferred not to be reminded of, though he acknowledged the well-meaning greeting from the craftsman.

'Are you bound to a ship?' Oliver asked.

'No, sir, just coopering in the yard here for the present. Apart from the constant demand for new barrels, there's a non-stop stream rolling on and off ships every day. Many of them are damaged and in need of repair. The ships come in for water or victuals, off-load the empties, refill the holds and they're off before you know it. Certainly no shortage of work here.'

'Then you have no desire to sail at the present?'

'You looking for crew, Capt'n?'

'Indeed.'

'Then I'll be happy to sail from here, and there's a few men I know'll be eager to sign. Am I right in thinking you'll not be heading back where we went afore?'

'I would think not, but do not let me keep you from your work.'

'No, sir. Thankee, sir,' the cooper said, reaching for his hammer and a length of iron.

A positive start, Oliver thought, as the two officers emerged into the bright sunlight.

Glancing back across the water, Algiceras Bay glittered under the Mediterranean sun. Sharing the anchorage were ships, cutters, schooners, sloops and brigs bearing various flags. The bay offered a sheltered haven from the turbulent currents of the Strait of Gibraltar through which they all had to pass. Amongst the British vessels in the roadstead was the frigate he had disembarked from only an hour earlier.

'I have no desire to return to *Isle of Lewis*,' Oliver said. 'I have had more than my fill of it, in more ways than one. Your suggestion of a clean lodging house appeals to me. What would you recommend?

'I have a room at the Rosia Bay Inn. The landlord once served as cook aboard a second rate. His anecdotes are quite entertaining, though I fear they stretch the truth a little. However, the food is good.'

'Then his tales will be a pleasant change from the wearisome stories I have been listening to this past week. But first I must collect my orders.'

The building occupied by the Royal Navy's representative on The Rock was a white colonial mansion whose furniture reflected a strong Spanish influence. The *décor* was certainly that of a fine house rather than a naval establishment but, as it was a location to which foreign diplomats were invited, the cost was deemed justifiable. With the Spanish border only a few hundred yards walking distance away, it was far more expedient to purchase such items made by Iberian craftsmen than to fill the holds of supply ships with heavy furniture made from English oak. Cargo space was too valuable, especially in times of war. Despite the warmth of the sun outside, the corridors and receptions rooms within the stone building were cool.

The meeting with the current senior naval officer in Gibraltar was a necessary formality that was quickly attended to, the waiting time being longer than the appointment itself.

'Your sealed orders, Captain,' the Admiral said, handing Oliver an envelope impressed with the familiar waxed seal depicting an anchor and twisted cable. It was that same image, carved in stone, that appeared above the entrance to the Admiralty building in Whitehall. Only two weeks earlier he had admired it there, but the time lapse seemed much longer.

'These only arrived yesterday,' the Port Admiral said. 'Bad weather on the Bay of Biscay dismasted the ship conveying the dispatches from London. You are indeed fortunate they arrived at all, for I heard that the captain had considered returning to Portsmouth. If that had happened, you could have been sitting here twiddling your thumbs for weeks.'

'Indeed.'

Shuffling through a pile of papers, the Admiral took off his wig and scratched his bald head before continuing. 'Your command, Captain Quintrell is His Majesty's Frigate, *Perpetual*. Some months ago, she fell foul of a pair of French corvettes off Minorca.' He shook his head. 'The dispute over that tiny scrap of useless land amazes me. Despite being soundly outnumbered, the frigate managed to limp in here dragging its sails like a swan with a broken wing. An unfortunate and embarrassing sight witnessed, of course, by our Spanish neighbours across the bay.' He sighed wearily. 'I am advised, however, that the wrights have done a remarkable job and the repairs have been fully completed.'

'And her crew?' Oliver enquired.

'Apart from the carpenter and his mates and a handful of marines who remained aboard, all the hands were paid off and most have already signed on other ships. With that in mind, I have taken the liberty of advertising for a crew. I have also given instructions for *Perpetual* to be victualled and watered as soon possible.'

Oliver thanked the Admiral. 'And the magazine?'

'Powder and shot has been ordered and will be delivered aboard once you are off the dock. I understand there is some urgency in your departure.'

The captain nodded. He would know more once the contents of his orders were revealed to him. The Admiral was obviously a busy man who had little time for pleasantries so, with no further questions, Oliver rejoined Mr Parry outside. The whole matter had been dealt with in less than five minutes. The next priority was to visit the naval yard and the frigate awaiting him.

Two days later, a crowd of sailors gathered along the quayside where *Perpetual* was moored. Progress of the disorganized line was slow, as the queue shuffled towards a table where a young midshipman was seated. Dressed in a finely tailored uniform and with face and hands scrubbed to a shine, the junior officer was recording the names in his book, taking note of any special skills and allotting the hands to various stations accordingly. Speaking in the best King's English, Midshipman Smith instructed each man where to sign or make his mark.

Standing a short distance away, Mr Hazzlewood, the recently promoted lieutenant, observed the proceedings. By comparison, his uniform was relatively old, of a poorer cut and ill-fitting, suggesting it had been handed down or purchased second-hand.

Pacing the wharf, Mr Parry cast a critical eye over the waiting men, discharging those who displayed the slightest sign of sickness, also any who looked too frail or unfit to withstand the rigours of a long voyage. Amongst the throng, a few faces were familiar, and occasionally, the first lieutenant would stop and acknowledge a seaman by name, without appearing over-friendly. Of the older men, he dismissed a few, advising them to attend on the following morning, stating that they would only get a berth if younger and fitter men were not available to fill them. *Perpetual* could not accommodate them all.

While some scratched an inky cross in the book others signed their full names forming each letter slowly in neat copperplate scroll. One of the adept writers was a naturally muscled black Jack. His bare shoulders were smooth as polished jet. They glistened, as if doused in whale oil. The indelible marks of punishment, however, criss-crossed his back – the pink keloid scars accentuated by the dampness of his skin.

'Mr Hazzlewood, bring that man to me, if you please.'

'Aye aye, sir.'

'Come along, you,' Mr Hazzlewood called, beckoning the sailor back from the table. 'The lieutenant wants a word.'

Mr Parry lifted his gaze to the man who, in bare feet, stood over six feet tall. 'Your name, Mister?'

'Ekundayo. But the men call me Eku.'

'Do you write more than your name, Eku?'

'Yes, sir.'

'And why do you choose to sail with us?'

'To leave this place,' he replied.

'Have you sailed on a navy ship before?'

'Yes, sir. Many times afore.'

'But you have no slops or dunnage.'

'They were stolen last night when I was sleeping. But I have these,' he said, opening his palms. 'That's all I need.'

Having stepped up onto the weather deck, Captain Quintrell was observing the proceedings from the ship's rail. He considered that the average size and general state of health of the sailors in the line was typical of any ship's muster, but when he looked at the black seaman, his recent conversation on the *Isle of Lewis* sprang to mind. Captain Slater had argued that even in poor health, through ill-treatment or malnutrition, Africans were fitter and stronger than white men of similar age and weight. It was an argument he had to agree with. A healthy black tar was worth two or three of any feeble-fisted pale-faced English sailor. It was an interesting fact and from experience he had found it to be true.

'Mr H, take this man to the purser,' Mr Parry said. 'See he is supplied with shoes and clothes and show him where the mess is.'

The sailor knuckled his brow.

'I trust you realize this is not mere generosity on the part of the Navy Board. The cost of the slops will be deducted from your wages, so I suggest you don't allow anyone to steal them this time. However, if you work hard and obey the rules, you will be well treated, I can assure you.'

The Negro nodded and followed the newly appointed lieutenant onto the frigate's deck.

With the only tall man removed from the crowd, the remaining sea of heads was of a similar height but displayed varying thatches ranging from blonde to brown, black to ginger, even peppery white. Some were bald but most had a mop of unkempt hair which was likely running with lice and in need of shearing. Some pates were hidden under knitted or felted hats but a plaited queue, dangling from the back of man's neck, was an indelible mark of his profession. Most stood around five and a half feet in stature, a few were taller, a few smaller, but hidden within the mob was a figure almost a foot shorter than the average. Clasping a rolled blanket under one arm, he shuffled towards the table with the others.

When he reached the head of the line, Midshipman Smith looked up. 'I am afraid we are not signing boys,' he advised eloquently.

'I ain't no boy,' was the bold reply. 'I'm fourteen. Besides, him over there said I could sail on his ship.'

'*Him*?' Mr Smith repeated emphatically. 'Firstly, young man, I would advise you that it is rude to point. And secondly, if it is Captain Quintrell to whom you are referring, you most certainly do not refer to the captain as *him*.'

'But that's *him* what knows me.'

'Does he now?' Mr Smith said, his right eyebrow raised. 'And where would he know you from?'

'From that Admiralty place in London.'

The Honourable Biggleswade-Smythe could not resist a smile. 'Am I to believe that you first became acquainted with Captain Quintrell at the Admiralty? Is that correct?'

'Sort of,' the boy said. 'But if you don't believe me, ask him. He'll tell you.'

Ignoring the last remark, the midshipman continued. 'Fourteen years of age, you say. Have you sailed before?'

'Yes, can't you tell from the slops I'm wearing?' I sailed from London on the *Isle of Lewis*. Same ship the captain come to Gibraltar on.'

'And, no doubt, you both dined together whilst on board.'

'Don't be daft.'

'I'll have less of your cheek, young man, or you'll not be sailing with us.'

'It's God's truth. The captain over there told me where to find his ship, and I found it and here I am.'

Midshipman Smith scratched his head in disbelief. 'What is your name?'

'Thomas Wainwright.'

'Can you write, Master Wainwright?'

'Of course I can write. And read too. I ain't dumb.'

'Hey – stow it!' Mr Hazzlewood growled, having just returned from the ship. At the same time, Mr Parry strode up to the table.

'What is happening here, Mr Smith? Why has the line come to a stop?'

'No problem, Mr Parry,' the midshipman said. 'Put your mark here, lad.'

'But I told you I could sign.'

'Then sign, for goodness sake, and be done with it. Next!'

Chapter 6

Mess Mates

Three days later, His Majesty's frigate, *Perpetual* weighed anchor from the roadstead in Gibraltar Bay and headed towards the Atlantic Ocean. From the coast of North Africa to that of southern Spain, the azure sea shimmered under the cool November sun. Though the Strait of Gibraltar concealed currents, which swept around the rocky promontory making it a perilous and deceptive stretch of water to navigate, it didn't deter the porpoises for whom it provided a permanent playground.

Oliver was not sorry to be leaving The Rock which was overrun by bands of vicious Barbary Apes. Their screechings and penchant for thieving was not only a constant reminder of their claim to residency, but of the proximity of the pirates of the nearby Barbary coast. He did not envy the small population of this far-flung British territory, residing on a tiny pocket of land almost completely encircled by water and frequently shrouded in a miasmic cloud of foul-smelling air.

'Take her out, Mr Parry, if you please. Set a course for Madeira. Let us show a clean pair of heels to the Dons of Cadiz.'

'Aye aye, Captain.'

With bare feet balancing on the foot-ropes, sails ungasketted, and canvas cradled in arms ready to loose, the topmen awaited the call to make sail. On deck the landsmen, idlers and waisters stood poised one hand on a line, sheet or brace, ready to ease or haul according to the call.

The fore and main courses clattered down noisily and the yards creaked as they were braced around but, once filled, the grey canvas submitted to the wind in silence. Aloft, the sailors toiled in unison without a word being spoken, and with the helm over, the frigate heeled like a stalk of ripe barley in the face of a steady breeze. *Perpetual* was under way.

'Madeira it is, sir,' Mr Parry confirmed.

Madeira. What memories that destination conjured up in Oliver's mind. It was about a year since he had visited Susanna. A long year of waiting, half of it without occupation. He considered how many times his thoughts had returned to the island. Too many times. For him, thinking of her was an escape from reality, a mental and physical self-indulgence, a retreat from the humdrum, but mostly a closely guarded refuge that no one but he could enter. At last he was returning in person and soon he would be with her again, albeit only for a short time. His one concern was that the ship carrying his letter had arrived safely. He wondered what her reaction had been on receiving the news. Positive, he hoped.

Then he questioned his presumptions. Was it possible she no longer resided on the island? Perhaps she was living in England or Portugal. Perhaps she had married again. She had served more than a respectable time as a widow and was a handsome, eligible woman, nay – in his eyes she was beautiful. What man would not think so? Casting the negative thoughts from his mind, he trusted she would be as pleased to see him as he to see her. The heaviness in his groin confirmed his own feelings.

As Oliver Quintrell headed forward, the men coiling lines moved aside and showed their obedience. A few hesitated, as if about to speak but thought better of it. The only word, 'Capt'n,' was mumbled by a few.

Oliver regarded each leathered face, remembering some, not as names, but as hands on the various vessels he had commanded. Some were easy to place, like the man with half a face discharged from the Haslar Hospital and foisted onto his previous crew by the Clerk of the Cheque in Portsmouth. And the man with the badly burnt torso, who when fully dressed displayed no sign of injury. Mr Parry had spoken up on behalf of both these men and, although he had been disinclined to accept them, he had conceded to his first lieutenant's request and neither seamen had let him down.

Smithers, a topman curled his lip showing a pair of crooked black teeth, the only ones in his head. He was a sailor, liked by few, who disparaged everything and everybody, yet he was as surefooted as a tailless ape and as agile in the rigging as any Captain of the Top could wish for.

When the bell in the belfry announced the dog watch, the starboard crew climbed down to the mess. Being the first night at sea, table mates had not been chosen though the cooper had already selected his seat and was particular as to the sailors who joined him.

After being spurned by one group who swore they'd choke if they had to share a table with a Chinaman, a Lascar or an African, Ekundayo wandered down the mess looking for a place to eat.

'Hey, you there,' Bungs yelled. 'You can sit yer body 'ere, if you ain't got bugs.'

The sailor nodded, slid along the sea chest opposite the cooper, but said nothing.

'You can talk, can't you?'

The Negro nodded.

'What's your name, then?'

'Eku,' the sailor replied.

'Eku. I never heard that one before. But you'll sit here with us, because I need to hear a few new yarns. I get tired of the same old stories day after day.'

John Muffin sitting in the corner didn't respond. That suited Bungs, who accepted him as one of his mess mates, not for the sake of new knowledge but, for the fact that, throughout the last cruise, he always ate his meals in silence and, even after finishing, said nothing at all. Muffin's choice of seat was against the ship's hull where he rested his head against the timber. Having sailed together before, Bungs knew that for the greater part of every mealtime he usually appeared to be sleeping.

'Hey, kid,' the cooper bellowed, grabbing the elbow of the lad passing the table. 'What are you doing on one of His Majesty's ships?'

The boy struggled to release his arm.

'Ain't you got a tongue in your head either?'

'I can talk,' Tommy argued.

'Well, I expects a straight answer when I asks a question. And none of your lip or I'll give you a taste of this.'

'Stow it, Bungs,' Muffin said quietly. 'Leave the lad alone.'

Bungs unclenched his fist and thumped it on the table. 'He's all right,' he said, indicating for Eku to slide along the bench and for the boy to sit next to him. 'I know why you're here. You're like all the other powder monkeys – you're looking for a quick passage to the hereafter.' Bungs laughed. 'Ain't that right? What say you, Eku?'

'I ain't saying nothing, Mister. I just listening. I learn quick.'

'Aye, well, so long as you don't get too clever for your boots.'

58

'The nigger ain't got no boots,' Muffin said, smiling. 'Didn't you see him on the dock when we came aboard?'

'Then we ain't got nowt to worry about, have we?'

Ekundayo shook his head.

Getting no argument, Bungs turned his attention back to the boy. 'So tell me, lad, what's a youngster like you doing on here.'

'I ain't a youngster. I'm fourteen, and I've been put to work with the gunner in the magazine.'

'Well, I can tell you, you'll not get much conversation from him. Deaf as a post he is. Same as all gun captains. It's the firing that sends 'em deaf. Mark my words, if we sees any action, you'll be running the deck with cartridges under your shirt like the other powder monkeys.'

'I don't care what I do. I can run and I learn quick too.'

'Aye, but you're no thicker than a streak of whitewash,' Muffin said. 'I doubt you're strong enough to lift a cartridge.'

'I'm stronger than I look, and I can work hard. I've been working since I was eight years old and I'm used to getting mucky. Me ma says, I got a decent brain between me ears and if I don't use it, it'll get rusty. She also said you only have to show me a chore once and I'll pick it up in quick sticks.'

Bungs leaned back and laughed. 'Listen to him. Now he's wound up, we ain't going to stop him.'

'Me ma always said, that if you don't ask, you never learn. That's what me ma said.'

'Well, you've got a flapping tongue in your gob, that's for sure, but don't forget your ma ain't here to hold your hand or wipe your arse for you.'

'I'll be right,' Tommy said, rolling back his sleeve and holding out his square plate for the knuckle bone which was dropped onto it. Bungs leaned across the table, grabbed the boy's arm and examined the long black scars running down his left forearm.

'What's this then? Looks to me like you've been a powder monkey before. Be wary lad, I don't take kindly to liars.'

Tommy looked puzzled. 'I told you, I don't know what a powder monkey is and I ain't never been one before.'

'Perhaps you should ask your ma, she might know.'

'Stow it Bungs, don't make fun of the lad,' Muffin mumbled.

After taking a closer look, Bungs released the lad's arm. 'So how did you get them marks? What did you do afore you came here?'

Tommy didn't answer.

'I reckon you was a sweep. That would account for the soot fixed under your skin.' Bungs laughed. 'And with that mop of hair, you'd have made a fine brush. I can just imagine you sliding up and down them great chimneys easy as a greased piston rod. Am I right?'

'I weren't no sweep,' Tommy said, 'but I worked hard.'

'Aye, and you'll work hard and long on this ship. But with all your cheek, I'll bet, you'll be kissing the gunner's daughter before the week is out.'

Tommy looked blank.

'Don't scare the lad,' Muffin said.

'Won't do him no harm. I'm just learning him a thing or two.'

'Oh, yes, I can imagine the kinds of things you'll learn him. Probably scare the living daylights out of him.'

Bungs' eyes widened. 'Don't scare easily, do you lad?'

Tommy hesitated and Bungs was quick to sense some apprehension.

'Afraid of falling overboard and drowning, are you?'

'Sea don't worry me,' Tommy answered boldly. 'I can swim.'

Bungs smirked. 'So, we've a got us a mermaid amongst us, have we? Flowing golden locks and swims like a fish. You ain't got a tail have you?' he said, leaning over to peer under the table. 'Well, I can tell you right now, swimming's not much good when the ship founders in the middle of the ocean. Best to drown quick smart, that's what I think.'

Tommy ignored him. He was more interested in ripping the last sinews from the knuckle-bone and sucking the marrow from the middle.

But Bungs wasn't done. 'I can tell you, if you float around for long enough, bobbing like a piece of cork, the sharks'll get you for sure. Bite your legs clean off.'

'Don't scare me,' the boy said.

'What about the millers that comes in the night, then?' Bungs added, with a sneer.

Tommy frowned. 'What's millers?'

'Rats, lad,' Muffin explained. 'Fat rats. That's what millers is.'

Tommy sucked the grease from his fingers then rubbed his sleeve across his mouth.

'Aye. They crawl over you in the night and chew your ears, or nip your nose, or feast on the fleshy bits you like to play with down your breeches. I'd keep me blanket tight under me chin, if I was you,' Bungs hissed.

'I'm not afraid of rats.'

'Me neither,' said the cooper, changing his tone. 'Quite partial to a bowl of fresh pink baby ones. Stew up nicely, they do, with an onion and a lump of butter. Beats salt pork any day.'

Tommy looked at the other men to see if their mess mate was joking. It was obvious he wasn't.

'So, tell old Bungs, what is it that scares you, lad? Most folk have something they're afeared of. Is it spiders? How about them that's as big as your hand with long hairy legs? Or bats – ready to latch onto your neck and suck the life-blood out of you? Or what about snakes – slithery blighters, full five fathoms long and thick as the foremast?'

Unperturbed, the boy shook his head.

'Must be something. What about ghosts then, or sea monsters?' The cooper's eyes sparkled. 'The ones with tentacles that slide over the rail, suck onto the deck and pull the ship down to Davey Jones' locker.'

'I'd like to see that,' Tommy said, grinning to the cooper's goading.

'Tell him about the Flying Dutchman,' John Muffin added. 'That used to scare the daylights out of me!'

'Later maybe. You're a Nancy, Muffinman. This lad here is made of stronger stuff, aren't you lad?'

Tommy nodded. 'My ma said, there's no point worrying about stuff that scares you – so I don't.'

'I might like to meet that ma of yours one day. What's her name?'

'Eliza Wainwright,' Tommy announced proudly.

'So tell me, young Wainwright, where did you get them powder burns from, if you've not served on a gun before.'

'Leave the lad.'

'I weren't talking to you, Muffinman.'

'Well, I were talking to you, Tinkerman.'

'So how come you're so talkative these days. Never used to say boo to a goose on the last cruise. Put your rags out to wash this week, have you?'

Muffin leaned forward on his elbows. 'Well, one thing's for sure. *You* haven't changed, Bungs. Still the miserable old fart, you always was.'

'That's it!' said Bungs, rising up from the chest and pushing the swinging table in Muffin's direction, but his mate was ready to fend it off.

'Watch out, Bungs, bosun's mate's listening!' The timely warning came from the next table.

'Why should I care?' Bungs said, flopping back onto the sea chest he'd been sitting on. 'I've been round long enough and served on more ships than they've ever seen. It's about time they learned to show a bit of respect.' He turned back to the lad. 'Not that I get any from the likes of this scum down here. But don't you worry, young Tom, if you stick with me, I'll look after you and you'll have nothing to worry about while you're on this ship.' The cooper grabbed his plate and wooden tankard and slid from the table.

'What are you looking at?' he demanded of the West Indian who hadn't taken his eyes off him throughout the conversation.

'You're a funny man,' Eku said, flashing a smile which revealed two decks of perfect teeth.

Bungs swung around and was about to reply when the sound of the ship's bell chimed from the belfry on deck.

John Muffin laughed and patted the black seaman on the shoulder. 'You'll fit in nicely,' he said. 'Bungs' bark is far worse than his bite, but he needs someone to bark at.' Then turning to Tommy, he offered some advice. 'Don't ever take him seriously, lad, and you'll be fine, I promise you.'

Once the last of the midshipmen arrived, having made an embarrassed apology and shuffled around to find a place to stand in the captain's cabin, Oliver was able to address all his officers, including most of the warrant officers.

'Gentlemen, let me formally welcome you aboard *Perpetual*. I have already spoken with Mr Parry and our sailing master, Mr Greenleaf, informing them of our ultimate destination. I am sure you are all eager to learn that fact.'

Almost everyone in the cabin nodded.

'You will have noted that our hold is filled to the deck-beams with supplies – sufficient to last us for a nine-month voyage. I can now advise you that after a brief watering stop in Madeira, we sail for the west coast of South America. Once we have navigated the Horn, we will head north to Peru. Hopefully, from the Cape, our only stop will be to replenish wood and water.'

After considering the mixed expressions on his officers' faces, Oliver continued. 'I can see those of you with an appetite for action appear disappointed. Perhaps you are under the impression that we are sailing beyond the reach of French ships. Heed my words – do not allow this preconception to make you complacent. The French will happily take the war into the Pacific to court the favours of the Crown of Spain. And do not forget that we will be crossing the sea-lanes of well-guarded Spanish treasure ships.'

The young midshipmen's eyes widened.

'As such, the dangers we face come from several sources – pirates, privateers, the French, and even the Spanish who exhibit an extremely patriarchal and proprietorial responsibility over their South American viceroyalties and, in particular, over the royal treasury in Buenos Aires.'

The captain continued. 'For those of you who have not sailed with me before, let me advise you that I have doubled the Horn many times. It lies in a fickle stretch of water that deserves respect but, as our passage will be in the months of the southern summer, I anticipate no major problems with snow or ice.'

Mr Hazzlewood and Mr Smith exchanged knowing glances.

'Our mission, Gentlemen, is to locate a ship of the line – *Compendium*, Captain Crabthorne. She is a 28-gun frigate, and on board is the new British Ambassador to Peru. *Compendium* sailed from Portsmouth several months ago, during the peace, and should have returned to England by now. However, she has not been sighted and there has been no word of her from ships returning from either Rio de Janeiro or Valparaiso.'

'Is she an ageing vessel?'

Oliver smiled. 'Most British frigates, including *Perpetual*, are relatively old but they are also reliable and fast – hence the reason so many are still at sea, and, I should add, more than any other class.'

'But if she was lost around the Horn, no one would know.'

'That is true, Mr H, but with no word of wreckage, we must assume she is still afloat.'

'Perhaps she's been taken by the French as a prize,' the sailing master said.

'Believe me, French pride would not permit them to keep such information secret for very long. Gentlemen, my orders are to locate *Compendium*, to provide assistance if she requires it, then to escort her to Peru in order that Captain Crabthorne can complete his mission. If she has been taken by enemy forces, then we are to make every effort to retrieve both vessel and crew. However, if no trace is found of either *Compendium* or her captain, we can only assume she has met will misfortune. We must then satisfy ourselves that there are no survivors. After that, our ultimate destination is Callao.'

Several of the junior officers were eager to ask questions. For most it was to be their first time around the Horn. For several the first time across the Equator.

'I thought the Spanish galleons were legends from the past.'

'You can be assured, gentlemen, that the treasure ships and the valuable cargoes they carry are real. South America, and Peru in particular, is the greatest source of silver in the world. And with only a few minor exceptions, the southern part of the Americas is also the greatest source of the world's gold. I am sure you have heard of *El Dorado*, the mythical man covered in gold dust.'

A few of the young officers nodded.

'The natives of the region have their own names for the precious metals, based on their colour, I assume. They refer to gold as the *sweat of the sun* and silver as the *tears of the moon*. Rather poetic, would you not agree? And from the vast stores of wealth held in the fortified strongholds of the viceroyalties, great quantities are regularly transferred to Spain. Perhaps not in the ungainly galleons of old, but in seaworthy ships possibly disguised as traders. The Admiralty believes that at least three or four major shipments of gold and silver bullion are consigned across the Atlantic every year.'

'But apart from the precious metals, what is Britain's interest in South America?'

'A good question, young man. The answer is both commercial and political. I am sure you are all familiar with the triangular trade, the route taken by the slaving ships. They sail from the major ports of England, to the coast of Africa, and from there to the West Indies, before returning to England. What you may not be aware of is that more slaves have been traded to South America than have been consigned to the Caribbean. While most have gone to Brazil, it is thought likely that 300,000 or more have been delivered to Peru on the west coast, mainly to work in the silver mines.'

The captain set his gaze on his junior officers. 'In my opinion, this is a triangle with four sides. An economic and geometric conundrum which you can discuss at length with the sailing master.'

He continued. 'Are you also aware that sixty per cent of Britain's trade is based on imports of sugar, tobacco and rum? While these commodities come mainly from the plantations in the Caribbean, South America is a growing source of these commodities, a fact Britain is not ignorant of. I suggest, to improve your minds, you extend your reading beyond the *Seaman's Almanac* and *Naval Gazette*.

'For the interim, however, I can advise that our immediate destination is Madeira, and thence Rio de Janeiro.'

Mr Hazzlewood asked a question that was on the tip of several tongues. 'Will the men be allowed ashore when we reach Brazil, Captain?'

'That decision I will make when we anchor in Guanabara Bay.'

Casting his mind back to the incident that occurred when he last visited Rio, he preferred that no one went ashore. But he knew the hands would be weary after their transatlantic crossing, and stepping ashore would provide an opportunity for them to work off their pent-up emotions before facing the challenges awaiting them at Cape Horn. Despite his earlier observation about that passage, Oliver was fully aware that even in summer it could prove slow, arduous and oft times deadly.

'Wherever we make landfall, I warn you now that should any man from your division return later than the specified time, the letter R will be placed against his name and he will be treated as a deserter under the Articles of War. You all know the penalty that offence carries. And the Articles apply equally to every one of you assembled here.' He paused studying the faces directed at him, noting the varying ages and the variety of expressions they held. 'I trust we will have a safe voyage and succeed in our mission.'

As the men streamed into the mess, it was quickly abuzz with the sound of muffled voices and clatter of wooden tankards.

'Eh, you, catfish face,' Bungs bellowed, pushing a man out of the way as he plonked his plate on the table and attempted to sit down next to the cooper. 'Find yourself another stall,' he bellowed, 'because you ain't feeding your face here!'

The man looked bemused, held his ground and rubbed his whiskers.

'Didn't you hear what I said,' Bungs barked. 'Go sit with the other warrants. You're not my mess mate and you're not sitting here at my table.'

'I don't see your name carved on it,' the man said, shrugging his shoulders. 'Looks like this is a spare place. Just thought I'd be sociable.'

Bungs shoved his own plate aside and raised himself till he stood a full six inches taller than the other man.

'Suit yourself,' the seaman said, turning away. 'I'll go find them what's got a civil tongue in their head.'

'Calm down, Bungs,' Muffin called quietly. 'He don't mean no harm. Just wants a chin-wag. You said yourself you wanted to hear some new yarns. Beside he's been aboard a lot longer than us. He's the chippie who sailed into Gibraltar with her. Him and his mates have been working on her while she was in the yard. Besides, he ain't done you no harm, has he? You've only been on board a couple of days. How do you know what he's like, if you don't give him chance to natter?'

'I don't care how long he's been aboard. He gets right up my nose. And you,' he yelled, pointing his blackened forefinger at the man seated against the hull, 'can keep your tuppence worth to yourself, if you value your teeth!'

Tommy fixed his eyes on the table and waited till the cooper was eating, before turning to John Muffin who had already relaxed against the hull with his eyes closed. 'What's he done to get Bungs all in a lather?' Tommy whispered.

Muffin thought for a moment. 'I think it because that fellow is the ship's carpenter.'

Tommy looked at him blankly. 'So, what's wrong with that?'

Muffin spat the lump of pork he was chewing into the palm of his hand, looked at it, fingered it, then stuck it back in his mouth and swallowed. 'I know what your problem is,' he said, looking straight at Bungs. 'He reminds you of Percy Sparrow. He even talks like Chips did.'

Bungs didn't reply.

Tommy waited for Bungs to explode, but he said nothing.

'So where's this Percy Sparrow now?' Tommy asked.

'Fiddler's Green.'

'Where's that – somewhere in London?'

Muffin huffed. 'You've got a lot to learn, lad. That's Davy Jones Locker at the bottom of the sea. Have you heard of that?'

Tommy nodded.

'You'd never believe it, by the way Bungs used to speak to him, but the pair was the best of mates. Bungs always used the same tone like he did just now. Argued all the time, the pair did, and Bungs always had to get the last word in. But Chips would just smile, or make a joke of it and ignore him.' He sighed deeply. 'But I never seen a man more broke up than Bungs was when Percy Sparrow died. But that's what you get all the time at sea – some make it home and some don't.'

'Aye,' a voice called. 'But it's different if you get killed in action, or if the ship goes down. No one can help that. But what happened to Sparrow was enough to turn anyone's stomach.'

'You lot trying to put me off eating?' Smithers complained from the next table.

'It don't seem to be stopping your jaw from flapping or your teeth from chewing,' Muffin said.

'Well I pity Smithers,' Bungs quipped, 'he's only got two left. You want me to chew your meat for you?' he yelled, throwing his bone across the mess at the topman.

Smithers ducked.

'Watch out, Bungs. Midshipman aft!'

Eku winked at Tommy, as the chatter died and the pair gnawed on their hard-tack in silence.

At night, the mess, where the men both ate and slept, was as black as pitch. The only light was shed from a single swaying lantern above the companionway at the far end of the deck. The familiar sounds, which the men ignored, were those of the ship – the creaks and groans of timber under stress, the constant thuds that reverberated back from the bow as it pounded into the waves, the rhythmic roll of something loose on the deck above, the bark of a man's cough, the rasp of continual scratchings by men irritated by bites, or the gnawing of rats' teeth scraping up the spilled meat-juices that flavoured the fibre caulking between the deck boards.

The high-pitched scream which broke the apparent silence could have come from a girl being ravished. It woke almost every man on the starboard watch, even the topmen who were exhausted after battling a stiff breeze to put reefs in the topgallants and topsails during their own watch after being called aloft to help the larboard watch for several hours.

'Who was that,' the bosun's mate yelled, unable to see through the darkness and the corrugated profile of men's bodies swaying in hammocks above the level of the tables. 'Speak up,' he yelled, raising his starter. 'Don't wait till I come in and get you.'

'Shut your yap,' a voice barked.

'Damn your eyes, we're trying to sleep.'

Swaying in his hammock, within two inches of Tommy Wainwright, Bungs' eardrum was still ringing from the scream. He'd never heard anything like it, not even when a man lost a leg or an arm. Often they said nothing.

With his right arm extended, the cooper parried the windmill of blows Tommy was swinging. Twisting in his hammock and reaching across, he found the boy's mouth and clamped his left palm firmly across it. 'Shut up, lad,' he hissed, into his ear. 'Stay still, else I'll thump you and then you'll have cause to scream.'

Beneath the weight of Bungs' arm, Tommy relaxed and from the sound and pattern of his breathing the cooper judged his nightmare was finished and he'd returned to normal sleep.

With no one answering his call, and because of the impossibility of moving between the hammocks to find the culprit, the bosun's mate aborted his search, allowing the men to return to their interrupted dreams. The seagoing sound of silence returned, punctuated only by snores and sniffles and the odd outburst of unintelligible gobble-de-gook mumbled in a sailor's sleep.

Tommy Wainwright had woken to his own scream but only momentarily. Just long enough to sense something pressing on his chest and finding it hard to breathe. He opened his eyes to the intense blackness but quickly closed them again. For a few seconds, a sense of panic overwhelmed him, before he drifted back into the recurrent nightmare he had woken from.

Chapter 7

The Nightmare

It began with an insidious low rumble which was followed by an eerie silence. Then the earth shook sideways collapsing the rock behind him and pelting him with grit and stones. Choking dust filled his eyes, throat, and ears. Though his mouth was open, he could neither scream nor shout, nor hardly even breathe. And when, after what seems like an age, he found a voice and called out for help – no one came.

The tunnel Tommy was working in was only a few yards long and not much broader than his shoulders. Lying flat on his belly on the wooden carriage, his body was only a few inches above the ground, and the roof of solid rock only a few inches above his head. As he had done every day for the past year, he'd pushed himself up the slight incline often scraping the skin from his knees on the hard ground and bruising his elbows on the hand-hewn rock walls. Today, an arm's length in front of him was the seam – a solid wall of coal. In his right hand was a charge of gunpowder. In his left – a wooden prod. His job was to place the charge in the hole made in the rock, then ram it in. When the task was completed, he'd call out to the man on the line who'd pull the cart carrying him, down the slight incline and back to the pit's main shaft.

But for now, he couldn't move. His left arm was jammed against the side. He dropped the charge from his right hand and swivelled his elbow so he could touch his face. After rubbing dust and grit from his eyes, he blinked away the tears, but whether his eyes were closed or open made not the slightest difference in the intense blackness. Reaching forward, he touched the rock face and felt the hole drilled in it ready to receive the charge, but when he ran his hand along the roof above his head, he discovered it was no longer smooth but criss-crossed with cracks broad enough for him to slide his hand into. He feared the roof was in danger of collapsing and if that happened it would bury him alive.

Five years ago, when he had first started work, the pit had claimed the life of his father. And his grandfather before that. Was he to be the next?

And what of his sister, Annie? She was two years younger than him and working in a different tunnel off the same shaft. Crawling on hands and knees, with a rope fastened around her middle, her job, like that of many of the youngsters, was to drag baskets of slack, or coal up to the surface. Where was she when the roof caved in? He wondered.

Saved by stout hob-nailed boots, Tommy's feet were jammed between fallen rocks and, despite trying to propel the trolley forward or back, not even the slightest movement was possible. He could neither move nor turn around. The only sound in his six-foot stone coffin, besides his crackled breathing, was the *drip*, *drip* of water splashing on his head. Turning his face, he manoeuvred each drop to run from his hair, across his temple, then down his cheek to the corner of his lips. Sticking out his tongue, he caught the drops one by one. The water was fresh, not salty like his sweat and, after spitting out a mouthful of muddy dust, he dampened his lips, but it did little to avert his raging thirst.

As time passed, the thought of sleep alarmed him – the fear of another rock fall, the fear of the air he was breathing running out, the fear of never waking up. Or worse still – of waking again and again to the inky blackness and the aggravating sound of the water tapping on his head. In trying to shake the liquid from his ear, he hit his head hard on the rock above. Recoiling from the pain, his chin banged on the edge of the wooden cart snapping his tongue between his teeth. He tasted blood and sobbed, and cursed at the same time, using all the foul words he had learned from the miners. Then he thought of his mother, and cried again. He screamed. He yelled. He cried out constantly till his mouth was dry. But no one heard and no one came to dig him out.

The hours dragged by till eventually he stopped calling, deciding he was wasting his breath. His left arm pained him and his eyes were sore from the grit he had rubbed into them. But his tears no longer flowed. His thoughts drifted to his mother, then back to his sister and the pain gnawed at his heart. He tried hard to imagine some other place far away from the pit and the blackened hovels of the coalmining village he lived in. Of the old men on the street corners, bent over, coughing up blood blackened with coal dust. *Would that be him one day?*

Then he thought of the sea, though he had never seen it, and tried to imagine how vast it must be. The only water he knew was the duck pond and the part of the river that had been diverted to turn the water-wheel that powered the pit. He'd seen a barge on a canal, but never a ship. Yet he remembered a whale's tooth that had been passed down in the family. Scratched on it was a drawing of a sailing ship. When he thought of that ship, he promised himself that if he was pulled out alive, he'd find one and sail far away from the pits and the grimy dirt that could bury a man far quicker than the local grave-digger could dig a hole in the ground.

Drifting in and out of sleep for what seemed like days, Tommy woke suddenly to a different sound. An irregular *click, click, click*. Was it more water dripping from another part of the roof? The sound seemed very distant. Then he recognized the *ping* of a pick striking solid rock, of shovels scratching at rubble, and felt a frightening shower of small rocks tumbling down on him.

Then came the voice of the gruffest angel he could ever imagine. 'Is anyone alive in there?'

'Help me! Get me out! It's me, Tommy. I'm stuck. Please, get me out.'

'Stop hollering, boy! Save your breath. We're working as quick as we can. Don't worry, we'll have you out of there in no time.'

It seemed like an eternity before the men were able to break through to the narrow tunnel and move the rocks lodged around his legs. Then, with stones still dropping onto him, Tommy felt the wooden wheels of the cart turn. Very slowly it was hauled down the incline, jerking and creaking as it bumped over the rubble along the way. Keeping his head low, Tommy stretched his right arm out in front of him and tucked his left arm close to his body holding it to him like a broken wing.

He didn't dare open his eyes until he felt rough hands on him brushing the dust from his hair, and heard voices. Opening his eyes, he saw light – the glow from a lantern a few yards away. He gazed at it and wanted to rise to his knees, but neither his legs nor arms responded.

'You'll be fit as a fiddle in no time,' one of the miners said. 'And you'll soon forget all about this. It weren't a bad fall. You were lucky. Don't worry, you get used to it after a few times.'

'Where's Annie, my sister?' Tommy asked. 'Is she all right?'

There was no answer.

Desperate for air, Tommy felt he couldn't breathe and feared he was being buried in the tunnel again. Throwing his arms about was all he could do to escape the nightmare gripping him.

'Stop fighting me, lad, or I'll thump you,' Bungs hissed again. 'It's watch time. And if you're not in the magazine in a couple of minutes, the gunner will be after you with a rope's end. Get out and I'll help you fold your hammock, but just this once. Now move!'

'Out or down!' was the cry from the bosun's mate. Those not wanting to get up were beaten out of their beds.

Rubbing the sleep from his eyes, Tommy swung down to the deck, slipped into his shoes, grabbed his hammock from Bungs and joined the line of men heading up to the weather deck.

Later that day, as tiredness began to sweep over him, he fought to keep the torment out of his mind. Above his head, the square sails billowed like bed sheets on a wash-day line. From the bow, the sea creamed along the beam and left a sweeping wake stretching almost to the horizon. Lifting his chin and opening his mouth wide, Tommy gulped the air like a fish gulps water. It was an involuntary habit he had developed of late. But he had kept to the promise he had made to himself and the further the ship sailed, the greater the distance he put between himself and those awful memories.

His sister had died that day in the mine. She was only twelve-years old. His elder brother, George had been lucky and survived the rock fall. At fourteen-years-of-age, skinny as a rake, and standing only six inches over four feet tall, Tommy Wainwright had been the ideal size to work in the narrow tunnels deep below ground. But his mind had been made up and he swore he would never ever go down the pit again.

'I'm going to London,' he had told his mother. 'I'm going to find me a ship and I'm going to fight the French and stop them coming to England.'

Eliza Wainwright understood and never once tried to stop him. As a girl, she had toiled down the pit herself, and had hated every minute of it. Five years ago she had lost her husband and now her daughter, and with no bodies to bury, there was not even a plot in the graveyard where she could mourn over them.

'Go,' she had said to her son, 'and if needs be, never come back here. Go with my blessing.'

'One day I'll come back,' Tommy had cried. 'I promise. And I'll make you proud.'

The following week, with his meagre possessions rolled up in a blanket, Tommy Wainwright had set off for London. His mother had given him five shillings which was the total sum of her savings. He had slept under the stars at night and when it rained found shelter wherever he could. He'd worn a hole in the sole of his shoe and got a ride part of the way on the back of a cart. But whatever happened along the journey nothing would deter him from the promise he'd made to himself.

Yet the fear he had felt when trapped underground was a memory that would continue to haunt him.

Chapter 8

Madeira

It was December already and a chilled mist hung in the deep valleys which ran down the worn volcanic slopes of the island of Madeira. Under the breath of a dying breeze, *Perpetual* had slid into Funchal road late the previous evening dropping anchor a distance from an array of ships – a sloop-of-war, a frigate, a big East Indiaman with a convoy of smaller vessels nearby, and an assortment of American, Portuguese and Baltic traders.

The following morning, the air was as still as an empty grave. There was little movement on the roadstead save for the local fishermen and ships' boats conveying sailors and water barrels to the beach.

Since before dawn, there had been an unusual eagerness amongst *Perpetual*'s crew to swab the decks, polish the brasses, neatly furl the flaccid sails and present the ship in an orderly fashion. All hands hoped that the sooner the daily chores were completed, the sooner they would be allowed ashore. Madeira was a favoured port for sailors of all nationalities – not for its scenic delights (although there were a few who spent time wandering the attractive bays and inlets with charcoal and paper), nor for its sweet wines, though many took advantage of a little too much of the smooth red liquor. The main attraction for the majority of sailors was the island's ladies. The local beauties were good-looking, swarthy-skinned, willing, and as tantalizingly sweet and juicy on the tongue as the island's luscious grapes. Madeira's *bordellos* were filled with both.

Although the group of islands belonged to Portugal, a cacophony of languages could be heard on the streets and alleys running off them. If they chose to, most vendors spoke English, but for hungry young sailors, the primeval sign language, used to purchase sexual favours, was universally understood.

Apart from refilling the barrels of water emptied since leaving Gibraltar, the other reason to stop at the Atlantic archipelago, was to collect firewood – sufficient supplies for several weeks of sailing. With forests covering the lower hillsides, there was a readily available source that was reasonably accessible. By contrast, Gibraltar had long since been stripped of its trees and all timber, including that for firewood, had to be purchased from Spain or shipped from England. It was, therefore an expensive commodity in the tiny British territory, and limited in supply.

From before dawn, lighters had appeared from the port to bob around every ship in the roadstead, plying their trade. To add to the *mêlée*, boats were swung out from the ships and lowered to convey men and barrels ashore and return later loaded with fresh produce, water and wood.

Armed with axes, saws, and ropes, *Perpetual*'s woodcutters were always first away. They had a long pull ahead of them and a hard day's work once they located a suitable stand of timber. Though forests blanketed the lower slopes, the woods near the town had long since been stripped bare, and though young saplings sprouted from the ground, it was dry dead timber the woodcutters wanted. Green wood was easier to chop, but it choked the galley stove, burned with less heat, and upset cook. And if cook was not happy, every man on board suffered the consequences.

Will all the necessary demands being attended to, Oliver was content to leave the ship in the hands of his first officer. He had full confidence in Simon Parry's ability. Should he be cut down in action, or succumb to some deadly disease, he felt Mr Parry would easily step into his shoes and assume command. His lieutenant had ability, confidence and grace, and the required experience and knowledge to captain a frigate, having once commanded his own. In Oliver's opinion, it was a travesty that a court martial had stripped him of his rank. But nothing he said or did could change that.

Sometimes, when he observed his lieutenant gazing out to sea, he wondered what thoughts were foremost in his mind. Was he jealous, envious or angry at his situation? If so, he didn't display such feelings. In Oliver's eyes, he deserved a command, yet Simon Parry accepted his step down as only a true officer in His Majesty's service should. Perhaps he was a religious man, though he had never seen him reading a Bible or heard him quoting the scriptures. Perhaps he was consumed by conscience and accepted his position as the penance he must pay for the loss of one of His Majesty's ships and the lives of many of its crew. But surely, as the war with France escalated, the Admiralty could not continue to ignore his ability and hopefully, in the fullness of time, he would receive the promotion he deserved. Oliver hoped that would be the case.

Jumping from the boat onto the beach, Oliver's feet sank into the wet grey sand composed of small pebbles, broken shells, pumice and volcanic dust.

'Return the boat at two o'clock,' he said.

'Aye aye, Capt'n,' Froyle replied, as the boat crew prepared to pull back to *Perpetual*.

'Not a moment later,' the Captain reiterated. His order was directed towards the four midshipmen, and the gunner and his mate, who were going ashore to sample the town and all it offered. The men acknowledged the order, grinned at each other and then argued over which way to head along the main thoroughfare.

Oliver's destination was predetermined.

Twenty yards from the beach, in a small paved square and under the shelter of some palm trees, a group of donkeys idled, flicking their ears and tails, while the owner sat cross-legged on the ground chewing a wad of tobacco. Seeing the captain approaching, he immediately jumped up, spat out the bolus of leaves and offered his services. After the captain indicated his intended journey up the side of the mountain, the cost of hire was agreed on and the business transacted.

Having chosen the largest of the animals, whose ears more resembled those of a mule than a donkey, Oliver swung his leg over the mount and made himself as comfortable as possible on the coloured blanket. With his legs dangling loosely on either side, he considered his appearance was less than dignified for a British Naval officer, however, no one on the street seemed to notice or even give him a second look.

It had been a year since he had visited the island and seen Susanna and unlike his previous visit, when he had arrived with apprehensions, this time he could hardly control his desires. In the privacy of his cot, she had slept beside him every night since

Perpetual had left Portsmouth and before that too. He still pictured her the way he had left her on his previous cruise, her long black hair cast casually over her left shoulder, her breasts heaving within the embroidered bodice and her long legs, hidden beneath the folds of her petticoats – so smooth and so willing to wrap around him.

A sudden thought that she may not be at the house, or may be entertaining visitors concerned him. He could steal only a few hours of liberty and could not extend his stay on the island any longer than it took to supply the vessel. His orders were to proceed south with all haste but if, and only if, there was no wind, he would be unable to sail and could possibly return.

Later he would reprimand himself for succumbing to temptation. Yet far from the ship, straddling a donkey, breathing the fragrant air of this verdant isle, he had only one thought in mind.

His mount stumbled, as it climbed the steep mountain path, throwing him forwards over its neck. At least, if he was dislodged, he would not have far to fall. But with no saddle or stirrups his seat was precarious and he had little control over the beast. However, like every other four-legged transport servicing the port and its surrounding hills, the donkey was familiar with the various routes up the mountainside and once pointed in the right direction proceeded without encouragement.

Despite that, the climb seemed arduously slow. At every bend in the zigzag track, Oliver hoped to see the path leading to Susanna's house, but every time it failed to materialize. For some reason, the climb felt steeper and was far more hazardous this year than he remembered from the past. Perhaps, it was because the recent rains had clawed gouges, the size of horses' hooves, down the centre of the track. One wrong step and the animal's leg could be broken. To add to the hazard, the track skirted an almost perpendicular cliff that dropped into a deep gorge. If a rider fell into such a ravine, he would never be found. Oliver's only consolation was that if the donkey stumbled on the track and he survived, he could travel the rest of the way on foot. This would allow him time to appreciate the panoramic views over Funchal Bay.

Then he considered his level of fitness and the additional layer of fat he had added to his waistline. It was not so much the lack of exercise he had suffered from on land, but a daily routine that had revolved around eating. The delicacies served with morning and afternoon teas had appeared obligatory, then there were the sumptuous meals for luncheon and dinner, plus the house parties. Over the indolent months of summer and most of autumn, his exercise had been limited to morning walks on the beach and, despite his wife's disapproval, to his regular swim in the sea near the mouth of the Bembridge River.

'How can you divest yourself of your clothing on a public beach and plunge into the foul silt of the estuary,' she had said, airing her disgust.

'You mean, in the presence of a flock of screeching gulls and terns?' he had questioned cynically. 'It is invigorating to the skin and allows me to taste the salt.'

'Surely,' she would reply, 'your months at sea provide you with enough salty air to last a lifetime, though you seem in need of being continually reminded of it. Why not stand at the end of the garden for an hour? I can assure you, you will receive all the sea breezes you need. Indeed, the wind near blows me off my feet every time I step outside the door. And besides, we have salt on the table and every exotic spice in the larder to satisfy your strange cravings? But to come home with your garments coated in sand is inexcusable. The laundress tells me there was an inch of beach sand in the tub the last time she washed your stockings and breeches.'

Oliver frowned. 'I hardly think the maid should be reporting on the condition of my laundry.'

'Well, I felt it was my duty to ask her.'

'Ah,' he replied sagely.

'Pray tell me, what does that sigh signify?'

'That I shall have Casson wash my clothing in future in the manner he does on the ship. Most satisfactorily, I might add. And he never mentions the colour or composition of the washing water. But you can be assured, my dear, I do not intend to refrain from my morning exercise.'

From thoughts of his wife's demands, his mind jumped to Casson, the sailor who was his steward at sea, and acted as his manservant when ashore. Already, he had repositioned the buttons on his jackets a full inch to accommodate the captain's expanding girth and apologized that they would go no further without spoiling the appearance of the uniform. Oliver hoped that by the time they reached Rio de Janeiro, as a consequence of eating naval fare, he would be requesting the buttons be returned to their original positions.

At last, he arrived at the pathway leading to the house. Sliding from the donkey, he secured the reins to a vine. The courtyard, like the air around it, was still. Leaves and flowers still glistened with moisture from the morning mist. A long-legged dog lying under a bush dragged itself up, stretched and barked twice. It looked at the visitor, barked again then lay down on a deep litter of fallen magenta flowers.'

'Pancho!' a voice called from within the house. '*Onde estás?*'

The dog lifted one ear but did not get up.

Oliver inhaled deeply. She was here.

As if answering his silent prayer, Susanna stepped out to the courtyard.

'Pancho!' she called again. Then she saw the naval officer standing beneath the stone archway.

'Oliver, is that really you?'

Neither moved as they gazed at each other.

'Are you alone?' she asked.

'I am. Are you?'

Susanna nodded. 'Are you able to stay?'

'Only for an hour or two.'

She smiled, rocked her head to one side tossing her hair from her shoulder.

Unbuckling his belt, he removed his sword and walked across the courtyard towards her.

'Come,' she said, taking his hand and leading him inside.

'Did you receive my letter?'

'Yes, over a week ago but, as the days passed, I feared you had not been able to stop. Every day I gazed out over the harbour and imagined each new arrival to be your ship. But this morning with the mist and lack of wind, I did not expect to see you.'

'Stealth and surprise can sometimes reap success in battle.'

'I can assure you, Captain,' she said, with a cheeky grin, 'you will have no difficulty in taking this prize.'

Her arms slid inside his jacket and his arms enfolded her.

'How sweet the air is here,' he said, burying his face in her hair. 'And how much I need you.'

The release of emotion pent up within him was hard to control. One day a year was not nearly enough. A week. A month, maybe. Why had he not visited her while waiting for his commission? There had been ample time to make the journey.

'I could have sailed here and spent time with you,' he whispered in her ear, as they lay together.

'And risked missing your commission?' she teased. 'It may have gone to someone else.'

But for the present moment, Oliver didn't care. He wasn't thinking about commissions or sailing orders, Admiralty boardrooms or ceremonial swords. They had no place in his mind. There was only one thing he longed for and it was here in his arms on the slopes of Madeira.

On returning to the town, the owner of the donkeys was nowhere to be seen – probably enjoying an afternoon *siesta*, Oliver thought, so, after tying the animal to a post, he returned to the beach. Checking his watch, he had arrived fifteen minutes early and was pleased to see the cutter being rowed across the water some half-a-mile away.

Further along the beach, not fifty yards away, another naval jollyboat was preparing to push off.

'A moment,' the officer called to his coxswain. Stepping out of the boat, he strode over to where Oliver was waiting. 'Captain Quintrell, *Elusive*, is it not?'

Oliver had not recognized his old friend, William Liversedge who he had served with aboard *Capricorn*, a 74-gun ship of the line when they were both midshipmen.'

'*Perpetual* – frigate,' Oliver said, indicating to the bay. 'Good day to you, William.'

'My apologies, I am not up to date with the latest commissions. But tell me, Oliver, are you sailing this evening or can I press you to dine with me? I have venison roasting on a spit as we speak. You and your senior officers would be most welcome to join me aboard *Imperishable*. Shall we say, eight o'clock?'

'I would be delighted,' Oliver said. 'I fear nothing will be sailing if this damned calm persists.'

Stepping aboard the frigate, *Imperishable*, anchored in Funchal road, Oliver was immediately aware the vessel was not carrying cargo but transporting troops who were taking up most of the deck space. After briefly reminiscing with his old friend on the quarterdeck, the two captains went below and joined the ship's senior officers who were already seated around the table.

'I am bound for Jamaica with troops,' Captain Liversedge said. 'They are urgently required because the danger of slave uprisings is increasing. Presently there are upheavals on several islands in the Caribbean, and it is said that on the island of Hispaniola the slaves are gaining the upper hand. To make matters worse, France and Spain are arguing over ownership and now the Americans are showing an interest. Britain had already sent thousands of men and landed supplies and guns, but I fear the French have sent more. The stories coming from there are horrific. It is hard to believe the reports of some of the atrocities committed – by all sides.'

'Is is wise then to be sailing alone, unsupported by a naval escort? French territories are some of the first islands you must pass when you enter the Caribbean. You could be sailing into a hornet's nest?'

'It was thought not politic to send a convoy – in other words, the defence of England against Napoleon's proposed invasion force was seen as a more expedient means of deploying Royal Navy vessels, rather than sending a convoy to protect a shipload of troops. Soldiers, like marines, are not highly regarded by the navy. And men are dispensable. However, were I transporting gold or specie then I believe I may have been treated in a more favourable light.'

'With spies in the English Channel, perhaps their judgment has some merit. Easier for a single ship to slip out unannounced than a convey that always attracts an unnecessary fanfare.'

'Perhaps,' Captain Liversedge said, sounding unconvinced. 'But, Gentlemen let us not dwell on such mundane matters. I trust you will enjoy your meal. The meat could not be fresher. It was shot and hung only four days ago. Not exactly the King's deer, but a fine stag from one of the nearby islands.'

'Might I enquire if this is your first commission since the war resumed?' Oliver asked.

'Indeed, it is not. I sailed to Buenos Aires in March when the Treaty broke. On that occasion I returned a contingent of marines to England. The Admiralty feared our presence on the River Plate could prove to be an embarrassment if Spain became inveigled into France's devious schemes.'

'A possibility that is still very real,' Oliver remarked.

'Indeed. It will only be a matter of time. But I heard that you sailed to South America last year. Is that correct?'

Oliver looked up from his meal and nodded. 'I touched on some of the ports but only briefly.'

Aware that there were matters about that voyage which his captain was not at liberty to discuss, Mr Parry interrupted the conversation. 'Sir, did you happen to encounter *Compendium*, Captain Crabthorne, anywhere on the South American coast?'

'Captain Boris Crabthorne? Certainly, and I was able to supply him with sails and cordage for which he was most appreciative. You must understand, he had just managed to limp back into Buenos Aires and his ship was in an utterly forlorn state.'

Oliver exchanged raised eyebrows with his first lieutenant.

'An unlikely place to have encountered French action being so far south,' Mr Hazzlewood observed.

'It was not the French or the Spanish that debilitated him, it was the weather.' He glanced around the table. 'Captain Crabthorne said that for almost a month he had attempted to round the Horn but, in the end, with his men exhausted and with his ship suffering more acutely from the conditions than his crew, he had had no alternative but to return to Buenos Aires.'

Oliver allowed Captain Liversedge to continue without interrupting.

'We had only entered the Plate estuary on the previous day. Our crossing had been totally without incident and having suffered no delays in the Doldrums, we had only used half our estimated supplies and the ship was sound. Therefore, I was able to assist him with sails, cordage, spars and even extra slops.'

'For his return to England?'

Captain Liversedge shook his head. 'No.'

'Are you saying that Captain Crabthorne intended to continue with his mission? Surely, with the worst of the southern winter still upon him, was that wise? It sounds a rather questionable decision to make.'

William Liversedge agreed. 'Foolhardy even. Those were exactly the thoughts that ran through my head. I was concerned he would not make it, but he was intent on trying. He said his mission was of vital importance and he would not return to England without completing it.'

'But to sit out the winter and wait for warmer weather would have been more prudent.'

'I agree, but Captain Crabthorne was insistent. Though not without apprehension, he was fully aware of the possible consequences. The weather was likely to be harsher than that which he had battled during the previous weeks. His crew was unhappy and when *Compendium* arrived in Buenos Aires a few of his men ran. Surprisingly though, the majority stood by him and swore they would sail anywhere with him. A good captain and a fine sailor, I am led to believe.'

'And a good gardener,' one of the midshipmen whispered.

The disdainful look from Captain Liversedge brought a rosy flush to the young man's cheeks.

'Before we weighed from the River Plate, Captain Crabthorne shared a meal with me. He spoke nothing of the purpose of his mission, save for saying he was sailing under Admiralty orders and was intent on carrying them out – whatever the cost.'

Oliver questioned that statement. 'But to chance losing one's ship and one's men to save a few weeks, achieves nothing.' He paused for a moment considering the ramifications for his own mission. 'Have you heard anything more of him since you left Buenos Aires?'

'No, and, like you, I can only trust in God that he succeeded in making the passage.'

'Amen, to that,' Oliver added, lifting his glass and swilling the dark liquor around before swallowing the contents.

Captain Liversedge did the same. 'However, perhaps I should add that he did not intend to sail around Cape Horn.'

'What? Surely he was not intent on sailing east and circumnavigating the world? Such a voyage would take a year.'

'No, he planned to sail through the Magellan Strait and navigate the maze of channels at the western end to reach the Pacific that way.'

Oliver shook his head. 'But what of charts? That passage is poorly mapped. My father ran a packet from Boston, and I sailed with him when I was a boy. He doubled the Horn many times and attempted that passage on two occasions, but each time had to abort it and turn south.'

Captain Quintrell had everyone's full attention. 'Though the island of Tierra del Fuego shelters those waterways from the worst of the Antarctic gales, it fails to stop the cold air infiltrating every stream and channel and, at times, freezing them solid. Then there are the enormous rivers of solid ice which flow down from the snowfields high in the mountains and deposit great chunks of ice into the waterways creating unseen hazards. Furthermore, some of the channels narrow unexpectedly providing insufficient width or depth of water to turn a ship around in. I fear that his decision may have not been a wise one.'

Captain Liversedge shrugged his shoulders. 'Crabthorne was confident he could get through. He had engaged two pilots, including a native Indian who convinced him he could guide him all the way to the Pacific.'

'I commend his confidence,' Oliver said.

The company around the table murmured their responses.

'If you should encounter *Compendium* on your travels, kindly convey my regards to Captain Crabthorne and compliment him on his tenacity.'

'I will, indeed,' Oliver said.

From the quarterdeck, Captain Quintrell watched as *Imperishable* weighed. The wind, which had blown in with the first rays of sunlight, was light, but sufficient to fill the topsails and carry Captain Liversedge and his consignment of red-coated soldiers from the roadstead. As soon as the watering was complete, he intended to follow.

But for Oliver, the news he had received the previous evening had left him with mixed feelings. *Compendium* had left Buenos Aires and had headed south intent on making the west coast of South America by one means or another. Yet that news was over six months old and the details of Captain Liversedge's encounter in the River Plate would have been recorded in his log and presented to the Admiralty on his return to England. So if the Admiralty was aware of the situation, why was he not advised of it when he departed Portsmouth? Oliver considered his mission – to sail half way around the world to locate another ship. But it was not for him to question the reason. He was under Admiralty orders.

Chapter 9

Imperishable

It was three days since they had sailed from Madeira, *Imperishable* having sailed two days earlier. *Perpetual's* delayed departure was due to a prevailing calm that had descended on the island group and had been disinclined to move away. Because of the lack of wind, Oliver had had little choice but to endure a frustrating wait. Having allowed the crew periods of time ashore, he had ventured up the mountain for a second time but had only stayed for an hour. But what a glorious hour that had been.

He had watched her undress. Stood behind her at the French window as she faced the bay, naked and beguiling. He had run his tongue down her back and she had tossed her hair over him. Turning her about, he had carried her to the bed, laid her down and admired her curves. The swell of the ocean was never as smooth or inviting as she. Climbing on the bed beside her, she had rolled onto him and straddled him, gently pinning his hands with hers. Swaying like the incoming tide, the waves of ecstasy had broken far quicker than he had wished and, like a piece of flotsam, they had carried him to some shore far from reality.

Lying there, allowing Susanna to rub her body against his, he had listened to the noise of the cicadas clicking their legs, and watched a moth entangle itself in a spider's web signalling its demise. But the sound of an infant crying and dull thud of a gun salute, fired from the battlements on the harbour, had returned him to reality and reminded him where his duty lay.

'Will I see you on your return?' she asked.

'I think not.'

'Will you write?'

'When I can.'

That was all she had asked. Nothing more. And he could offer nothing more. Slipping a loose gown around her shoulders, she had watched while he dressed, helped smooth his stockings over his calves, brought his shoes and slid them onto his feet.

When he left, there had been no words of good-bye or even *au revoir* just an embrace which neither had wanted to break. Then began the bumpy donkey-ride down the hill to the town knowing it may be another year before he was able to return, and with no guarantee of that.

Four days out from Madeira and it was time to exercise the guns. The shortcomings of the *Isle of Lewis*'s gun crews were still fresh in Oliver's mind. He did not intend to tolerate a similar situation on *Perpetual*. But as yet, he was not cognizant of his own men's capabilities or the capacity of his junior officers who would be in charge of the divisions. While the sailors appeared responsive to orders and most of the gun crews were experienced in action, it was the distribution of sailors within the divisions that had led to the disappointing performance on Captain Slater's ship.

Addressing his concern to his senior officers, midshipmen and warrant officers, Oliver stipulated his requirements.

'I want a list of every man on every gun crew for each division. I wish to know if they are idlers, topmen, able or ordinary seamen and their experience on a gun. I need to be advised if they are fully fit or carrying old injuries. I want a list of what other tasks they are employed at and where their capabilities best lie. Where a topman is a member of a gun crew, I want him relocated to a position from which he can quickly be replaced by an idler. I realize this will not be possible in all cases. However, when we go into action, I do not want a single gun growing cold if hands are called aloft to make sail. Is that understood?'

The answer came in chorus, 'Aye, sir.'

That afternoon, smoke belched from the waist of the frigate as the starboard guns fired repeatedly and the westerly wind insisted on returning the smoke to the crews through the gun ports. After an hour of constant effort, the men were exhausted. Arms and legs ached, hands wept from blisters, eyes were reddened, tears flowed, throats rasped, lungs heaved and ears rang continually.

Several crew changes had been made to the disgruntlement of a few gun captains but, overall, Captain Quintrell's demands had been met and most divisions could now operate according to his stipulations. But, should the necessity arise for all 32-guns to be fired simultaneously, then every man on board, irrespective of his role, would be called on.

Oliver was satisfied with the men's performance and was about to order they be stood down, when a call came from the masthead look-out.

'Deck there!'

'What do you see,' Mr Parry replied.

'Sail. Three points off the starboard bow.'

'Distance and bearing?'

'Perhaps six miles. Heading south.'

'Can you see her colours?'

'British, I think. But there's a lot of smoke. Looks like she's on fire.'

'Do you recognize her?'

'Could be the frigate that sailed from Madeira afore we did.'

Captain Liversedge and his consignment of red-coats, Oliver thought. 'All hands to make sail. Helmsman, three points to starboard.'

Then another call from the masthead. 'There's another ship. It was hidden by the smoke. A French corvette, I think.'

The sound of distant gunfire carried on the westerly breeze.

'She's taking fire, Captain.'

Oliver had heard it. 'Mr Tully, get up and report. I pray we are not too late to assist.'

As the sand ran through the half-hour glass, there was little the captain could do but watch and wait. With *Perpetual* already cleared for action and the guns still warm, he was ready.

'At least she's not hauled her colours,' Mr Parry said, trying to be positive. 'But, as we are downwind, I doubt Captain Liversedge has heard our guns while he's been under fire.'

The news from aloft was not unexpected. 'The corvette is closing again.'

'Then let us pray the marines aboard her are capable of assisting on the guns and the troops she is transporting are able to fend off boarders.' He turned to his first officer. 'I think we should let them know we are here and announce our intentions. I want every second gun on the starboard side fired. I am certain they will hear us from this distance.'

As *Perpetual* sailed closer, even through the haze of smoke, the damage to the British ship was clearly evident. Her mizzen mast had gone while the sails she still carried had been shredded with canister and chain. With no forward momentum, she was dead in the water.'

'The Frenchy's reducing sail, looks like he is preparing to board.'

'He thinks he has a juicy prize, but he is mistaken,' Oliver mused. 'Let us take him before he has the opportunity to board. No doubt, he will expect us to sail alongside and we will not disappoint, but first we sail under his bow, rake the deck and fire for the foremast. Then, take her around and clew up the mainsails. Slow us down sufficiently to provide time to deliver two or three broadsides when we sail by. Double shot the guns and fire for her hull. I do not want to see shot skimming over the French deck and inflicting any more damage on the British ship. Then, when we are clear of her, hard over the helm, rake the stern and take down her rigging.'

Approaching through the smoke and from the lee side of *Imperishable*, the French corvette proceeded undeterred. Had he not seen or heard Perpetual? Or was he confident he could take the troop carrier and then transfer his attentions to the other British frigate? While he pondered those questions, the appearance on deck of over a hundred red-coats helped turn the table.

The shots aimed from *Perpetual*'s forward guns were accurate, cutting the shrouds on the enemy's fore-channel. When the mainstay was severed, the corvette's foremast crashed to the deck. Finding his vessel immobilized and sandwiched between two British hulls, the French captain hauled down his flag.

'There were two corvettes when the action began,' Captain Liversedge explained later. 'They came up on me at first light. I put up a fight and tried to out-manoeuvre them, but one took out my rudder and put a hole in my hull just on the waterline. Though the carpenter managed to plug it, I thought I was done for. The French must have come to the same conclusion for after exchanging signals one headed away, leaving the other to board and claim *Imperishable* as his prize. I kept him at bay as long as possible, but I was coming close to hauling my flag. That was when we heard your guns. And what a welcome sound that was.'

'But what of your men?' Oliver asked, having seen the wounded still waiting to be taken below. 'It would appear from the type of shot they were firing, they were aiming for heavy casualties.'

'The men in the rigging and on the rails didn't stand a chance. The deck ran red.' Captain Liversedge sighed. 'In this sorry state, it will be impossible for me to proceed to Jamaica, in fact, I fear I shall be going nowhere.'

'William,' Oliver said quietly to his old friend. 'When Captain Crabthorne was in desperate need, you supplied him with sails and spars, now we shall do the same for you. While this weather persists, my men will assist you to make repairs to your steering and mizzen and bend new sails. Once in the wake of the trade winds they will carry you to the West Indies.'

'And what of your prize, Captain Quintrell – the corvette? That also is in a sorry state. And you have now acquired a mob of French prisoners to contend with.'

'The same will apply regarding repairs to her foremast and rigging. Hopefully she will have her own spares on board and a willing carpenter to lend a hand. My men will ensure she is sufficiently seaworthy to make the passage with you to Jamaica. Regarding prisoners, I cannot volunteer to take any aboard *Perpetual*, as they could jeopardize my mission. It will therefore be necessary to confine them below deck in their own ship.' Oliver turned to the officer recently passed for lieutenant.

'Mr Hazzlewood, the prize and the prisoners will be your responsibility. You will deliver them both to Kingston. Your first command, I believe. Congratulations.'

'Thank you, Captain.'

'Mr Smith will accompany you, while Mr Parry will request two dozen volunteers to sail with you. The biggest danger you could face is meeting a French convoy when you enter the Caribbean. However, the main French and Spanish involvement is around the Mona Strait and Santo Domingo. It would be wise to sail well to the south.'

'Thank you, Oliver,' William Liversedge said. 'Without your timely arrival, I would have been facing a court martial in Jamaica – if not meeting my Maker.'

'God willing, we shall meet next year in Portsmouth,' Oliver said. 'But let us first attend to the repairs.' For the present, he prayed the smooth conditions would continue in order that the work could be completed as swiftly as possible.

For three days, repair work went ahead, the three ships heaving and pitching and slowly drifting in a south-easterly direction on the broad Atlantic swell. Crews from *Imperishable* and *Perpetual*, plus a handful of French carpenters and their mates, worked around the clock snatching only brief interludes of sleep. The bosuns of all three ships attended to the rigging, while the sailmakers and any sailor who could palm a needle sat around the decks sewing new sails or patching old ones. Not until the sails were bent was a little time allowed for rest.

By now, the group of vessels had drifted into tropical waters. The air was warm and the sweet breath of the south-east trade wind was blowing in their faces. Though a long way from Jamaica, that wind was guaranteed to carry Captain Liversedge and Quintrell's prize over a sweeping arc of ocean to the islands of the West Indies.

Before the distance lengthened between the frigate heading south-west, and the two vessels sailing east-north-east, there was a round of huzzahs from *Perpetual*'s crew for Lieutenant Hazzlewood. As commander of the prize vessel, he stood proud on the quarterdeck of the French corvette now sailing under the union jack.

'All sail, Mr Parry,' Oliver said. 'We have been delayed long enough.'

Chapter 10

Sailing South

'Enter!' Oliver called, in response to the tapping on his cabin door.

Midshipman Tully lowered his head and entered.

'What is it, Mr Tully?'

'Excuse me, Capt'n, but the men have been talking and asked me to pass a request to you.'

Any occasion for the men getting together to discuss an issue sufficiently important to require it to be presented to the captain, was always a worry.

'Come in and close the door,' he said, snapping the lid closed on his ink well. 'Tell me, what is the men's concern?'

'Nothing serious, sir, only I mentioned it to Mr Parry first and he said it was not a decision he could make and said I should put the question to you.'

'Well, out with it man.'

'Mr Greenleaf said that two days from now, if the wind holds, we'll reach zero degrees latitude. The Equator.'

Oliver shifted in his chair. He had expected the question several days ago.

'The men want to know if they can perform the usual crossing-the-line rituals.'

'Rituals!' Oliver hissed, cynically. 'No. Categorically no. They may not!'

'But sir, it's just a bit of fun. And it's important to the foremast lads. It's tradition.'

'Damn tradition!' Oliver yelled. 'Did you not sail with me on my last command? Do you not remember the outcome of that foolish tradition?'

'Aye, sir. How could I forget it? Me and Mr Wood berthed together. But most of *Perpetual*'s crew didn't sail with us a year ago, so they just hold by tradition.' He paused. 'I can assure you,

Captain, this time it'll be different, I'll make sure it is and I'll make sure no one goes near the water.'

'Mr Tully, you served many years before the mast before you entered the service as a midshipman, am I right.'

'Yes, sir.'

'Then by now you should know that the day-to-day welfare of the men is the responsibility of the first lieutenant, while the safety of the ship and the success of this mission is a responsibility which sits squarely on my shoulders.'

'I know that, sir.'

'I have crossed the line many times more than most sailors aboard the ship and, like you, I am aware that the crew derive a strange pleasure from subjecting the newest, and usually the youngest hands to this rather ridiculous and sometimes deviant form of irreverent play-acting.'

Oliver leaned back in his chair and considered his outburst especially in front of a junior officer. Despite his prejudicial views on this issue, he had to concede that for some sailors such activities acted as a safety valve through which men released their pent-up emotions. He was also keenly aware that in equatorial latitudes the crew was often hot and tired, and that in these zones when the wind failed and the ship was becalmed for days or even weeks, sailors became bored. At sea, boredom was the flintlock which could spark mischief.

Furthermore, the men were far from home with the uncertainty they may never return to England's shores. And in the present political climate, if and when they did return, what would they find? Their homes burned, their crops destroyed, their wives raped and their children speaking with a French accent?

'Tell the men my answer is, no.'

'Aye, sir,' Mr Tully replied, his voice revealing nothing of his disappointment. Knuckling his forehead in the manner of a common seaman, he turned to leave.

'Pass a message to Mr Parry,' the captain called. 'I wish to speak with him right away.'

'Aye aye, sir.'

Within a matter of moments, Mr Parry was at the cabin door. 'May I enter?'

'Come in Simon. Sit down. I am sure you know what I wish to speak with you about.'

'King Neptune's Court?'

'The very same.'

Skirting the table on which various charts were rolled out, the first lieutenant sat on the seat beneath the gallery window.

'Simon,' Oliver continued, 'I trust you know that I am not entirely without heart, but some memories serve as poignant reminders that prick the conscience and make decisions more difficult to arrive at. While I cannot change the past and the future is in God's hands, I do have some control over the present.'

Mr Parry nodded.

Thinking for a moment, Oliver sighed before he spoke. 'If the present conditions continue for the coming two days, then at noon on the day we reach the Equator, I will grant the men half-a-day's ease. You will order an extra ration of grog to all hands and permit merriment on deck. Song and dance will be tolerated but within reason. That is of course providing there are no adverse changes in wind or weather. But there will be no shaving, no tarring and feathering, no pantomime, or any other form of theatricals. And certainly no dunkings! And if any man disobeys that order, no matter what his rank, let him be keel-hauled and see how such a dunking appeals to him. Do I make myself clear?'

'Perfectly, sir.'

Two days later, as midday approached, all eyes were on the midshipmen as they concluded their morning lesson under the watchful eye of Mr Greenleaf. Word had spread and every sailor on deck was waiting for noon to be called, for the sand glasses to be turned, and for the marine at the belfry to ring the ship's bell eight times.

As soon as the hour was announced the topmen followed each other from the yards, sliding down the stays like pearls spilling from a broken necklace. Within minutes a queue had formed near the scuttlebutt to be served a double ration of grog.

Accompanying the high-pitched peeping of a fife was the whine of a violin and the tapping of shoes jigging to a jolly tune. Most hands, congregating in the waist or on the foredeck quickly forgot the reason for the break in daily routine. Many didn't care, they were just happy to amuse themselves at their leisure. The handful of sailors who had never crossed the Equator before were relieved to hear the Captain's order for it excused them from being subjected to the discomforts of the traditional sea-going initiation. Only a small group, who had never sailed with Captain Quintrell previously, were peeved that their sadistic performance had not been permitted. The old *Elusives* were grateful to take their ease, a few reflecting on the past, but saying nothing.

In the bow, leaning against a mat of coiled lines, Eku and Tommy listened to the music.

'You're lucky, lad,' Eku said. If it weren't for the captain's orders, you might have found yourself kissing a fish, or being sprinkled with the droppings from the manger, or even having to crawl across the deck and kiss Smithers' feet.'

'Is that what happened to you when you crossed the line.'

'Shhh!' Eku said, holding his finger to his lips. 'I ain't crossed the line either. No one but you knows it, and I don't plan to tell anyone else.'

After a brief stop at Recife to take on water and collect fuel for the fire-hearth, *Perpetual* headed south and Oliver revealed his intentions to his officers.

'We have wasted enough time already and will proceed directly to the Horn. I do not intend to venture into Guanabara Bay or the River Plate, as a visit to each port will add another two or three days to our sailing time. The ship now has sufficient drinking water aboard and the purser advises me, we have ample provisions to last more than six months.

'It is time, therefore for you to inform the men of the conditions they can expect as we move into the higher latitudes. Our timing is favourable as mid-summer in the southern hemisphere is upon is. However, do not allow the men to become complacent. Even in summer we can be confronted with ice and snow and blizzard as we sail further south.'

He continued, 'You are at liberty to inform the men that I have chosen to sail west through the Strait of Magellan. This decision is not to avoid the Horn, but to follow the route taken by Captain Crabthorne in the naval frigate, *Compendium*.

'It will not be easy navigating a passage through the myriad of channels as our charts are probably incomplete, but I have discussed this matter with the sailing master and we are confident of success. If any of you young gentlemen have had the privilege of wandering through the sculptured hedgerows of Hampton Court's maze, I can warn you that navigating through this maritime puzzle will not be nearly as simple.'

Glances were exchanged between two of the midshipmen.

'Let me remind you, however, that Ferdinand Magellan made the passage nearly two-hundred years ago, with a crew half-dead from scurvy, during the wrong season of the year, and with only the stars to guide him. In comparison, we have charts, a sound ship, a favourable season, and modern instruments of navigation to assist us. However, no ship can function well without every man performing his duty. All hands must be alert whenever on deck and must report any unusual sights or sounds. If Captain Crabthorne has foundered in these waters, I intend to find him.'

After struggling to round Cape Virgenes, *Perpetual* headed west across the sheltered expanse of water which separated the south coast of South America from the Island of Tierra del Fuego. To the north was the uninviting barren coast of Patagonia sparsely inhabited by brigands, Indians, strange animals and wild horses. To the south the desolate island of fire – named by Magellan himself, for the columns of smoke he saw rising from its precipitous gullies.

The voyage along this early part of the Strait was uneventful, the sailing good, the only noteworthy items were obvious to everyone. The tall kelp which rose from a great depth of sea, formed a tan-coloured forest visible just inches below the surface. Though it swayed easily with the currents, it slowed the ship's forward momentum and could endanger the ship if it became entangled around the rudder. The colonies of seals taking possession of some of the rocky outcrops were also remarkable. Covering almost every square inch of them, the indolent creatures appeared disinterested in the passing ship. The cormorants, however, squawked noisily from small islands not selected by the seals. The dropping of tens of thousands of black-winged birds had transformed the rock from grey to white - the same colour reflected in the snow and ice cloaking the mountains that dominated the scenery ahead of them.

Reduced to reefed topsails and staysails, *Perpetual*'s speed slowed to barely a few knots as the frigate entered the passage cutting through the tail of the Andes – the ancient mountain range stretching the full length of the South American continent that crumbled into the sea at Cape Horn. Within the maze it created, channels extended in all directions presenting the captain with a nautical conundrum. Which was the safest way to go? Some passages were too narrow. Some were blocked with ice. Some led nowhere. Others were too shallow. Some initially appeared inviting but on closer investigation masked underwater hazards waiting to claw the bottom from an unsuspecting ship.

Oliver knew that his transit through the channels would take many days, but insisted *Perpetual* only sail in daylight. Even then, much of the distance would require men on the lead on both port and starboard sides, and another in a boat sailing, or being rowed ahead of them.

Captain Quintrell prayed for light airs, sufficient to carry his ship safely through. A gale of wind could dash the frigate upon the rocks and in that location there would be no passing ships to come to their aid. In any case, it would be unlikely anyone would survive in that region long enough to be rescued.

Chapter 11

The Shipwreck

With no experienced pilot aboard *Perpetual,* navigation was a headache for the sailing master and Captain Quintrell. Referring to the only Admiralty chart available, its shortcomings soon became apparent. Not only was the mapping incomplete but it soon proved to be both inaccurate and misleading. It also lacked details relating to depths, channel widths and the gradient of the slopes sliding into the water.

To gather some information, a boat was lowered and rowed ahead of the frigate, but as the convolutions of the channels and distribution of the hundreds of tributaries could not be seen from water level, observations had to be made and reported from the masthead. Like the fickle winds in the region. The strength, direction and rate of flow of the currents concealed beneath the pocked-pewter surface were also unknown factors. Estimations of the tides bearing in from both the Pacific and Atlantic Oceans could be made from prior knowledge, but the insidious undertow, swept in from the wild seas whipping around Cape Horn, was totally unpredictable.

'Deck there!'

'What do you see?'

'Looks like a mast-head.'

'Where away?'

'Around yon starboard headland. Just coming into view.'

The first lieutenant looked along the deck, 'Mr Tully, you've got good eyes, get up top with a glass. Tell me if it's a naval frigate.'

There was little point in shortening sail, with virtually no discernable wind, the courses were furled and the topsails barely luffing. *Perpetual* was lucky to be making two knots but with the number of rocks and scattered islands littering the channel, the snail's pace was quite acceptable.

'It's a ship all right,' the lookout called, as the frigate swam slowly around the headland. 'Not a frigate. Three masts Square rigged on all three.'

'She must have foundered,' the first lieutenant said.

'Anyone aboard?' Oliver called.

'Looks deserted. Looks like she's been there a while. Sails are in tatters.'

A disturbing picture quickly formed in Oliver's mind. He thought it unlikely a storm could have beaten so fiercely in this location to have shredded a ship's sails. Yet, if its canvas had been torn to shreds in the Southern Ocean, it would have been impossible for it to navigate this distance through the channels. It puzzled him.

'What you do make of it, Simon?'

'A wreck, no doubt. Do want me to order the boat to investigate?'

'No. Recall the boat for the present.'

The captain hailed the masthead again. 'I presume she is showing no colours.'

'No colours,' the masthead confirmed.

He spoke his thoughts aloud to his first lieutenant. 'So we have no idea if this is friend or foe. I feel caution is the best policy in this inhospitable part of the world. Let us show our colours, if you please, Mr Parry.'

'Mr Lazenby, run up the colours.'

'Aye, aye.'

'And all hands on deck,' Oliver requested. 'But quietly does it. And run out the guns on the starboard side.'

'Mr Nightingale, you heard the captain. Quietly now. No pipes. No whistles. No calls.'

A wisp of wind filled the topsails for a moment. They quivered then fell away, but it was sufficient to carry *Perpetual* forward a full ship's length, leaving behind barely a ripple on the slate-grey water.

High above, several black specks dotted the clear blue sky. Resting on the air currents, they appeared lifeless – their size, type and purpose indeterminable.

Condors, Oliver thought. *Scavengers*.

On the gun deck, the crews toiled methodically in the well-practiced routine. The re-shuffle of the gun crews had been achieved without complaint, as it didn't matter if a man worked alongside a mess-mates or a sailor he had never spoken to before. Each man knew his role and though he performed it independently, he was merely a spoke in a well-worn wheel.

'Report, please, Mr Tully. Anything remarkable?'

'I thought I saw some movement on the cap-rail but she looks deserted. There are barrels and swivel guns on deck and her hatches are closed. Strange though, the lines have been loosed from the pin rails and are hanging free. Looks like they've been sheared off.'

Mr Tully was a good man, a bit rough around the edges, had served less than two years as a midshipman, but had logged several years before the mast. Having acted as a bosun's mate, he knew rigging better than the veins on the back of his hand, so neither the Captain nor Mr Parry questioned his opinion.

'Sergeant,' Oliver called. 'I want sharp shooters aloft and ready by the time we have the wreck in full view.'

With the order relayed to the marines, the thumping of boots and the clatter of muskets fractured the silence. 'Quietly, sergeant! And no firing unless we are fired upon.'

With snow covered peaks rising steeply from the channel surrounding them and unknown depths hidden beneath the hull, the frigate drifted slowly around the headland, bringing the wreck into view.

'Mr Parry, I want a shot placed a dozen yards from her bow. Perhaps that will draw a response.'

Two minutes later, amidst a cloud of smoke sliced by a blue and orange flame, a gun resounded and bounded back to the twang of the preventers. *Perpetual* shivered, while on deck all eyes waited for the loud *thwack* as the ball shattered the rock face before spinning off into the water. While a few spontaneous cries of huzzah were uttered from the gun crew, much to the annoyance of the division's officer, there was no response from the ship sitting uncomfortably astride a submerged rock.

'Lower my boat, Mr Parry. I intend to go aboard. I will require my regular crew plus a couple of marines. Kindly issue pistols and cutlasses to every man – and to the other boat also.'

'You have a bad feeling about this?'

Without answering, Oliver sniffed the air. The smell was unmistakable. Sweet. Sour. Putrid. The smell of death.

While the second boat was being swayed out, Casson appeared from below, the captain's sword and pistol in his hands.

'Thank you,' Oliver said.

'Go careful, Capt'n.'

Though he did not answer and showed no response, Oliver Quintrell appreciated his steward's genuine concern. Pushing the pistol beneath his belt, he crossed the deck and stood for a moment waiting till his boat crew had taken their places and the marines were settled in the boat. But, as he descended the ladder, a shot rang out from the crosstrees. The puff of smoke hovering around the head of one of the marines made it easy to identify the culprit who had fired his musket.

'Get that man down here immediately,' Oliver cried, stepping back onto the deck. 'I want to know what he was firing at. I explicitly ordered no shots.'

The youth, afraid of heights and unused to the ratlines, climbed awkwardly. It was more difficult to climb down carrying a rifle than to climb up. The sergeant was waiting impatiently at the gunnel. 'Tell the captain why you discharged your musket,' he ordered.

Shaking so badly, the pimple-faced youth could hardly hold his rifle still.

'Have you never been into the top before?' Oliver asked.

'No, sir.'

'Then a spell in the rigging would be recommended punishment, but that is for your sergeant to determine. Now tell me, did your gun go off accidentally or did you fire at something in particular?'

'I fired, sir. I thought I saw a brown head pop up from behind the rail. Then it disappeared, but when I saw it again, I was afraid that whoever it was might have spotted me, so I fired.'

'Mr Tully, did you see any movement on the wreck?'

Everyone was eager to hear the midshipman's response.

'Aye, Capt'n, plenty of movement. Rats, sir. Lots of rats. Moving along the length of the cap-rail like waves on the far horizon. They're even up on the yards.'

Captain Quintrell was satisfied. 'Heave to. Let go the anchor, Mr Parry. Have the guns secured but keep the men at their stations. Mr Nightingale, be so good as to accompany me in my boat and bring your pencil and paper. Mr Tully you will take charge of the second boat.'

'Will cutlasses still be needed?'

'Yes,' Oliver replied, 'and grappling irons.'

'I doubt you'll find anyone aboard her,' the sailing master said, knowingly.

'I am quite cognizant of that, Mr Greenleaf.'

'Hope there's a chance of refitting her and floating her home.' The chance of prize money was never far from the master's thoughts.

'I shall only be able to ascertain that when I have stepped aboard and determined the whereabouts and welfare of her crew, the damage to her hull and the amount of water she has swallowed. Then, and only then, will I make a decision as to her fate. Let me remind you, sir, I am under Admiralty orders, and capturing prizes is not my priority.'

There was nothing to be gained by raising the sail on either the pinnace or the cutter, as there was insufficient wind to carry the boats and the distance to be rowed was only two cables' lengths. When the boats swam closer, the name carved on the ship's stern came into view. It was a long time since it had benefitted from a coat of paint but it was still legible – *Adelina*.

As soon as the captain's boat bumped alongside the part-submerged hull, grapples were thrown, but before anyone could haul themselves up the side, a rat scurried down the rope and fell into the boat between the men's legs. The infantile squeals and curses from the usually orderly crew raised a slight smile on Quintrell's face. The men of his boat crew, whose faces showed no emotion when faced with a full broadside, displayed the response of a group of women when confronted with a mouse in the parlour.

'For goodness sake, sit still!' Oliver called. 'Once on board, however, you have my full permission to dispose of as many of these creatures as you care to. But don't let them near you. I'll not suffer their lice aboard my ship.'

With the offending rat grabbed by the tail and tossed overboard and the grapples secure, Froyle was the first man to climb aboard. On reaching the rail, he carefully lifted his cutlass and watched as another rat measuring over a foot from head to tail, ran towards him. One slice from his blade cleaved it in two.

'Thought you were a canny blighter, did you?' Froyle yelled, 'Well you're not so lively without your head.'

The spontaneous cheering from the men in the boat was not condoned by the captain.

'Silence,' the coxswain cried, and not another word was uttered. Within minutes, rope ladders were rigged, one forward and the other aft, then both crews clambered to the deck.

Stepping aboard *Adelina*, Oliver was astounded at the amount of damage the rats had done. Marks on the deck lockers indicated where the rodents had gnawed the timber in an attempt to reach the contents. They had also chewed the wooden blocks, cleaning every morsel of fat from them. They had even eaten through some of the greased standing rigging and severed the hempen lines from the pin rails. But more obnoxious than the rodents' smell was the unholy stench exuding from the gratings.

'I warn you,' Oliver repeated. 'Don't let them bite you.'

A sound on the deck, like the click of a heel, alerted everyone. It came from the stout handle of a whip which rolled when the ship lifted slightly on the pulse of the distant Pacific tide. While the tip of the whip had been eaten away, more than a yard of its tail was stuck firmly to the deck by a streak of hard black matter. 'Rhinoceros hide, if I am not mistaken.' The captain commented. 'Mr Nightingale, I would like a sketch, if you please.'

'Take a look here, Captain,' Mr Tully called, pointing to a pile of stripped bones and scraps of cloth which had once clothed one of the crew. It appeared that the hand that had wielded the whip had received its due deserts either from the rats or vultures. Preferring carrion to live prey, and caring little if the meal was human or animal, sharp beaks and talons would have ripped the skin from their victim in a matter of minutes. Following the scavengers, the rats would have waited their chance to pick the remaining meat from the scattered bones.

'I wonder what killed him,' Oliver murmured. 'Disease? Dehydration? Starvation? Cold?'

'And what of the rest of the crew?' Mr Nightingale asked.

'Her boats are gone,' the coxswain called. 'There must have been survivors.'

'Then they were the lucky ones,' Oliver said.

A sudden gust of icy Antarctic wind blasted a broadside causing the wreck to groan with the strangled croak of a dying sea bird.

'You men will remain on deck,' Oliver ordered. 'Mr Nightingale, come with me. Froyle, find a lantern, if you can.'

At the bottom of the after hatchway was the door to a large cabin with stern windows which allowed ample light to spill inside. Until recently, it had obviously been the domain of the ship's master, but now it was empty. The tired furnishing remained but there was nothing of value. No sextant. No logbook. No inventory. No telescope. Not even a compass. And no trace of the captain. Not even his coat. The small cabins adjacent to it were likewise empty, however, a lantern hanging outside still had oil in it and was quickly lit.

'Let us examine her cargo,' Oliver said, heading amidships. Descending to the orlop deck, he discovered the hatch to the hold had been padlocked. An iron bar soon prized the lock from the timber. As the solid cover was removed, the air from the hold escaped in an overpowering whoosh of vile vapours.

'Get back! Don't breathe this foulness.'

'Dear God,' Mr Nightingale cried, 'what is in there?'

Oliver covered his nose with his neckerchief and warily took three steps down the ladder, kicking out at the rats that ran over his shoes. At first glance, as his eyes adjusted to the dim light, it appeared the water which had penetrated the hull was swirling about, but the movement on the surface was a sea of vermin swimming in haphazard circles. These were well-fed rodents grown fat on the cargo chained within the hold of the ship. The scene confronting him was alarming.

'Pass me the lantern,' he ordered.

Holding the ladder with one hand and the lantern in the other, he gazed around knowing his worst fears had been realized.

It was impossible to count the remains. The hundreds of bodies, lying flat, packed tightly into tiers that would have allowed little more movement for the occupants than lifting the head a matter of inches. For those carcases above the water, their African faces were unrecognizable. Not even their blackness was evident. Skulls were white. Teeth were white. Even the sinews and bones not chewed were also white. But the fear and agony they had suffered still registered on their open jaws. Their silent cries were almost audible.

Oliver climbed back to the orlop deck and inhaled deeply, filling his lungs with less-foul air.

'Mr Nightingale, if you have no stomach for this, I will understand, but if you can bear to view this scene, I would appreciate a sketch to support my log. Such desecration of human life cannot be described in words but the picture should be recorded. It will certainly be etched in my memory for as long as I live.'

Tying his neckerchief over his nose and mouth, the young lieutenant descended into the hold lashing out with foot and elbow at the line of rats racing for freedom.

On deck, the sailors made sport of the vermin, slashing at them as they popped up from below, chasing them across the deck, hacking at them repeatedly with their cutlasses leaving a trail of deep gouges in the ship's rails and pools of blood on the deck. Their games ended abruptly when then captain appeared on deck.

'Send a message to the gunner. Tell him I want linstocks, slowmatch and powder.'

No one questioned what for.

'You there, Foss and Froyle, the magazine is half flooded but there is canister and grape-shot on the shelves – about the only thing the rats haven't eaten! Take four men and carry what you can. And the two swivel guns, Mr Tully, kindly have them lowered into the boats. They may come in handy. I'm sure I don't have to remind you to lower them carefully.'

'Anything else to transport, Capt'n?'

'I think not. The stores which aren't below the water have been eaten by the pests, even the spare sails and cordage. Anything made of vegetable fibre has been consumed. The sooner we send this ship and her occupants to the bottom the better.'

By the time the transfer of various items between the wreck and *Perpetual* had been completed, it was growing dark. Mr Nightingale's drawing pad of sketches was handed carefully down into the boat along with a chart box which the captain had found in a cupboard after a more thorough search in the main cabin. The maps it contained of the coast of Chile and Peru were more recent and detailed than those supplied by the British Admiralty, and Oliver was certain they would prove useful as their journey progressed. He considered that the master of the *Adelina*, if he had survived, would have cursed himself for forgetting such an item, when he abandoned his ship.

Finally, with the Captain in the boat, the gunner and one of his mates each draped a long length of slowmatch over the gunnels, one forward and one aft. These led to a generous stream of gunpowder which snaked across the deck and ran down the ladders to the lower decks.

With all the men safely aboard the two boats, Oliver gave the signal. With flames spitting from the sizzling matches, *Perpetual*'s boats pushed clear from the side of the slave ship and pulled for the frigate. Fearing a sudden explosion and bombardment with flying splinters, the men lowered their heads and rowed for their lives. But the captain had indicated to the gunner, when he laid the powder, that he wanted a slow blaze. His aim was to engulf the ship in flames capable of consuming everything above the waterline. As to the sodden hull, he would be satisfied if it broke up, slipped from the rocks and slid to the bottom of the deep channel.

Though questions were put, little was said when Captain Quintrell, his officers and boat crews came aboard and the business of hoisting the boats was quickly attended to. From the rail, Oliver watched the fire take hold. Red tongues licked the dangling ribbons of shredded sails and raced up the tar-soaked shrouds far faster than any sailor could climb.

Voluminous clouds of black smoke vented into the cold colourless sky hiding the masts as they leaned and finally fell, crashing across the burning deck. From the gunnels and taff rail, rats plopped into the water and paddled feverishly for the nearest land.

'You mark my words, this coast will be infested with them before long. They'll multiply like roaches.'

'Shame to burn a prize,' the sailing master commented to the quartermaster, in a voice loud enough to the overheard by Captain Quintrell. 'Do you know what her cargo was?'

Oliver shivered in the chill wind and turned and addressed him. 'Slaves, Mr Greenleaf. Human souls. Hundreds of them. Mark my words, it would have given me great satisfaction to tow her back to Bristol. Not for the prize money, but to present her to the rich merchants in their plush offices, to show them what their fat profits are derived from.'

Heartily sickened, he turned back to his first lieutenant. 'I should say a prayer for them,' he said. 'But it can wait. On Sunday, I will remember them in our service. However, I fear, when the men learn the details of the *Adelina*'s cargo, they will become unsettled. They are already wary of this god-forsaken passage, afeared we will get lost, or become frozen, or wrecked like that ship and her unfortunate cargo. For the moment all they see is their prize-money being scuttled. This will lead to some dissatisfaction.'

'Then let us pray for a breeze to deliver us to the Pacific Ocean and let that sea be as peaceful as its name implies.'

Oliver agreed. 'The sooner we depart this place, the better. Cape Horn may have a violent temper, which it finds hard to control, but at least we know its vices. This passage is deceitful. Contrary. Misleading. Take my word, Simon, on our return from Peru, we will double the Horn, no matter how long it takes us and we will leave this region to the rats and its indomitable natives. How either manages to survive in this hell-hole, I do not know, but they are welcome to it.'

Gazing up to the black specks suspended high in the air, Oliver wondered what was carried in the roiling black smoke swirling skywards. Was it delivering the dead slaves to the condors or carrying the spirits of the departed to their ancestors?

'Pray for that breeze, Mr Parry,' he said, 'a gentle breeze to carry us safely through to the open sea.'

Chapter 12

Ekundayo

'Didn't I warn you?' Smithers boasted, 'cursed it was, that ship. Cursed with the ghosts of them slaves before they snuffed it. See the way that smoke's reeling round and round like a spinning top. I tell you, it's their black souls dancing. I've seen it before in the West Indies. Seen 'em twisting and turning and swaying their hips about like their bones are not joined together. And listen to the spitting and crackling. That's the echo of the whip lashing them that took 'em.'

Most chose to ignore Smithers' rantings, but Tommy shuddered. Behind him, the windlass creaked, as it was turned, hauling the anchor up from the depths of the channel. The staysails rattled when they were run up and the yards creaked as they were braced around. Then slowly, almost imperceptibly at first, *Perpetual* swam forward, turning her face from the wreck and heading back to the relative safety of one of the broader channels.

'But Foss told me they were all dead,' Tommy said. 'Ain't that right?'

'Never can tell with them blacks,' Smithers added. 'There's those among 'em that never die. Ghouls and witchdoctors and such like that come back to haunt you. Just like the Dutchman. Maybe that's his ship – looks like it with its shredded sails and rigging. '

'Shut you mouth, Smithers,' Muffin squawked. 'You'll give the lad more nightmares.'

'Me? Not me,' he claimed, the right side of his face contorting in an evil sneer. 'I'm learning him stuff he needs to know.'

'I don't know no Dutchman, but I ain't afraid of him,' Tommy boasted.

'It ain't a man,' Muffin explained quietly. 'It's a ship. A Dutch ship. A ghost ship. The captain's name was Vanderdecken.'

'So, what happened to him?'

The sailor cast a glance over his shoulder before continuing. 'The truth is, he was battling constant storms. Trying to round the bottom of Africa but his ship couldn't make the passage.'

'Did he sink?'

'No, worse than that, he made a pact with the Devil swearing he's round the Cape if it took him from then until Doomsday. But instead of helping him, the Devil cast a spell on him so his ship had to roam the seas forever from that day on.'

'That ain't scary,' Tommy said.

'It's all in the way the story's told,' Muffin mumbled.

'Telling it ain't nowt,' Bungs said, eager to add something to the tale. 'It's seeing that ghost ship coming out of the blue and steering straight at you afore she disappears. That's enough to curdle your blood. One instant you're gazing at an empty horizon with not a billow of cloud or a sail in sight then, all of a sudden, you blink because you think you're imagining it. But it's there all right – all a-shimmering and a-glowing in the distance, not even sitting on the water but hovering full six foot above it and bearing down on you.'

'You've seen it?' Tommy asked.

'Not personal, but I've heard from them that has, and I don't mind admitting, I'd piss myself if I saw the Dutchman.'

Tommy laughed.

'You might laugh, boy,' Bungs scoffed, 'but why do you think you see a horse-shoe pinned to the foremast. And you're likely to spy one on most ships. It's to ward off evil spirits, like the Dutchman, that's why.'

Muffinman smiled. 'I reckon you'd be scared of your own shadow on a moonlit night, Bungs. In fact, looking at you across a table is enough to send the shivers down anyone's spine, don't you agree, young Tom?'

'I ain't afraid of spooks, especially on the sea.'

Eku said nothing. There were things he had witnessed on the Caribbean islands that were enough to turn any man's legs to jelly.

At breakfast, the next morning, Bungs studied the Negro sitting opposite him, scraping the last of the burgoo from his wooden bowl. 'You didn't look upset that your people got burned up in that ship,' he said.

'They were not my people,' Ekundayo answered.

'But they were black slaves, and blacks are all the same, aren't they?'

The sailor laughed.

'What's funny?'

'You are. You think all black men are the same. But you are wrong.' He glanced down the mess table at Muffin, sitting in his usual position, leaning against the hull.

'There are many sorts of black men, just as there are many types of white men. Some good. Some bad.'

Muffin opened his eyes and leaned forward to listen.

'First, there are the black men in Africa who catch the tribesmen in nets like wild beasts and carry them to the ports to sell to the white Portuguese traders. Then there are the blacks themselves who are manacled and loaded into the ships and sent to the plantations where they're worked till every ounce of life is beaten out of them. Then there are the rich black plantation owners. Free-born blacks who have bought land from poor white farmers and become even richer. They are educated men who behave like white men and think like white men. Then there are the mulettoes – a mixture of colours. And finally there are the black rebels. These are mainly escaped slaves. And these are the blacks who are feared by both black and white. The French and Spanish have reason to be wary of them because there are thousands of them now and they will stop at nothing to get what they want.'

'Tittle-tattle. I've heard it all before.' Smithers said, turning his back on the West Indian.

'Well, I've known plenty of black Jacks and I ain't never seen no difference in any of them,' Bungs argued.

'Me neither,' Muffin added.

'Then you have witnessed nothing,' Eku said, pushing his empty bowl across the table.

'So what makes you different from them black slaves?' Tommy asked.

'Slaves come from Africa in chains. I was free-born on the island once called Hispaniola. New slaves do not speak my language. They do not live the way I live. They are not Christians. They are not educated. They do not read or write. And when they run away from their owners, they often revert to their wild African ways.'

'But there are many black tars on ships who were once slaves.'

'I know. I have sailed with them. But I am speaking of the worst of the black rebels on Santo Domingo. They kill in the most ferocious manner, rape and murder women in front of their men folk, string children up from trees and slice off their heads with machetes.'

'Is this true?' Muffin asked.

Eku nodded. 'The owner of the plantation where I was raised was a rich man, but he was a black man like me. One day, the rebels arrived and grabbed him. For no reason, they tied him to a tree, stuffed his mouth with gunpowder then tied a rag across it. After they had pushed a length of slowmatch under the cloth, they lit it. They laughed out loud when he danced to the flames running up his clothing and searing his chest. They jeered and laughed louder when he tried to scream with no sound coming from his mouth. For a second, they were silent when his head was blown clean from his body. Then the rebels cheered and laughed some more.'

'But I thought Santo Domingo was Spanish,' Bungs said.

'Spanish first, then French, now – who knows? Napoleon has sent a vast army to hold onto the island. England has also sent soldiers. Even the Americans have sent ships.

'Why would they want to win such a wild place?'

'Because they want the coffee and sugar which is grown on the plantations there. Didn't you know that Santo Domingo or Saint-Domingue is the richest colony in the West Indies?'

John Muffin shook his head. 'Did you see these things you talked about?'

'Not all, I left before the killings got any worse. But I was born on a plantation owned by a rich black man. Unfortunately, men like him know little of Africa or the old ways. They pretend to be white. They wear fine clothes and ride in fine carriages, and import the best European horses and English leather saddles. They smell of perfumes and pomades, wear wigs and are surrounded by servants. My master dressed his daughters in the finest gowns sent from Spain and decorated the house with paintings and pottery shipped directly from Italy.

'When I was a child, I lived in a small white-washed building not far from the big house. My mother was a free woman and was educated and was engaged as companion to the owner's wife. Because of this, she was treated almost like a member of the family and was given fine dresses to wear when she accompanied the mistress to town. Of course the family spoke French and Spanish, not the language of the slaves that is made up of many African tongues. But because I was the same age as the plantation owner's youngest son, I was allowed to attend classes with him. I played games with him, wrestled with him, rode with him, and learned to speak the King's English with him.'

'So why are you here?' Bungs asked. 'Why did you leave the island?'

Eku sighed. 'Because I saw the cruelties I told you of. Neighbour fighting neighbour. And, I heard of many terrible things done by both blacks and whites alike. I left my home and my mother on the day the rebels attacked. I hid and watched when they dragged the fine furniture from the house and made a great bonfire on the lawn. After drinking lots of rum and getting very drunk, the rebels grabbed the servants and threw them onto the fire also. Alive. Screaming. So I ran, first to the garden, then to the sheds where the cane was processed. But when I saw them coming carrying flaming torches, I ran through the cane fields before they set them alight. I didn't know where to go or what to do, so I climbed up the hillside and hid in a cave. I stayed there for several days and waited until the smoke and noise had died. I had nothing to eat or drink, only the water which trickled out of the ground. But always in my mind was the thought of the sea. If I could reach a port, I was certain I would get on a ship and it would take me to freedom. I didn't care where I went – to France or Spain or America, I just wanted to leave Santo Domingo far behind.'

Tommy could understand that feeling.

'I was twelve-years old and already tall and strong, so when I reached the quay I joined a line of men rolling barrels of rum onto a schooner. I heard it was bound for Boston, so before it sailed, I sneaked aboard and hid till the ship was clear of land. The captain was an American and a fair man. He gave me a whipping but, because of my size, he didn't put me ashore and he added my name to the muster book. Everyone thought I was a run-away slave so I talked like a slave and pretended I knew nothing. That was easy,' he said, looking at Bungs, 'because no one expected anything more from a black man. When the ship reached Boston, it unloaded and then headed to Barbados.'

'And you stayed with it.'

'Yes.'

'And from there?'

'After a while, serving on a schooner trading with the American ports, I joined a West India Company vessel bound for London. But when it arrived, I learned it was returning to the Caribbean, so I signed on a 74 heading for the Mediterranean.'

'Fighting for England against the French,' Bungs laughed. 'And is that how you came to Gibraltar.'

'Yes,' Eku said. 'The ship came in for fresh supplies.'

'So,' quipped Bungs, 'here you are, pretending to be a common black tar, yet talking more like a toff with every breath.'

'I don't pretend to be anything I am not, and I care not what others think of me. How I speak is my business but for the present, I am a sailor, a black Jack, and that is how I earn my bread.'

'But them black slaves who died on the wreck, don't you grieve for their souls?'

'As men of any colour, I pity the misery they suffered,' Eku said. 'But as slaves, I say they should thank God that their fate befell them before they were branded, sold in the markets like cattle and whipped till the skin was peeled from their backs and their minds turned against their masters and themselves. I have no more feeling for the men who perished on the ship than you do, but I have a burning hatred for the black men who captured them and traded them in Africa, and for the white men – English, French, Dutch, Spanish and Portuguese who transported them in irons over the seas. It is a hatred which simmers in my breast and I fear one day it will explode.'

From the deck, the ship's bell rang calling the starboard watch back to work.

'Your mother,' Bungs asked, as they headed for the companionway. 'What happened to her?'

'I don't know,' Eku said. 'She was with the women who were dragged from the house by the rebels. I can but guess her fate. My only prayer is that her end was quick and that her suffering was short.'

'I'll say amen to that.'

Perpetual's progress was painfully slow – only two to three knots – but with the aid of *Adelina's* Portuguese charts, the frigate navigated the maze of channels and myriad of islands littering the western end of the strait which Magellan had first navigated. As the ship swam towards the Pacific Ocean, Captain Quintrell was drawn by the water's pulse and thrust of the distant tides flowing in from the open sea many miles away.

In this part of the passage, strong wind was something he did not want. Yet he had to ensure the frigate kept moving because the channels were so deep that the lead failed to find bottom, and without hope of a secure anchorage at night, there was always fear they would run aground and be unable to get off. Navigating was difficult enough by day. By night it was impossible.

From the small rocky islands, seals barked at each other or yawned lazily, ignoring the frigate drifting by. The penguins, more wary of the trespassers, paddled violently to escape the approaching leviathan. High above, the condors hung motionless, their enormous wings resting on invisible columns of air. At times, their constant presence was intimidating. Were they following the frigate?

'Canoes, dead ahead!' the lookout cried.

The men on the forward deck jostled for view.

'Native Indians?' Quintrell asked.

'Aye, Capt'n. Three canoes. Crossing our bow.'

From the deck, all eyes gazed at the dark-skinned natives; the men wrapped in warm fur-skin cloaks; the women, daubed only in white markings, naked from the waist up.

'How come they don't freeze,' Tommy asked.

'I guess they are used to it,' Muffin said.

'Maybe the fire in the boat keeps them warm.'

Smithers laughed, then looked. 'Well I'll be. Wonder how long afore it burns though the bottom. Fools,' he cried.

Despite calls from the sailors on deck, the Indians showed no response or interest, paddling speedily from the path of the great ship to the sanctuary of one of the many inlets.

As the channel narrowed, the steep-sided mountains closed in on *Perpetual*. Above the layers of rocks skirted with grey tangled scrub, thick snow covered the peaks. In places, great tongues of ice, several fathoms thick loomed over the water's edge revealing deep cracks and inner caverns of intense cornflower blue.

Later in the day, when rain and sleet wet the deck, solid sheets of water poured over the scoured mountainsides transforming the dull rock faces to tear-streaked cheeks of shiny steel. Waterfalls appeared everywhere offering an abundance of fresh water. But with no stretches of beach to run a boat onto, refilling the barrels with crystal clear water was not possible.

'Does anything survive here?' Tommy asked.

No one answered.

'How many more days?' Mr Parry enquired.

'If these charts are correct, according to my calculations, we will slip into the Pacific tomorrow. Then we will stand away from the coast and head north.'

'And what of Captain Crabthorne?' the lieutenant asked, pulling his boat cloak around him.

Oliver sighed. 'If the good captain is lost in this maze, we could search for a year and never find him. I can only pray that he has navigated a course without incident.'

Oliver didn't fail to recognize the quizzical expression on Simon's brow.

'What puzzles you?'

'Unanswered questions,' Simon Parry said. 'It puzzles me why Captain Crabthorne was so insistent on sailing around the Horn?'

'Orders, Simon. Like me, he carries Admiralty orders and it is his duty to comply with those orders to the letter and not to question the reasons behind them.'

'I understand that fact but, from the information you have provided, his mission is to deliver a diplomat to Peru.'

'The new ambassador. Indeed. Continue.'

'But the captain chanced losing both ship and men by attempting to round the Horn at the most unfavourable time of the year. Surely it would have been more sensible to disembark the ambassador at Buenos Aires in order for him to travel overland to Valparaiso. From there, he could have taken passage on any ship and sailed north to Lima?'

'It is possible, but I see two obstacles to your argument. Firstly, a journey over the Andes is fraught with danger no matter what the season. There are few known routes and in winter the high passes are blocked with snow. Secondly, apart from the dangers from avalanche or melt water, that inhospitable countryside is inhabited by Indians, brigands and mountain cats. I'm not sure which would be the worst to encounter.

'However,' Oliver continued, 'I must admit, a similar notion had crossed my mind. If Crabthorne had sailed north to Panama, he could have sent a party across the isthmus by land. For more than two centuries the Spanish have been using that route to transport silver from the mines in Peru. Had the ambassador followed *El Camino Real* – the old Royal Road, he would have arrived in Lima far quicker and safer than by taking the perilous sea voyage round Cape Horn. Captain Crabthorne is obviously no fool and his dogged determination speaks to me of something more important than merely accompanying an official representative of the British Government.'

'Then perhaps there was more than one supercargo aboard *Compendium*. A regiment of troops, perhaps, or a consignment of specie, certainly something of significance that he would not have trusted to anyone else's hands.'

'But the chance of losing everything in the Southern Ocean was a big gamble to take.' Oliver paused for a moment. 'Tell me, what is currently known of the viceroyalties of Chile and Peru?' He needed to clarify his own ideas.

The lieutenant considered the question. 'At present the people of Chile are itching for their independence. Peru wants it also. However, it is said that while the Chileans are united in their efforts to gain freedom, the Peruvians are less organised or committed. Even if they decided to rebel, I'm afraid the firm grip which Spain holds over them will be difficult to dislodge.'

'And of course, Spain does not wish to lose control of such a valuable territory, which has provided it with immense wealth for well nigh on three-hundred-years.'

'The gold of Incas,' Mr Parry added.

'Not only that, but silver and emeralds, plus quicksilver, copper and other minerals from its mines. It is hardly surprising French noses have been drawn in this direction. Britain and France are both aware of the treasure ships that carry precious cargoes to Spain two or three times a year. What the spies do not know, however, is when they sail and by which route.'

'Is it known which ports they are dispatched from?'

'Mainly from Callao in Peru. At other times from the Viceroyalty of Río de la Plata at Buenos Aires. That was one of my reasons for not entering the River Plate. French ships are never far away.'

'But to take a treasure ship from an ally would be an act of piracy.'

'Correct. But who is to tell?' Oliver asked.

'So with the war waging in Europe, wouldn't it be safer for Spain to leave its wealth in the treasuries in South America?'

'Spain cannot afford that luxury,' Oliver said. 'It knows full-well that Napoleon is its greatest threat. He has the power to overrun Spain with his ever-growing army. The alliance Spain made in May was to keep Bonaparte at bay. And its guarantee was secured with Peruvian silver.'

'But the time may come when Spain can no longer meet France's demands.'

'Then Spain will be invaded and its people, its monarchy and its wealth will fall into French hands. Mark my words, Napoleon will waste no time in usurping the Spanish throne and the government's only option to safeguard its sovereignty will be to enter the war on Napoleon's side.'

'What I cannot fathom,' Simon said, 'is what connection, if any, exists between the war in Europe and Captain Crabthorne's mission to Peru?'

Oliver shrugged his shoulders. 'Nor can I. *Compendium* is a single ship, probably an ageing frigate, not a second or third rate with a naval escort. It will be carrying only twenty-eight or thirty-two guns, and by the time it reaches Callao, it will probably be in need of a refit. I understand a handful of marines are aboard, but certainly not many, and I am not aware that the ship has any other additional crew. Boris Crabthorne is an experienced seaman and,' he said, with a smile, 'we are told, he is a good gardener to boot. But I fear he has little experience in action.'

'Perhaps that is one reason he was dispatched to the Pacific and not to Admiral Nelson with the Mediterranean fleet.'

'Perhaps,' Oliver mused, realizing he too had been consigned to the far side of the world.

'Do you think we will find him?'

'I can only pray so,' Oliver said, taking a chart from the box he had seized from the slave-ship and rolling it out on the table. 'We know he was delayed. We also know that there is a vast expanse of ocean before us still to sail.'

'You intend to sail all the way to Callao, Captain?'

'If necessary. Only then will we know whether he reached his destination. In the interim, I intend to quiz the Governor or *Intendant* at Valdivia, and if *Compendium* has not ventured into that port, then I will do the same at Conception and Valparaiso. Captain

Crabthorne would need to stop to take on wood, water and victuals after his arduous passage and, hopefully, somewhere along the coast, we will receive news which will allay our concerns.'

Having completed their meal, Oliver waited for the coffee to arrive.

'Gentlemen, it is regrettable that we have not located His Majesty's Frigate *Compendium*, however, because we found no trace in the straits, I am presuming the captain successfully navigated his passage and, like ourselves, is now being tossed by the rollers of the Pacific Ocean.

'Captain Crabthorne's orders are to sail north and I anticipate he will have set a course some miles from the shore. I intend to follow. Valdivia is the first major port on the Chilean coast that offers a safe harbour and I feel certain the captain will have stopped there. I will enter the harbour, providing we meet with no objection from the Dons. The town itself is on a river, several miles inland from the coast. For your information, it is possibly the best protected settlement in all of Spanish America.'

'Can we be certain that if we enter the harbour, we will not place ourselves in danger?'

'We cannot be sure. If there has been a change in the fortunes of Europe, since we left England, news would have been passed to the viceroyalty in Buenos Aires, and from there word would have travelled overland and reached Valdivia before us. Until we are advised to the contrary, we must assume we will be safe, but I will not enter the harbour until given a guarantee by the Governor or *Intendant* of the region. I intend to take a boat into the port and speak with these officials personally.

'You have visited Valdivia before?' Mr Parry asked.

'Several times but long before my days of naval service. As a boy, I sailed with my father. As master of a coastal trader he visited all the ports on the coast of South America. His voyages then took him north to San Francisco, but that is not our destination on this cruise. However, it was during those visits, I learned many things and gained much knowledge from my father's charts. He painstakingly recorded information about every harbour including the depth of water, the currents, tidal flows, landing places and, most importantly, the position of the ancient fortifications.'

Oliver turned to the young midshipmen around the table. 'I would advise you to stay on deck when you are not on watch. Keep your eyes and ears open for one day you may have command of your own ship and, who knows, next time you sail into these waters you may be seeking a safe harbour to refit, or searching for an enemy ship hiding in one of the many inlets.'

'You said ancient fortifications, Captain. Does this mean they have been abandoned?'

'By no means. They are old but heavily armed. They were built by the Spanish *conquistadores* two-hundred years ago to protect the coast from foreign invaders who were eager to relieve them of their treasure. Over the years, new forts and battlements have been added and all are armed with heavy cannon. These defences are impregnable against attack as they are located on the cliff tops. Believe me, when I say, the mouth of the Valdivia River is better guarded than the River Thames or any other port in England. From memory there are ten forts located on various points around the bay.'

The midshipmen were amazed. 'Is the treasure stored there?' one asked.

'Not now. Not since the early days of Spanish conquest. But that does not mean that either Chile or Peru is devoid of wealth. It is considered by unspecified authorities, claiming to be more astute that even the Admiralty, that once or twice a year a ship loaded with the riches of these regions is consigned to Spain.'

The eyes of the young men around the table sparkled.

'Are we going to take a treasure ship?' Mr Lazenby asked eagerly.

'Ha!' laughed Oliver. 'And on what grounds can we take a friendly ship sailing from its home port, no doubt under the escort of a man-of-war or a pair of frigates. A tempting prize, maybe, but taking it would be an act of piracy.' He turned to the young men at the table. 'Be mindful of your allegiance to the Crown and curb any thoughts of gross avarice. If you are sailing with that thought in mind, then I suggest you adopt another garb and I will thank you not to grace my table.'

Oliver's expression mellowed. 'Patience, young man, sea war will bring prizes when you least expect them. But remember that death also lurks over the next wave.'

The midshipman shuffled down in his seat.

'In answer to the question that is teasing the tips of your tongues, the treasure ships sail mainly from Callao, the port which serves Lima in the north. Also from Buenos Aires on the east coast.

118

If we do not locate Captain Crabthorne in Valdivia or Valparaiso, then Callao is where we are heading. So, Gentlemen, I suggest we drink a toast to Callao and our voyage north.'

Chapter 13

Valdivia

When *Perpetual* emerged from the western end of the Magellan Strait, it stood out to sea, clear of the fragmented jigsaw of islands that stretched northwards for almost eight-hundred miles.

As the frigate headed to Valdivia, sailing parallel to the coast, the colours of the land changed from dull grey and white to verdant green and rich brown. Gone were the fjords and frozen inlets of the south. Gone too the icy winds blowing up from the Southern Ocean. With the sun growing warmer each morning, along with the mercury, spirits rose bringing welcome relief to everyone aboard, especially the topmen.

Though the land was still part of Chile's long coastline, it appeared like a different world, the only constant feature was the line of distant mountains. By day the serrated peaks of the Andes melded in a haze of mauve on the far horizon. By late afternoon, the backdrop of snow-capped peaks and volcanic cones glowed golden in the dying rays of the evening sun.

'It's amazing,' Oliver mused over a glass of brandy, 'what a difference a few degrees of latitude make to the men's temperament.' It was a statement which demanded no answer, and the captain was comfortable with his first lieutenant's silence.

Like the crew, both officers welcomed the changed conditions but knew that as *Perpetual* sailed further north to the arid coast of the Atacama Desert, the stagnant heat would have as much of a detrimental effect on the men's demeanour as the cold. However, there was some consolation. Providing there was ample drinking water, the men were unlikely to die from excessive heat, whereas bitter cold could wreak havoc on a ship, freezing men's fingers to the rigging or turning their toes black.

A few days in port would be welcome by everyone.

When a break in the coastline was observed, Oliver recognized the broad entrance to Corral Bay that led to the Valdivia River on which the old Spanish colonial town had been built. Though the fortifications surrounding the bay could not be seen from the deck, he was certain his vessel would have been sighted from the land and news that a British frigate was closing would already have been relayed to the authorities.

Calls from the masthead announced that a ship, flying Spanish colours had left the bay, rounded the northern headland and was heading to the north-west. Shortly after, this was followed by a small cutter bearing south-west towards the frigate.

'Boat heading this way.' The call came from aloft and confirmed Oliver's suspicions that *Perpetual's* presence had been noted.

'Reduce sail,' he called, slipping the glass under his arm. 'We must prepare to receive a welcoming party. How is your Spanish, Simon?'

'Tolerably poor.'

'About equal to mine then. Let us hope our guests speak English.'

It took almost half-an-hour from the first sighting of the cutter to it sailing to within speaking distance. After a short exchange between the two vessels, the Spanish naval officer was invited aboard. He was greeted formally with the appropriate squeaks from the bosun's whistle and salutes from the officers.

The meeting, conducted on deck, was brief, as the officer's command of English was on a par with that of both Captain Quintrell and his lieutenant's familiarity with Spanish. In anticipation, Oliver had prepared a letter outlining his requirements – permission to enter the bay, and the request for a pilot to escort *Perpetual* into the mouth of the Valdivia River. He further begged an audience with the Governor or *Intendant* of the region.

At the conclusion of the interview, the officer tucked the envelope into his jacket pocket, bowed in a courtly fashion and returned to his boat. Although, Oliver was eager to receive news of Captain Crabthorne, he considered it pointless asking the Spaniard if he had seen or heard of *Compendium*, as both the question and his answer could easily have been misinterpreted.

Suffice to say, *mañana*, was a word which the Englishmen understood, so when the cutter departed, Oliver felt assured that a pilot vessel would arrive the following morning. He knew that once they entered the bay, the distance to Valdivia was about fifteen miles, though Oliver was careful not to reveal his prior knowledge of the area to his Spanish visitor.

His recollections of the port he had visited with his father were of cordial encounters extended in a most gracious manner, for though Valdivia was a long way from Europe, the customs, protocols and behaviour of its officials reflected that of the affluent families of Spain.

'When I go ashore, I will require an interpreter to accompany me,' Oliver said. 'A man who speaks Spanish. Preferably a midshipman or warrant officer. If not, I will settle for a sailor, but one who is reasonably presentable.'

At supper time, Mr Tully descended the companionway leading to the galley, stopping on the second-last step.

'Do any of you men speak Spanish? And I don't mean cursing and swearing in that language,' he called. 'The captain wants someone to go ashore with him.'

'I know how to get me a señorita,' Smithers smirked, opening his legs and cupping both hands over his crutch. 'But you don't need much Spanish for that.'

The men at his mess table ignored him. They'd heard all Smithers' jokes before and quickly returned to the conversations that had been interrupted.

'Hey, you,' Mr Tully said, pointing to the West Indian. 'Didn't I hear the men say you escaped from Santo Domingo and shipped to Barbados?'

'Ha! Knew it!' Smithers cried. 'We got us an escaped slave onboard!'

'I'm no slave,' Eku replied, defiantly. 'I was free born.'

'Shut your mouth, Smithers,' Mr Tully yelled, hopping down to the deck and moving through the mess looking at each table in an attempt to find a volunteer.

'Didn't you tell us you spoke French and Spanish?' Bungs crowed, leaning across the table till his nose was almost touching that of the black sailor. 'Or did you forget all of a sudden?'

A line of straight white teeth flashed back at the cooper from between a pair of dark wine lips. 'How could I forget? That was my mother's language. That is the language I spoke when I was a boy.'

'So why didn't you answer the call?' Muffin asked.

'I don't think the captain wants no black tar.'

'He didn't say what colour a man should be. Go after him,' Bungs said, prodding the Negro from his seat. 'Tell the middie what you can do. Who knows, it might be worth something to you, or maybe something you can bring back here and share with us. If nothing else you'll get a trip in the captain's boat, see the sights and maybe even get a sniff of some women, then you can come back and tell us all about it.'

Eku was reticent.

'Go on. Don't be daft.'

'Mumbo jumbo, that's all he can speak,' Smithers hissed, from the next table. 'I've heard them blacks, clicking and clacking to each other like a gaggle of geese when their necks are wrung.'

'Aye, well, you'd be an expert at that, Smithers. Shame you can't turn your hand to something useful. I've watched that lad up on the yards. He puts the rest of your watch to shame. Near hauled the t'gallant in single handed. Strong as an ox, he is.'

'Bah,' Smithers retorted, jabbing his spoon back into his bowl. For once, he had no answer for Bungs because he knew the Negro was worth any pair of topmen on the yards.

'Pardon, Captain,' Mr Tully said, 'I have a man here says he knows Spanish.'

'Then bring him in, I wish to speak with him.'

The broad shouldered West Indian bowed his head and knuckled his forehead, as he entered.

'Your name,' Oliver asked.

'The priest gave me the name Antonio but my mother gave me my grandfather's name. His name was Ekundayo. Eku is the name I am called by on this ship.'

'Then I shall call you, Eku. I am told you speak Spanish?'

The Negro nodded.

'Castilian Spanish?'

'I do not know. I speak the Spanish of the rich white people of the island on Santo Domino where I was born. I also speak the language of the slaves but they are quite different, you know.'

'If you are capable of understanding and conveying a message in Spanish that will suffice. When we anchor in the bay, I intend to take a boat up-river to the town and I will require you to accompany me as my interpreter. Are you capable of doing that?'

'Yes, Captain.'

'That is good,' Oliver said, glancing down from the sailor's naked chest to his bare feet. 'Did you not get supplied with slops when you came aboard?'

'Aye, Captain.'

'Then I would be grateful if you would wear them on this occasion.'

The following morning, with a local pilot aboard *Perpetual*, and the Spanish cutter sailing alongside, Captain Quintrell and his officers were able to observe the fortifications that surrounded the grand harbour as they sailed between the broad headlands and into Corral Bay.

The scene had been well captured by the wet fingers of the sculptor who had formed the *papier mâché* model that he had admired in the reception room at the Admiralty. Oliver had been impressed with the accuracy of the overall features, though some of the fine detail had been lacking.

In miniature, the model had exactly replicated the grand harbour located on the Pacific coast offering a broad anchorage with several large inlets from it including the estuary of the Valdivia River that snaked into the hinterland under the shelter of several mountain ranges. In particular the model had shown the exact location of the forts built on almost every promontory. Ten in total.

When he had visited the port previously, his attention had never been so keenly warranted. Now he was alert to all the sights, sounds and smells. The forts were no longer the ageing buildings decorating the headlands that he had admired as a boy, but live battlements housing iron guns, powder rooms, weapons and soldiers. They were poised with guns aimed, always ready for action. And because of their locations, they were invulnerable. With the only access by steep goat-tracks that wound around the rocky headlands, any advance on the garrisons on foot would be virtually impossible.

Between them, the forts not only protected the bay's entrance from the ocean, but the inner bay. Any enemy ship foolish enough to attempt to penetrate those waters would not survive the bombardment which could be directed at it. If sea war came to the

South American coast, Valdivia would be one port which would stand its ground.

The only enemy the fortifications could not hold back was the sea itself. Fifty years earlier, a great wave had swept in from the Pacific, rushed up the river, drowning the town and sweeping away both its houses and its people. From the battlements the soldiers could only watch in horror, and the shots fired from the cannon to warn the inhabitants that the sea was about to engulf them, came too late.

'Mr Nightingale, I am sure the Admiralty will appreciate your artistic eye as much as I do. While we are in this port, I would like you to sketch every bay and inlet, every stone tower, even the tracks cut into the hillsides climbing up to them. The time will come, and quite soon, I fear, when your work will be a boon to our navy. That is your duty for the period of time *Perpetual* is in this harbour. Are you able to do that for me?'

'Aye, Captain.'

Turning away from the midshipman, Oliver addressed his first lieutenant.

'When I go ashore, I will purchase some cattle. They can be slaughtered on the shore. What is not eaten during our stay can be salted and sealed in barrels. The men will appreciate a serve of fresh beef. Speak to the cook and cooper about that. I am sure they will not object to leaving the ship for a few hours. Also arrange suitable volunteers to go with them.'

Simon Parry nodded.

Oliver continued, as if thinking aloud. 'Fresh fruits also,' he said. 'Apples, oranges, lemons and limes if they are available. The soil here is rich and the produce of the region excellent. And for my own indulgence,' he added, smiling, 'a few bottles of the local wine. I hope you will share some with me.'

'Indeed,' Simon said. 'I look forward to it. How long do you intend to remain in port?'

'Three days at the most. Time only to take on the supplies. When I am ashore, I want a masthead lookout posted in case *Compendium* should enter the river. I am also interested in the traffic on the roadstead – a record of any vessel and its flag.'

'It will be done,' Simon said. 'But what of the rest of the men? Are they allowed ashore?'

'No. I am sorry. I know my decision will not be popular. But this port has many distractions which could entice men to run.'

'You're a lucky sod,' Smithers moaned, when the captain's boat was being lowered. 'You get to go ashore and we've to stay here. You'd think, after all these weeks on board, the captain would at least let us taste the local produce.'

'The women you mean?' Froyle said.

'That's what you get for being on the captain's boat crew,' Foss added. 'But I can tell you, if the wind don't pick up it'll be a fair pull battling against the river's outflow and the tide on the ebb. Do you want a seat in the boat?'

'Don't be daft,' Smithers said. 'You never know with these foreign ports what to expect. If the natives is unfriendly, we could end up with us throats cut.'

'Don't talk silly. This place is civilized. See the ships over yonder. Them's traders and they look to be in good trim. And if you cast your eyes up stream, you can see shipyards and boats in the making. But I don't see any natives with shrunken heads hanging from their belts.'

Perpetual's anchorage was at least three miles down-river from the town and, as expected, the boat's crew had a hard pull against the tide and current of the Valdivia River. After passing the township and several small jetties where boats were busy loading fresh produce, the captain's boat ran up on a narrow stretch of beach. Waiting to meet it were two Spanish soldiers, two grooms and six sound horses.

'Mr Nightingale, I would like you to accompany me,' the captain said, while waiting for the boat crew to heave the boat further up on the sand. 'And you will come also,' he said, turning to Eku. 'Do you ride or do you prefer to walk?'

'I ride,' Eku answered.

'That is well. Foss, kindly remain with the boat and make sure none of the men are tempted to wander.'

With one of the soldiers stationed near the boat, the servants assisted the visitors with their horses before mounting up and escorting the captain's party. Their destination was the *hacienda* of the *subdelegado* to the *Intendant*. After half and hour, riding east along the flat marshy banks of the river, the party turned inland across several miles of farmland. Cattle, horses and llamas grazed on the estates, while the peasants, working in the fields, showed no interest in the riders.

Eventually, a single-storey white building came into view. Perched on a low rise, it was set against the snow-clad peaks of the high Andes. Built in the Spanish style, the house was fenced by a high wall and surrounded by old established orchards. On reaching it, the party slowed and Captain Quintrell, Mr Nightingale and the seaman were led through a pair of elaborate iron gates into the broad courtyard where they dismounted. Despite the summer heat, the lawn was green, while the broad sweeping fronds of several palm trees created an area of shade.

'This way, please,' a liveried servant indicated, meeting them at the door and directing them along a short colonnade. From there, they were ushered into a large reception room that was lavishly furnished. Glass chandeliers hung from the ceilings while ornaments made from glass, stone and silver decorated the side tables. Scattered across the tiled floor were several large cow-hides in various colours, while the velvet upholstered chairs looked both comfortable and inviting.

With difficulty, their host stood up and turned to greet them. His weight rested on a walking stick. 'Welcome, gentlemen,' he said.

It was immediately evident to Oliver he would not require the services of an interpreter. He bowed.

'Captain Quintrell, His Majesty's ship, *Perpetual,* I presume,' their host said. 'My name is Señor Michael McGinty and as you will detect from my accent, and perhaps the colour of what little hair I have left, I am Irish by birth. But, I trust you will not hold that against me.'

Oliver smiled politely and introduced the other two members of his party.

'Please sit, gentlemen. You will have to excuse me for I am unable to stand for long periods.'

He rang a small bell and a girl immediately appeared from the corridor with lemonade which she offered to the group. The visitors were grateful.

'I trust you like what you have seen of our river and harbour. We are very proud of our region.'

'It is a delightful area, and a pleasant change from the sea,' Oliver said.

The Irishman continued. 'I must tender the apologies of the Governor. He and his wife are visiting Buenos Aires, but I am sure he would have been delighted to receive you. The *Intendant* is also absent. He had business to attend to in Valparaiso. However, I trust you will accept an invitation to dine here with me and my family. Perhaps tomorrow if that is suitable.'

'Most kind of you, Señor.'

'But I imagine you are not here to sample our local wines, but to supply your ship. I presume you are sailing north, as there had been no word of you before yesterday.'

'Your lookouts have keen eyes, Señor McGinty.'

'Indeed, it is necessary. You may be aware of the cavalier antics of the pirates on the coast of South America. They come mainly from India and the East Indies. There are also the French, who patrol the Pacific seemingly innocently but their intent is yet to be determined. And we also suffer seasonal visits from whalers and sealers, American and British merchants, Dutch and East India Company vessels, along with the slavers who hide under various flags.'

'Your harbour is a busy one, Señor, and, I am sure, your fortifications afford excellent protection from the sea,' Oliver commented.

'Indeed, but today our concerns are not only from the ocean. They also come from the land.'

Oliver was eager to hear more.

'This country, like the new colony Britain is attempting to establish in New Holland, is made up of new immigrants, but free men, not convicts like you British prefer to send. Chile is a country made up of people from many nations. Though its white population is predominantly Spanish, there are Swiss, Irish, Norwegians plus many Englishmen. Cornish tin miners, Yorkshire engineers, and Scottish cattle breeders who have made this country their home. The government is not averse to attracting foreign investors who wish to set up large farms here, or skilled artisans, or surveyors seeking to discover more precious minerals in the ground.

'But unlike New South Wales, where the British claimed they had acquired an empty land – a *terra nullius*, the Spanish *conquistadores* arrived in South America to find a land already populated by native people; intelligent civilized people who were farmers, miners, millers, metalworkers; industrious people who had worked the land for centuries and valued its many gifts.

'Naturally, the *conquistadores* were attracted to these riches and proceeded to relieve the natives of them. But also, because the primitive beliefs of the Incas did not conform to the teachings of the Jesuit priests, they used force to convert them to Christianity. Of course, when their valuable treasures were looted, their temples burned and their high priests tortured and murdered, the native inhabitants lost all regard for the Spanish invaders.'

The Irishman glanced at the captain's black sailor. 'I see from the expression on your face, young man, that you have some understanding of the type of treatment to which I am referring.'

Eku nodded in acknowledgement.

'But this country also has a large number of black slaves, does it not?' Oliver asked.

'Indeed it does. There are many here who were transported over the seas. And of those many have mixed with the native Indians. But unlike the plantation slaves of the Caribbean, who have faint hope of freedom, the slaves brought to Chile can work and save to purchase their freedom and farm their own land. Unfortunately, however, Spain has observed the product of their industry and is greedy. It takes advantage of their work, levies high taxes and sends the profits from their labour to Europe.

'Today, the peasants you see working in the valley, the descendants of the Incas and other native races, are uniting against the viceroyalty's hold over the various regions. Believe me, Captain, Chile will be the first of the Spanish colonies to seek and gain its independence. Already there are minor skirmishes in the countryside and the underlying feeling of resistance is strong.'

'Will it come to civil war?' Simon Parry asked.

'One day, perhaps.'

'But you, Señor, are a representative of the government, are you not?' Oliver observed. 'Does that not place you in an unfortunate position?'

'That is a matter I will discuss with you over a glass of wine. I have spoken too long and said too much, and you have your own problems to contend with. Order what you will of live stores or fresh produce and I will ensure that your requirements are met quickly and efficiently.'

'Thank you, Señor. I am honoured to accept your generous hospitality and look forward to joining you tomorrow for dinner.'

'And my wife and I will look forward to entertaining some English guests.'

As he rose to leave, Oliver turned to his host. 'Just one question, Señor McGinty, did an English ship, *Compendium*, Captain Crabthorne, visit your port recently perhaps to replenish its supplies?'

'Indeed it did, and what a delight it was to entertain the good captain. He allowed me to conduct him around my various estates and even took a ride with me into the foothills of the local *cordilleras*. I thoroughly enjoyed his company.'

'Ah,' Oliver responded, relieved to hear that *Compendium* was still afloat and its captain obviously in good health, but surprised and a little perplexed to learn that a British captain, engaged by the Admiralty on an urgent mission, was idling his time away galloping around the Chilean countryside. 'Captain Crabthorne was in no hurry then?'

'He had little option, sir. His ship had suffered much damage on its voyage around the Horn and he was lucky to limp into Valdivia unassisted.'

'Strange. I had word from Rio de Janeiro that he had intended to travel through the Magellan Strait.'

'Your information was correct. Captain Crabthorne attempted that passage but failed. He thought he had an experienced pilot aboard, but the man proved unreliable. As you are no doubt aware, the Strait is not an easy waterway to navigate and when he became lost, he had little option but to retrace his steps, sail south and face the Cape for a second time. But from what he told me, the sea was no kinder to him than it had been several weeks earlier, and when he arrived off our coast, he was minus half his main mast and had lost much of his rigging. He was most grateful to utilize our shipyards and the skill of our wrights to assist with the repairs.'

'Might I ask how long Captain Crabthorne stayed in Valdivia?'

'More than three weeks. He sailed about a week ago. He would have gone earlier but a few of his men decided they preferred our warm climate to the cold waters of the Pacific Ocean. I later heard that all the deserters were rounded up.'

'The Admiralty is indebted to you, sir.'

'Think nothing of it. Both my wife and I enjoyed the pleasure of his company.'

Oliver smiled and bowed. 'Until tomorrow then, Señor.'

After struggling to his feet, their host did not accompany them outdoors, instead he choose to sink back into his chair.

During the ride back to the waiting boat, Oliver was deep in thought and said nothing.

His conversation with Señor McGinty had answered some questions, but raised even more. That the man currently left in charge of the region was Irish had surprised him, but whether that man had arrived in the country as a naval commander, military officer, pirate, adventurer, investor or itinerant worker would remain a mystery. The most positive aspect of the meeting, however, was the news that Captain Crabthorne was alive and heading north as intended. For the present, however, Oliver was looking forward to an interesting conversation during the meal on the following day.

Chapter 14

Señor McGinty

Having removed their coats for the ride, due to the sweltering heat, the two officers dismounted in the courtyard and attended to their dress. As they were led into the grand reception room which Oliver had visited the previous day, the smell of sweet orange blossoms pervaded the portico. Waiting to greet them was the acting *Intendant*, Señor McGinty and his family.

'Welcome, once again, Captain,' he said, not rising from his chair. 'Let me introduce my wife, la Señora McGinty and my daughters, Isabella and Charlotte. As you will see from their names, I show allegiance to both Spanish and English queens.'

Stepping forward in turn, his wife and daughters curtsied to their guests – their satin gowns, fashioned in the style of the Spanish Court, rustled to the slightest movement. The jet black hair of the *subdelegado*'s wife contrasted with the aquamarine of her gown reflecting the sea's colours by night and by day. Fortunately, the girls showed nothing of their father's ruddy Irish features, their elegant pale necks complimented by the exquisite emerald necklaces that adorned them.

Unlike her husband, Señora McGinty spoke with a marked Spanish accent. 'I trust you had a safe passage, Captain Quintrell,' she said. Appearing twenty-years younger than her husband, her smooth olive skin had a warm glow about it.

'Thank you, Señora. Rounding the continent is always a challenge but, on this occasion, not a soul was lost to the sea nor a single barrel dislodged.'

'Then I trust, when you return to England, you are equally blessed.'

'Thank you, Ma'am.'

Mr Parry broke the moment of silence that followed. 'Have you resided in Chile for long, Señor?'

'My family has been in this country for many years and have established several successful estates in this particular region. We are fortunate,' he said. 'Our soil is fertile and our land quenched by the pure melt-water from the *cordilleras* that almost encircle us. In springtime the valley is ablaze with a profusion of wild flowers. Which reminds me,' he said, turning his attention to Captain Quintrell, 'of our conversation, regarding Captain Crabthorne. He displayed a rare knowledge of flowering plants and their propagation, and was kind enough to give my wife and daughters some practical instruction. Is that not so, my dear?'

The señora smiled.

'Captain Crabthorne was very interested in the possibility of growing grapes here, but I believe this region is too cold in the winter time. Further north around Valparaiso would be more suitable.'

Oliver acknowledged with a nod but it was not a line of conversation he could entertain for any lengthy period. Fortunately, the talk of grapes prompted a call to sample a glass of Chilean wine. When it had been served the acting *Intendant* suggested that his wife and daughters take their leave.

'Yesterday, I spoke briefly of the political unrest simmering here. Not only in Chile, but throughout Spanish America.'

Turning to Mr Parry he added, 'Our country is preparing for the day when it will gain its independence. For far too long, Spain has squeezed its territories in South America dry – from Peru in the north to Chile's frozen south, over the Andes and across the vast open pampas to the fertile lands of the River Plate. I hear that the viceroy of Río de la Plata lives like a king on taxes collected from our peasants, while our gold and silver is melted down and sent to Spain. Today men burrow like *tucu tucu* – desert rats – to find more precious minerals and gemstones, not for our benefit, but to satisfy the overlord. I fear Spain will only grant us independence when every ounce of ore has been stripped from our mines.'

He sighed. 'And if and when that day arrives, Spain will turn its back on us. Then we will have no protector and no means of protecting ourselves.'

'Forgive me for asking, Señor, but is this country ready and able to rule itself?'

'I believe Chile is almost at that stage. But not so Peru. The capital, Lima, with its port at Callao, is an outpost of the Spanish

Court, just as Buenos Aires is. Throughout Peru, bribery and corruption are rife, and even the influence of the Jesuits, though the sect was expelled long ago, is still felt. Sadly the people there are weak, because their financial and familial ties to Spain remain strong. They lack leadership. Lack Hope. Spain will not release its grip on Peru, because the rich silver mines of Potosí are within its boundaries. For Chile, however, yes, I believe we are almost ready for independence and the next few years will prove me right or wrong.'

'Señor, if you will pardon my candour in pointing to the obvious, but you are an Irishman by birth and Chile is only your adopted land.'

'On the contrary, sir, I am of the people and for the people, because I grew up here and have lived amongst them for fifty years. They trust me, despite my position. But because of my position, as a representative of the government, I am privy to all that is happening both here, in Valparaiso, Santiago, Conception, Lima and in Buenos Aires. And even across the Atlantic in Madrid.'

'I am a little puzzled,' Oliver said. 'Why you would wish to share this information with us? Surely, in some circles such expressions of opinion would be regarded as treason.'

Señor McGinty smiled sadly. 'I am an old man but I speak to you in all honesty because I love my country and I fear for my people. This land may be rich, yet most of its inhabitants are poor. The peasants toil ceaselessly to pay their taxes, and Spain is a hard taskmaster.'

'And the future?'

'No one knows what the future holds. But soon, I fear, Spain will crumble under the weight of obligation it has to France and when it throws its lot in with Napoleon, sadly our two countries will be at war. That will be catastrophic for us. Already we are stretched to the limit and, if we are called on to find more money to fund the fighting, it will bankrupt this land. Believe me, Captain, before long the people of Chile will rebel and, like the French and American revolutionaries, they will gain their independence. And when that glorious time arrives, this country will need a friend and ally, and Britain could be our saviour.

'But, I must be mindful of what I say. While there are those in this town who would gladly rise up against the old order, there are many here who are loyal to the Spanish Crown. The difficulty is knowing where individual allegiances lie.'

'I am obliged, Señor, for your forthrightness and for your most cordial hospitality. If there is any way I can reciprocate, please feel at liberty to ask.'

The Irish immigrant, *subdelegado* to the *Intendant* of the region, was about to struggle from his seat, when he hesitated. 'There is one matter, I will broach. However, I am a little reticent to do so for fear of breaking a trust placed in me by Captain Crabthorne.'

Conscious of his host's quandary, Oliver was puzzled.

'Mr Parry, would you be so kind as to entertain the ladies for a moment. My wife would be most happy to show you the wonderful view we have of the Río Valdivia. You can see as far as the Bahia de Corral. I promise I will not detain your captain long.'

'It will be my pleasure,' Simon Parry said, bowing his head to his host before heading in the direction of the cooking smells drifting from the dining room.

'Please sit for a moment, Captain. What I must share with you relates to one of your men.'

'My men?' Oliver retorted. According to the explicit orders he had given, none of his men had been allowed ashore since they had arrived in port, and he trusted there had been no inappropriate behaviour from members of his boat crew. Or was it possible a man had jumped ship and run without him being aware?

'I am referring to a young British officer – a midshipman brought ashore during the time Captain Crabthorne was in Valdivia. I was told he had been unwell before the ship arrived and I understand his condition had deteriorated while the vessel was undergoing repair.'

'An infectious malady? A contagious disease?' Oliver was concerned. 'Scurvy perhaps? What ailed him, Señor?'

'From my limited knowledge, I gather he was suffering from an irritation of the brain which made him completely unaware of his surroundings.'

Oliver tensed slightly. Firstly, he was relieved to learn that the officer in question was not one of his own. However, the mention of brain fever, reminded him of the spell he had endured as a patient in the Greenwich Seamen's Hospital which had robbed him of many months of his naval career. Because of that experience, he felt sympathetic towards the poor unfortunate sufferer.

'Did the young man recover?' Oliver enquired.

'Indeed he did, but unfortunately not until after Captain Crabthorne had sailed.'

'So, he remained in Valdivia. In your hospital, I presume?'

'Not quite so. He was brought ashore soon after the ship anchored in the river. I am told Captain Crabthorne's surgeon thought his removal from the ship was for the best. I understand the young man was in a confused state, though I never met with him myself. However, as we do not have a hospital to equal your British standards, the captain asked if there was a private dwelling where he could be lodged until he returned from Peru. Because the captain had some relationship with the young officer, he generously offered a substantial fee to ensure he received the best of care. In response to the request, a widowed lady of good breeding was happy to provide her house and offer personal care for the period of his recuperation.'

He paused and explained. 'The arrangement was most satisfactory, as it was not considered politic to have him cared for by an official body. As a result, Captain Crabthorne asked that this matter remain confidential between us. I would have honoured that promise, but for the fact I heard yesterday that the young man had completely regained his mental capacity and was anxious to return to his ship with all haste. Even in the last day or two, he has been seeking arrangements to travel overland to Valparaiso where he intended to take passage to Peru and thereby rejoin *Compendium*. Your arrival, therefore, is opportune, for I fear the young man's presence has led to some awkward enquiries. There are those amongst the community who question the intentions of an English officer residing in the viceroyalty. I am sure you understand the types of rumours I am alluding to.'

'Indeed, and, if it will save any further embarrassment, I will be happy for this officer to sail with me.'

The *subdelegado* looked relieved. 'I am beholden to you, Captain. I will arrange for him to be transported to your ship tomorrow.'

'Thank you, Señor. In turn, I will deliver him safely to Captain Crabthorne who will be delighted to learn of his full recovery.'

'Now, Captain,' Señor McGinty said, 'it is time to join the ladies. And I can guarantee that after months at sea dining on a diet of salted pork and beef, my table will offer some local produce that is sure to tempt your appetites.'

Oliver waited until the Irish-born gentleman had struggled to his feet. The worn joints in his knees were obviously painful and a problem to him.

'Might I ask the young man's name?' Oliver enquired.

'Mr Edward Atherstone.'

The smartly dressed midshipman, who climbed nimbly aboard *Perpetual* late the following morning, was sallow-cheeked and appeared a little breathless, but otherwise appeared sharp-eyed and eager. Mr Parry, who had been advised of his imminent arrival, was on deck to receive him.

After saluting the quarterdeck, the young man announced in an elegant tone, 'Edward Atherstone, midshipman, recently of His Majesty's frigate *Compendium*, Captain Crabthorne. Permission to come aboard?'

'Welcome, Mr Atherstone. Mr Nightingale, here, will show you to the midshipmen's berth. Once your dunnage is stowed, kindly present yourself to Mr Greenleaf, the sailing master, on the foredeck. His morning class is almost finished but he will be taking the sightings at noon and I see,' he said, glancing at the sand in the hour glass, 'that will be very soon.'

'Aye aye, sir. Then, may I speak with the captain?'

'The captain will speak with you when the captain requires.'

'Thank you, Lieutenant.' With that, the midshipman was directed down the forward companion to the galley and thence along the length of the mess deck to the midshipmen's quarters.

Strolling the weather deck with Mr Parry, Oliver felt revitalized after his brief time in Valdivia. The welcome extended to him and members of his crew had indeed been a warm one, and he would have accepted the Acting *Intendant*'s offer of a ride to the foothills of the mountain ranges had he not been obliged to continue on to Callao. Things may have been very different if he had been received by the *Intendant* himself or the Governor of the region. But as they were absent, that was a matter for speculation.

'What are your first impressions of our new arrival?' Oliver asked. 'I am told, he has been severely ill for some time.'

'He appears surprisingly well,' the lieutenant commented. 'A little pastey in complexion, but well-mannered, neatly attired and obviously intelligent. And is eager to speak with you.'

'In due course, but for the present, I will enter his details in the ship's log. He will fill one of the positions made vacant by the officers dispatched with the prize in the North Atlantic. In the meantime, have all our requirements been met?'

'The last of the cattle has been slaughtered and Bungs assures me all the barrels have now been sealed. Cook is happy, which is remarkable, and the other supplies are aboard. Only one more boat still to return.'

'Well done. Then, if there are no other matters to be attended to, I plan to sail with the tide tomorrow in the forenoon.'

'Do you intend to stop at Valparaiso or Conception to enquire if Crabthorne is there?'

'That will not be necessary. We now know his ship is sound and he is well stocked with fresh supplies. Therefore, the captain has no reason to break his journey again and I am certain he will head directly to Callao.'

'And our course?'

'The same. I will speak with Mr Greenleaf. We are but a week behind *Compendium* and have more than two thousand sea miles ahead of us, so there is a possibility we may be able to close the gap.'

'Would you estimate a month of sailing ahead?'

'Perhaps. Depending on the wind.'

Simon touched his hat and was about to oversee the hoisting of the newly arrived midshipman's chest, but the frown on Oliver's brow told him the conversation was not yet over.

'Even though this man appears well and fit for duty,' Oliver said, 'I want you to keep a close eye on him.'

'Might I know what concerns you?'

'Everything and every person aboard this ship concerns me. But to be delivered of a midshipman of fine background and with several years' service to his credit, possibly on the point of sitting for the examination for lieutenant, a man whose immaculate appearance resembles that of a middie arriving at his first ship after being fitted out by the finest tailor in London. Those sorts of things concern me.

'Plus, Señor McGinty told me Mr Atherstone was a relative of Captain Crabthorne. Strange. From the little I have learned of Boris Crabthorne, I gather he was no more than a Lord Mayor's boy from a modest background and certainly not an officer raised up through the ranks by patronage. Judging by the cut of this man's uniform and the size and weight of his sea chest, I would suggest he is from an affluent family.'

'But should we judge a man by the cut of his cloth, his carriage and the content of his dunnage?'

'Indeed, we should not,' Oliver said. He was about to add more, but refrained when he cast his mind back to his first meeting with Simon Parry at the Admiralty almost two years earlier. On that occasion, he had formed a similar view. But he had been proved very wrong in regard to every aspect of his lieutenant's character and seamanship skills.

Then he thought back to the image his grandfather always presented, that of a dishevelled herring fisherman whose offensive smell preceded him wherever he went. A man whose Cornish accent was so broad it was sometimes hard to understand him. Yet a man whose knowledge of boats and the sea, and whose alertness of brain surpassed many a naval officer who eventually rose to the rank of admiral.

Pre-judging people because of their appearance was a failing that Oliver found difficult to control.

'Once we are at sea, I would like to practice the guns. Allocate a division to Mr Atherstone and let us see how he performs.'

'Aye aye, Captain.'

Chapter 15

Mr Atherstone

After weighing anchor from the Valdivia River, *Perpetual* headed across the sheltered waters of the Corral Bay, sailing beneath the gaze of the old fortifications located on every headland. Ahead, the blue water of the Pacific shimmered beneath a cerulean sky while behind them the green undulations of the local *cordilleras* were set against the hazy mauve backcloth of the high Andes.

The following day, when the ship's bell sounded the end of the afternoon watch, the topmen slid down the shrouds while the newly called watch spewed up from the forward-hatch and climbed to the yards.

A small group of young middies joked as they made their way to the after companionway to return to their berths. Edward Atherstone followed behind them. His face was expressionless, but that was not unusual for he appeared to demonstrate little emotion. He had little in common with the other middies of his age and though, on his first night aboard, he had listened to their bawdy jokes, he had never responded with any of his own.

Carrying a brass glass under his arm, he turned to go down the ladder.

Waiting at the bottom, Tommy Wainwright had stepped aside to allow the group of middies to pass. He was about to place one foot on the step when he noticed Mr Atherstone climbing down.

'What have you been up to?' the midshipman demanded.

'Nothing, I was doing an errand.'

Atherstone scoffed, 'You will address me as, sir.'

'Yes, Mr Atherstone. Sorry, sir.'

'So why are you using this companionway, when the forward companion is nearer to the mess?'

'I just returned a bag of flour to the wardroom pantry – it was from Mr Nightingale's private supply. Cook baked him some scones this morning.'

'So you were lurking in the wardroom, were you?'

'No, sir, I weren't. I delivered the flour, like I was told, and now I'm going up on deck. You can ask any of me mess mates or cook, they'll tell you.'

'We shall see about that. If I find anything missing in the midshipmen's berth,' Mr Atherstone warned, as he stepped down, 'I shall know who took it.'

'That ain't fair,' Tommy mumbled under his breath. Fortunately the midshipman did not hear him.

Next morning, the ship's company was mustered on deck to witness punishment.

'What are the charges this morning?' the Captain asked, addressing Mr Parry.

'Three men for disorderly behaviour. Two drunk. The other late for watch. All regulars, Captain.'

'Let them step forward.'

The three offenders were immediately paraded before the captain. One swaggering as bold as brass. The other pair presented with their heads bent, but Oliver didn't need their names, he was familiar with all three.

'It appears to me,' the captain said, 'because you deliver yourselves for punishment on a weekly basis, you two must derive some strange delight in being flogged. Perhaps if I stop your grog ration for a month, that might clear your heads long enough for you to ponder over the job you have signed on to do. And for any man who cannot drag himself from his hammock,' Oliver continued, looking directly at the third sailor, 'the same punishment applies. Sleeping with a clear head should allow you to hear the bosun's call in the morning. Anything else on the list, Mr Parry?'

'Thomas Wainwright – accused of willful damage to property.'

'A serious charge,' Oliver said, with a frown. The name had a familiar ring, but he could not place the seaman who owned it.

'Step up, lad,' the bosun called, giving Tommy a sharp prod with his rope's end.

Oliver blinked, but otherwise showed no change of expression when the accused was presented to him.

'Mr Parry, kindly read the details of the charge.'

'Entering the wardroom and midshipmen's quarters without permission and removing two pages from Mr Atherstone's private journal.'

Oliver questioned the youth. 'Do you realise that deliberate damage and theft are serious offences?'

'But I didn't do it. I didn't go there without permission. And I didn't touch no journal. It's a lie.'

'Silence!' Mr Parry warned.

'Be careful what you say, young man,' the captain added. 'Making accusations against an officer could make matters far worse.'

'Tell him,' a voice whispered, from the crew.

Not knowing whether he was at liberty to speak, and lacking all his usual cocky exuberance, Tommy remained silent.

'Speak, boy,' the captain demanded.

Tommy looked forlorn. 'I went to the wardroom and I had to go through the midshipmen's mess to get there,' he answered, 'but it was just to return some flour to the officers' pantry. Nothing else. Cook will tell you. That's the honest truth.'

Oliver glanced along the sea of heads and picked out the cook's bald pate amongst them. 'Is what the boy says correct?'

'Aye, Captain. What he said about the flour is right.'

'And what of the book?' Oliver asked the boy, in a less threatening tone. 'Did you tear pages from the midshipman's journal?'

'No, sir, of course I didn't. I know better than to touch anything what's not mine.'

'Enough. Does anyone have anything to add to this charge?'

The deck was silent, save for the creak of a block and luff of a sail. Glancing up at the main topgallant, the Captain turned his head to the quartermaster, who was already adjusting the helm.

'Mr Atherstone, you brought the charge against this boy. Do you have anything to add?'

'The boy might deny the charge, Captain, but I know it to be a fact. I have the book right here as proof and can show where the pages have been torn from it.'

'That is not necessary,' Oliver said. 'Is this the boy's first offence?'

'It is.'

'Then, a dozen at the gun, bosun.' He inhaled deeply. 'Is that all, Mr Parry?'

'Yes, sir.'

Replacing his hat, Oliver glanced across the ship. 'The deck is yours, Mr Parry. You may dismiss the men.'

Instantly the crew replaced their hats and scattered. Those standing on the lowest ratlines jumped down to the deck. The sailors not on watch headed below and those on the larboard watch returned to the daily chores of swabbing and polishing, armed with some fresh gossip to mull over.

'You come with me, lad,' the bosun's mate called. 'You should thank your lucky stars that you got off lightly. Captain was in a good mood today.'

'But I never did what he said. That midshipman is the one who's the liar.'

'Belay your tongue, lad, or it'll get you into more strife. You're not the first who's swung for someone else's crime and you'll not be the last. Take my word for that.'

'But I didn't do it.'

'I believe you, but you'll ne'er prove it, not so long as Mr Atherstone wears a uniform and has the captain's ear.'

Tommy wiped his sleeve across his face. 'I thought Captain Quintrell was a good man.'

'Stow it, lad. The captain's all right. He's just doing what he has to. Like us he has to abide by them Articles that get preached to us every Sunday. Believe me, I've known captains that'll string a man up in the rigging and let him freeze to death just for looking at him. Hurry along,' he said, prodding the boy down the ladder to the frigate's waist, and the line of thirteen 12-pounder cannon lashed to each side of the hull. He pointed to the nearest.

'The sooner we get this over with the better. It'll only sting for a bit, but in a couple of days you'll have forgotten all about it.'

The days which followed were as boring as the scenery which presented itself off the starboard beam. Sailing north, *Perpetual* hugged the coast of the Atacama Desert which stretched for almost eight hundred miles. But unlike the winds which blew from the Sahara, this vast expanse swallowed the wind and stilled the sea. And when mixed with the cold waters of the north-flowing Humboldt Current, it created a moist blanket of mist which ironically floated along one of the driest and most inhospitable coastlines in the world. Yet it delivered not a singe drop of rain to it. Like the Doldrums of the South Atlantic, it was the nemesis of ships passing through it. The only consolation Oliver could draw was that Captain Crabthorne would have encountered the same insidious adversary.

Suddenly the silence of the deck was broken. Through the haze came a dull thud which sent a shudder through the timbers of the hull and a frisson of fear through the spines of the unwary. Another thwack followed, then the splash of something hitting the water close by.

Sailors, who had been lounging on deck quickly jumped to their feet and looked to the sea, while the young midshipmen, fearing that the ship was under enemy attack, looked to the lieutenants for orders.'

'Do we beat to quarters?' one cried.

Captain Quintrell's broad smile was reflected on Simon Parry's face.

The sounds were familiar. They had encountered them in the Southern Ocean.

'Stand easy,' Oliver said.

A few moments later, and no more than ten yards from the frigate's side, a huge white-crusted head, rose vertically almost to the height of the main yard. From behind its barnacled nose, a small round black eye fixed its gaze on *Perpetual*. Then, as if satisfied with what it saw, the leviathan threw itself onto the sea with a thunderous clap, showering the sailors gathered at the gunnel. Thirty yards away other members of the pod breached and blew noisily then, after an awesome display lasting several minutes, the whales sounded – their gigantic flukes slicing the water in silence and leaving barely a ripple on the surface.

For Oliver, the long day had been made even longer by the lack of wind, lack of activity on deck, indolence of the men on watch, and the miasmic fog which surrounded them. At times like this, when he had the luxury of leisure, his cot was not an attraction for he did not sleep well.

With his present frustrations weighing on him, he had eaten alone and drunk more wine than when he dined in company where conversation reigned. The Chilean grapes, grown from vines imported long ago from Spain and France, produced excellent wines, and he had savoured the best part of two bottles.

When he mounted the companion ladder, he found the deck quiet. It lacked the usual daytime noises. Most of the larboard crew was in their hammocks taking a well deserved rest after the arduous efforts of the preceding weeks.

Alerted by the sound of approaching footsteps, Mr Lazenby, officer-of-the-watch, turned from the rail, 'Good evening Captain,' he said.

Oliver wondered. Was it a good evening? From his observation of the haloed moon, it was evident that the mist still hung heavily over the sea and unless it cleared by morning and a wind blew up, they would be in danger of drifting towards land with the next tide.

From past experience, a stilled sea bore its own perils and could lull a sailor into a false sense of security. Flat water had no breakers and could hide a reef. Mist could envelop an enemy ship. Unseen currents could carry them onto a lee shore. As to the pirates – the known predators of this coast – the mist provided a veil of invisibility to hide behind.

'Look lively, there,' Oliver said, kicking the sole of a seaman's boot whose legs protruded from under a boat. 'Which watch are you?'

'Larboard watch, Capt'n. I came on deck to sleep, cos it's too hot to sleep below.'

'Humph,' Oliver snorted. In the waist, a group of seamen sat cross-legged mending their clothes by the light of a lantern.

Ding, ding – ding, ding, sounded the bell from the belfry. Oliver wondered if any other ships were nearby, as the distinctive chimes would carry for several miles over water.

Wandering back to the quarterdeck, he bade the officer-of-the-watch goodnight before retiring below.

Spread out across the table in his cabin were the charts he had been studying earlier in the evening. He sorted through them again, selecting the coast of Peru and sliding it onto the top. Sitting back in his chair, he gazed at the pile for a while till his eyes began to droop. Then he got up, removed his jacket and shoes, and swung into his cot.

Almost immediately, his eyes closed, but the charts remained foremost in his mind. They were flat images. One dimensional. Devoid of any contours. Then his mind jumped to the *papier mâché* model of Valdivia he had seen at the Admiralty, with its undulating hills, steep valleys, promontories, inlets and flat marshes running beside the river.

With his consciousness flickering like a dying candle, the shapes swirled in his mind. Now the lines belonged to Susanna lying naked across the polished mahogany. The charts, hills, coastline were now her rounded contours. They fought for his attention. Teasing him. Confusing him. The headlands, the hidden inlets – he could see them all. He could sense the rising sea. Feel the current of emotion flowing through his veins. Gliding with the ease of an albatross, he imagined himself pulling her towards him, drawing her across the ocean of white-capped charts that rustled beneath her loins, warping her closer and closer till he entered the port he had been absent from for too long.

Oliver savoured the vision for as long as his mind would hold it, but like the devastating tidal wave which had struck the coast many years before, the tide of his passion could not be held at bay and the sea rushed in. Only then did he allow himself to succumb to sleep.

Chapter 16

Gun Practice

Dodging around the men from several gun crews, Tommy raced along the deck, almost knocking Old Silas from his feet.

'What's your hurry, boy? Gun practice is over. You missed it!'

'I'm looking for Hobbles. He's one of the gun captains. Which is he?'

'With a name like Hobbles! Can't you guess? Walks like he's got a peg leg – only he ain't.'

'Try calling his name,' Old Silas said, with a wry smile, 'and I'll bet you a shilling, he's the only one who don't take any notice.'

Tommy was oblivious to the sailor's joke.

Silas's mate explained. 'His gun's abaft the waist, but you'll have to talk loud 'cause he's deaf.'

'Like all bloody gunners,' Silas added.

'Hobbles!' Tommy shouted, when he found the man with the limp. 'Hobbles,' he repeated, tugging on the gun captain's sleeve.

Knocking the boy's hand from his shirt, Hobbles placed the square of sheet-lead carefully across the breech of the gun, fastened it securely and dusted it carefully, before troubling himself with the boy's interruption.

'What do you want?'

'The gunner in the magazine sent me. He said I'm to serve this gun.'

'What's that you say? Look me in the face when you speak so I can hear you.'

'I'm to be your powder monkey,' Tommy yelled.

'What's you name, lad?'

'Tommy Wainwright.'

'Well, Tommy Wainwright, this here is Betsy,' he said, affectionately stroking the grey mottled iron. 'She's *my* lady and she's a real fine Walker lass. She answers to the slowmatch not a flintlock – they can be too temperamental. And fires twelve pound balls like the others down here do. Reliable, she is. Never fails. That's because I takes good care of her.'

The crew working the gun jeered.

'All right, he said. 'And because I've got a good crew working her.'

John Muffin and Ekundayo nodded to him from the other side of the gun. Tommy was pleased to see two familiar faces as he didn't know the other hands who made up the rest of the crew.

'You'll learn who they are, if you live long enough!'

Tommy took no heed. It was a relief to be on the gun deck after spending the last few days in the magazine scraping rust from the round shot hauled up from the hold. It was not only a heavy job that left him with aching arms, but it was painful, too, when fine metal splinters stuck in his fingertips. Aside from that, the magazine was a dark, dismal, dusty hole to be stuck in. No one was allowed to visit without the gunner's say so, and with him being stone deaf, it meant there was no one to talk to.

'Did he tell you what you've got to do?' Eku asked.

Tommy shrugged. 'He said when the cannons were being fired, either in practice, or for real against the Frenchies, I was to grab a cartridge from the magazine, stick it under me shirt and run like the hounds of hell was after me and deliver it here to Hobbles. Then I'm to run back and collect another.'

'And why do you think you stick the cartridge under your shirt?'

'To keep it tight so the gunpowder don't fall out?'

'Not quite, lad,' Muffin said, casting a glance at the big West Indian. 'It's to stop sparks or bits of burning sailcloth floating down on top of it and blowing you and the rest of us to Kingdom Come.'

'What?' Tommy asked, not knowing if his mess mate was joking.

'Don't worry, you'll not feel a thing,' Grimes said, leaning down to check the breechings were tight.

'So what do I do with the cartridge when I get here?'

'You stuff it in that box over there, close the lid tight, then run back to the magazine and fetch another.'

'That's easy,' Tommy said.

'Not so easy with the guns going off all around. You watch yourself when they're firing. A gun's got a kick ten times worse than an angry mule.'

'Aye,' Tom said. 'I noticed.'

'And what if the powder monkey on the next gun, is cut down?' Hobbles shouted.

'I'm to run twice as fast and bring powder to that gun too.'

The gun captain nodded. He was satisfied to have a lad who seemed to have a grasp of the rudiments of the job. Better than them, not much older than bairns, who'd hide in a corner snivelling after their mothers, or the ones who'd get lost on the deck forgetting which gun they were serving. In his years in the navy, he'd seen hundreds of them come and go – some cheeky little mongrels, some cocky scoundrels, some wimps, and plenty of youngsters who never deserved to be stitched up in an oversized hammock and sent to the bottom. But, whilst ever there were enemy ships on the high seas, the rules were unlikely to change.

'Are you scared of the noise?' Hobbles asked.

'No, sir, I've heard powder explosions before.'

'You served on another ship?'

'*Isle of Lewis*. I sailed with Captain Quintrell to Gibraltar.'

'Did you now? Then you should know what to do.'

Tommy shook his head. 'I was sent to the manger when the guns were being fired. I had to make sure the animals didn't get loose.'

'Then you've not heard the sound of a broadside on the gun deck. Stuff your ears with damp oakum, that's my advice, or you'll end up deaf as a door post, like me.'

'I'll make sure he does.' Eku said.

Oliver swished the last drops of his brandy around in his glass, savoured the aroma then swallowed.

'The timing was remarkably good,' he said, returning his attention to the afternoon's gun practice. 'Were you satisfied with the divisions, Simon?'

The first lieutenant paused before answering. 'Reasonably, though several of the gun crews are not yet performing to their best.'

'Then, while we have ample sea room, I suggest they practice every day until that is achieved. Tell me, did Mr Atherstone's division meet with your expectations?'

'Indeed, his gun crew performed admirably,' Simon said, but his tone lacked conviction.

'Why is it, then,' Oliver said, 'that you are not convincing me of your opinion? Perhaps I should rephrase my question. Would you say that Mr Atherstone is capable of discharging his duties most expediently on such occasions?'

'I cannot say, sir. He begged to go below to report to the surgeon just prior to the practice.'

'What?'

'Mr Steele, one of the master's mates led the gun practice for Mr Atherstone's division. I have recorded that fact in my daily report.'

Oliver scratched his claw-like finger along the peeling varnish of the tray in front of him. 'Pray tell me,' he said cynically, 'what malady beset Mr Atherstone so suddenly that he had to leave his post? Is he not aware that this type of behaviour is not permitted in action? You disappoint me, Simon. I am surprised you permitted him to withdraw.'

'He claimed he had a pain in the head which made it impossible for him to think or indeed see clearly.'

'And you believed this?'

'I did, on this occasion, because there was an expression on his face which convinced me all was not right with him.'

'Then I shall say no more until I have spoken with the surgeon. But in future, I expect nothing less than he behaves like a seasoned midshipman should, and a gentleman to boot. I care not whether he has a pain in the head or in any other organ of his body. In future, I expect to see him remain with his division even if his head has been blown clean off his shoulders!'

Hobbles picked up the length of slowmatch from where he'd rested it on the edge of a half-barrel. Lifting the smouldering end to his lips, he blew across it till the embers flamed and sparks spat from it.

'Fire!' was the distant call coming from the quarterdeck.

'Fire!' repeated the midshipmen in charge of the other divisions.

'Fire!' yelled Mr Atherstone to his gun crew.

The men were ready and standing clear. Hobbles, having watched the word *Fire* mouthed by the midshipman, touched the slow-match to the black powder in the bowl. A quick step backwards, despite his stiff leg, took the gun captain clear of the carriage's path.

Instantly, the powder flared sucking the flame down the tube to the cartridge which he had ripped open to allow for instant ignition.

In a flash, the gunpowder exploded within the cast-iron bore, the force of the blast shooting the ball out from the barrel on a tongue of orange flame, followed by a burst of thick acrid smoke. The sound was deafening.

As if alive, and with a mind of its own, the gun jumped from the deck and recoiled, throwing itself backwards on its wooden trucks till halted by the restraining ropes that prevented it from careering across the deck and colliding with a gun on the larboard side. The twelve pound ball hissed, as it flew over the water for almost a thousand yards, but any view of the shot, from the gun port, was blanketed by the choking smoke depriving the men the satisfaction of seeing the results of their labour.

'Reload!'

'Reload!'

On the second firing, the gun leapt back with greater ferocity, as if to bite the hand that had touched it. The breechings twanged, snapping tight, the blocks squealed and the carriage creaked, thumping down on the deck, after jumping several inches. The eight men, who made up the crew, knew to keep their distance until the gun had calmed itself, then they grabbed the lines and hauled it back to reload. The smoking chamber was quickly wormed and swabbed to snuff out any residual flames, then a new cartridge was pushed into position, a wad of rags added and rammed home, and a ball rolled into the barrel. Now all that remained was for Hobbles to clear the touchhole with his priming iron and pierce the new cartridge. A sprinkle of black powder into the bowl and the gun was ready to fire.

'Keep your distance,' Eku shouted to Tommy, who was about to place another cartridge into the box on the deck nearby. 'Beware! The gun's getting hot and, if she's fed too much powder, she can kick so hard she'll leap up and touch those beams above your head.'

'You,' Mr Atherstone called, pointing at the Negro. 'Stop your yap. And you,' he yelled to Tommy, 'stop dilly-dallying and get back where you belong. I mean now! This instant!'

Tommy ran from the gun, weaving back along the deck just as the order to fire rang out. The ferocity of the cannon amazed him, each one punching out like a huge piston, but belching smoke not steam. After each firing, the gun was dragged forward, instantly swabbed and reloaded in a repetitive routine. It was noisy, exhausting, exciting and dangerous. The searing flames flashed like lightning bolts and the thunderous roars were worse than any storm he'd ever heard. The smoke caught in his throat and eyes and, at times, he couldn't see where he was stepping. After a while, he was relieved to be heading below to the relative quiet and safety of the magazine.

The pimple-faced marine, stationed outside the powder store, asked his name, which Tommy thought was stupid as he'd been in and out at least half a dozen times that morning, but those were the rules. Like the fact he had to wear felt slippers, which he was obliged to pull on over his shoes whenever he entered. But when he had a moment to himself, he thought about the noise a single cartridge made and tried to imagine what the sound would be if the magazine, stacked high with barrels of powder, exploded. If that ever happened the ship would be blown to smithereens – and everyone with it. With that thought in mind, he decided if he had to wear slippers to keep the ship safe, he wouldn't complain.

The following morning when Captain Quintrell received the daily reports from his officers, which included observations on the previous day's gun practice, he discovered three charges laid by Mr Atherstone against a seaman in his division. The first charge was for failing to follow orders, the second for talking when he should have been silent, and the third for insubordination.

When asked to explain the charges, Mr Atherstone was adamant that the sailor was a regular troublemaker, a chatterbox and that his constant mutterings had disrupted the firing of the gun.

'And what is the name of this man,' Oliver had asked.

'He goes by the name of Eku. He's a black Jack.'

Without any other information regarding the events that had occurred, it was Captain Quintrell's duty to address the charges and dispense the appropriate punishment based on the midshipman's accusations. But Oliver had his reservations. Prior to this, the accused sailor had never proved to be a problem. He had never made mischief, been drunk or disobeyed orders and, from his own experience of the man on the day he had accompanied him ashore in Valdivia, he considered the Negro to be polite, well-mannered and obliging. Therefore, the charges laid against him appeared to be out of character.

But at sea, especially if under pressure, men were known to change their colours. He'd seen fearless seamen wail inconsolably.

He'd seen timid hands sing and dance hysterically in front of other men. While, at times, such abhorrations of behaviour were attributed to excess grog, at other times men were adversely affected for no apparent reason. But with a written report in front of him, Oliver had no alternative but to accept Mr Atherstone's word, however, this being the seaman's first offence, he was lenient with the punishment, stopping the sailor's grog for a month.

'Perhaps that will render his tongue less lively in the future.'

'But, Captain,' Mr Atherstone said, having anticipated a much harsher penalty.

'But nothing, Mr Atherstone. I have made my decision and there is no more to be said on the matter.'

'Gun ready!' the gun captain announced, as another morning's session of gun practice was about to commence.

The same cry was echoed right along the gun deck. Standing poised, every member of the crew knew what was expected of him. Whether nervous or excited, tired or bored, each man waited for the order to come from the quarterdeck and to be repeated by the division officers at the guns.

The distant call to fire broke the anxious silence, but before the word could be repeated by the midshipman in charge of Hobbles' division, a deep voice boomed, 'Hold your fire!'

Almost instantly the orders on the other guns were answered with a cacophony of blasts which thundered from the side of the ship. But Hobbles' gun remained silent.

Despite his deafness, Hobbles had been alerted by Eku's cry and stood for a moment, the slowmatch fizzing in his hand above the priming bowl. Glancing from the West Indian to the midshipman, he held his pose.

'Fire!' Mr Atherstone called.

'No!' Eku cried.

'You dare countermand my order! Fire, I say. Fire this instant.'

Hobbles read the words formed on the midshipman's lips and lowered the slowmatch. Instantly, the burning ember touched the powder, the flame whooshed down the quill into the cartridge and the whole bag of powder erupted. Belching smoke and fumes, Betsy spat her twelve pound shot across the water directly towards the imaginary enemy. But instead of leaping straight back, the gun carriage slewed sideways, dislodging one of the cannon's trunnions, splitting one of the rear trucks and almost turning itself around ninety degrees. In its vicious rebound, the wooden carriage knocked the legs from under one of the sailors, and before he could even blink, the front wheel ran over his leg. The seaman screamed but the gun crew was more concerned when the other trunnion slid from its groove leaving the cannon teetering and in real danger of crashing to the deck.'

Gun practice was immediately halted and Mr Parry was at the gun in an instant. Working as quickly as possible, men fought to release the man's legs from beneath the carriage wheels, while others attempted to prevent the barrel from overbalancing. But without handspikes or mittens, the heat of the gun burned their hands when they strove to prevent further damage or injury.

'Get this man below,' Mr Parry ordered, when the sailor was pulled clear.

By now, the smoke from the guns had settled and the men from the other crews strove to see what had happened, and find out which of their mates had been injured.

'Secure all the guns!' Mr Parry ordered. 'And pass word for the captain.'

But Oliver was already descending the companion ladder to the waist. 'What happened here?' he demanded.

Mr Atherstone was quick to answer. 'This man failed to secure the preventer.' He pointed to the Negro. 'It was his fault. He purposely tried to disrupt the practice. And succeeded. He disobeyed my direct orders. He did not perform his duty on the gun and this is the result of his insubordination.'

'Enough, Mr Atherstone!' the captain cried. 'Marines, take that sailor below. I will deal with him later.' For the present he was more concerned with the welfare of the injured man and the state of the gun deck than the rantings of an irate midshipman. 'Get the carpenter to attend to the broken truck, then have the gun reseated, the carriage repositioned and everything lashed securely. Mr Atherstone, I want a written report of this incident in my cabin this afternoon.' Then, turning to Hobbles, he shouted directly at his face. 'I will speak to you in my cabin, as soon as this mess is cleaned up.'

'What's going to happen to Eku,' Tommy whispered, as John Grimes was carried away on a make-shift canvas stretcher.

Muffin shrugged. 'Three dozen at the grating for all the charges Mr Atherstone's levelled at him.'

'But that's not fair.'

'There's nowt fair when it comes to the Articles of War, lad. And it don't matter whether we are at war or not, them rules are set in stone and if they're broken, it's up to the captain to decide what punishment to mete out. Captain Quintrell can only judge on the report he gets from the middie in charge of the division.'

'But it weren't Eku's fault,' Tommy said, not realizing the midshipman had come up behind him.

'Bosun's mate, start that lad,' Mr Atherstone called. 'I'll have no more insolence from another person in my division.'

Tommy tried to run, but with a throng of sailors gathered around to help secure the gun, he was unable to get away from the blows of the rope's end which beat down on his bare head and shoulders.

'Come in,' Oliver called.

Taking off his hat, the bosun entered, rather sheepishly. The captain's cabin had a different smell to his own dingy locker cluttered with buckets of pitch, tar brushes, bowls of kitchen grease and barrels of brimstone.

Without a greeting, Oliver asked the bosun for his opinion of the afternoon's *débâcle*. 'Did the breechings or preventer ropes cause the accident?'

'No, Capt'n, it was a loose eyebolt in the hull next to the gun port. The eye was ripped clean from the timber. I called the carpenter to fix it, but he said the whole length of planking – more than eight-feet long – was rotten with dry rot. He said he didn't know how it had held so long with the stresses it was under every time the gun was fired. He said it was the wrong wood for the job and must have been fitted by a blind shipwright when the ship was built.'

'And once it was painted, no one noticed.'

'Only good thing is that it was above water level.'

Oliver raised his eyebrows. 'Thank you bosun, I will speak with the carpenter. Let us hope we have no more planks from the same tree or any more loose rings in the hull securing the guns' breechings.'

'I can assure you the rings are firm, Capt'n. I've been right around and checked them all.'

Oliver wondered how a man could put sufficient pressure on an eyebolt to equal the recoil of a cannon weighing several tons, but he did not dispute the bosun's statement.

'Begging your pardon, Captain, but Hobbles said the crew man had noticed some movement in the ring when the gun was hauled up ready for firing. He said the Negro tried to alert the midshipman, but Mr Atherstone wouldn't take any notice of him. Then he tried to stop Hobbles from firing, but of course Hobbles couldn't hear him, so when he saw the middie mouth the word, *fire*, that's what he did.'

'Had no one checked the eyes bolts recently? Isn't that one of your regular duties?'

The bosun nodded. 'We do check, but we can't really judge.'

'Then I suggest you find a way of doing so in future. It is likely John Grimes will lose his leg because of this malfunction, that is, if he survives. Perhaps you and your mates will pay more attention in future.'

'Aye, Capt'n. We will.'

'In the meantime I will speak with the carpenter and have him check all the planking.'

Shipworm, borers, mice and rats were the elements a sea captain learned to share his space with in tolerable harmony, but dry rot was something he could well do without.

Eku winced as a sailor from the next mess table, brushed across his weeping back.

'Are you all right?' Tommy asked.

'Don't concern yourself with me, I heal quick. Don't you know we blacks got leather skin just like that of a sea lion or a right whale?'

'Aye,' Muffin laughed, 'and your back looks like a carcase that the whalers half-flensed before throwing it back. I reckon them pink stripes will look real pretty when they're healed.'

The laughter stopped abruptly when Bungs joined them at the table. It was unusual for him to be late for a meal.

'Have you seen Grimes?' Muffin said.

Bungs nodded.

'How is he?' Eku asked, wincing as he leaned forward.

156

'The surgeon says he's not good. His leg's broken to splinters, and his ankle bones will be good for nothing but a game of jacks on the deck. He says if the leg goes bad he'll have to take it off, but that he's never likely to walk on it again as it is.'

'Best have it off then and have done with it, I reckon.'

'Bloody bad luck,' Muffin said. 'His leg looked a bloody mess.'

'He told me, he tried to jump out of the gun's road but he wasn't quick enough. But he asked me to thank you for trying to stop Hobbles from firing.'

Eku shook his head in frustration. 'I should have grabbed the match from Hobbles' hand, but I wasn't close enough.'

'It weren't right you getting a flogging for it,' Tommy argued. 'Why didn't you tell the captain what happened. You should have stood up for what you saw and what you tried to do. That's what my ma always told me.'

'Them rules might work back home, lad, but on a ship it's different. The navy's got its own set of rules and I don't mean the ones we are always reminded of. Remember this – rule number one – never argue with an officer. See where it got me.'

Bungs nodded. 'Eku's right. On His Majesty's ships, it's best if you keeps your trap shut, you does your duty and you don't question anything them in the blue uniforms say. Stick by that and you'll be all right – but even then, there's still no guarantees. Sometimes,' Bungs explained, 'one of them officers takes a dislike to a foremast Jack – like Atherstone has with Eku here. Hard to know why he'll pick on a particular tar, maybe he don't like the colour of his skin, or where he comes from, or maybe the man reminds him of someone who once offended him. Seems there's neither rhyme nor reason for it, but when it happens, that young upstart, who thinks he's somebody, can make a man's life a misery. I've seen it before on other ships. One sailor, I knew, was so picked on, he tossed himself overboard. At least that's what was said, as he disappeared one night and no one ever saw him again.'

'So it don't really matter if you keep your nose clean and do as you're told, because you're damned anyway.'

'Ignore what Muffin's saying,' Bungs advised. 'Eku can look after himself, and you've nothing to worry about, lad. You told me yourself the captain did you a favour once before.'

'That's more than he's done for anyone else aboard this ship,' Muffin added, cynically.

'Hey! Shut it, you. Captain Quintrell's a fair man. He might have dragged us to hell and back but he always brought us through it safe and sound. And if we're lucky by the time this cruise is done, there'll be a pocketful of prize money waiting for us back in Portsmouth.'

Tommy looked at his black friend.

'Don't depend on it, lad. We haven't seen an enemy ship since we left the North Atlantic, and right now there's no war in the Pacific because all the ships are busy fighting in the Channel or Mediterranean. Only chance we'll get of prizes is when we're heading back to Europe.'

'Don't be too sure. They say Napoleon is building a fleet of ships that'll be faster than ours. I reckon it won't be long before he's sending some to the Pacific.'

'Didn't you say, he'll not come here to fight?' Tommy asked.

'It'll not be the fighting that brings him,' Bungs said. 'It'll be the Spanish treasure ships loaded with silver bars, and chests full of doubloons and dollars from the sale of slaves. As tempting as rind to a rat. You mark my words, we'll meet some Frenchies afore long.'

'You wanted to see me,' Simon Parry said, as he stepped into the captain's cabin.

Oliver nodded but barely lifted his head from the stack of papers, logs and account books scattered on his desk in front of him. 'This aspect of my work is tedious. I am sure you can relate to that.'

'Indeed, I can.'

'Please, sit,' he said, sorting through them to retrieve the piece he required. 'This is Mr Atherstone's report. I ask you to read it and offer your comments. I understand you were not witness to the event which occurred yesterday.'

'Unfortunately, no. I was forward at the time.'

'Unfortunate, indeed,' Oliver said, handing the paper to his first lieutenant. 'As you know, Mr Atherstone laid charges against Ekundayo. This is the third time he had accused the sailor of insubordination. The first time was associated with a charge of theft, but when the item turned up, he agreed to withdraw the allegation. The second time was insubordination and disobeying orders during practice, and this is the latest incident which occurred

158

with the gun.' Oliver shook his head. He could well do without this type of problem. 'Remind me,' he said, 'how long has this young midshipman been aboard?'

'It's ten days since we sailed from Valdivia.'

'Ten days!' Running his claw-like forefinger through his greasy hair, Oliver tucked the stray strands behind his ear. 'Do you know of anyone aboard who has sailed with Mr Atherstone on a previous voyage?'

'No, but I can make some discrete enquiries, if you wish.'

'What puzzles me,' Oliver said, ignoring the question put to him, 'is that a well-bred, intelligent and efficient midshipman of a relatively mature age, having already served almost six years, appears to be undermined by the presence of one particular seaman in his division.'

Simon nodded.

'As captain, I had no alternative but to address the charges, and deal judiciously with them. Yet, as a man, I could find no fault with the sailor. Similarly, and more puzzlingly, I find no fault with the midshipman who brought the charges.'

He thought for a moment and then continued. 'Mr Atherstone is always punctual, polite and dispenses his duties efficiently. He writes an excellent log and presents his daily reports in a remarkably noteworthy fashion. I understand he performs well in the sailing master's classes and climbs the rigging as nimbly as any topman. Besides those things, he stands out from the other middies both by the cut and neatness of his dress and by his mannerisms.'

Despite his own dislike of the Admiralty's adherence to patronage and privilege, Oliver had to admit that it was often men of such breeding who rose to become great Admirals.

Was it because of his apparent breeding that Atherstone appeared aloof regarding fellowship and was not an integral member of the midshipmen's berth? Perhaps if the Honourable Algernon Biggleswade-Smythe had not been dispatched along with Captain Liversedge in the North Atlantic, the pair might have a found common ground, if not through their respected families, then at least through the common pursuits enjoyed by members of the upper class.

In Oliver's estimation, Mr Atherstone needed some distraction. His preoccupation with duty was admirable but it was all consuming, to the extent it blocked out any hint of good humour, *bonhomie*, chivalrous thoughts and mateship. The gulf between officer and men had to be maintained, but it was a fine line to tread. And it was a problem all officers encountered at some time in their careers.

To maintain discipline on his ship, a captain must discourage familiarity between senior officers and seamen, but the rift must not be so great as to breed contempt, jealousy or hatred. And it was not for the captain of any ship to try to change a man's nature. He must accept both officers and men for what they were. But allegiances were important and, in Oliver's opinion, true friendships formed in the midshipmen's mess and wardroom were important bonds that an officer would carry with him from the day he passed the examination for lieutenant, to his first command, and later to his appointment as Admiral.

Oliver smirked at his own conclusion. He had arrived back at the question of privilege between friends that carried with it an unwritten obligation that could be called on at any time. A favour to the son of a fellow officer who you had sailed with for twenty years. Or for the nephew of a long-dead post captain, whose esteemed brother you had messed with as a fifteen-year-old midshipman a decade ago. It was of some consolation to Oliver that Earl St Vincent held a mutual feeling of disapproval of promotion through privilege and patronage within the service.

For his own part, his path had been unconventional, to say the least. He had been born on the heeling deck of a stinking herring boat, and cut his teeth on the gunnels. He had thrown and lost his first lead-line by the age of five and suffered the due consequences. And he had doubled the Horn several times before his tenth birthday.

Times of toil and terror had faded from his memory, but the thrill of a rolling sea and the sound of the rigging singing in the wind had never left him. Aboard his father's packet, he had sailed from Boston and plied the Americas both north and south, and crossed the Atlantic several times. He thanked his father for all the practical things he knew – and for ensuring that in the winter when the ship was out of the water, he attended nautical school to learn all that his father and the sea could not teach him.

On entering the Royal Navy, he had learned to adapt to a regimented way of life and had become intimately familiar with the rules to which the navy stringently adhered, though he did not agree with them all. He had seen the impress gangs at work, had even mustered men for ships on which he served. But he also remembered running from the Press as a lad and hiding in the cellar of an inn. At a tender age, running from the gang was a challenge. The ones who were caught were the old hands, the drunks, the sick and those who had been injured, not the fit young coves that the navy really needed.

By the time he entered as a middie, there was nothing about the sea with which he was not familiar, either practically or theoretically – he had been well schooled – which aggravated the ship's schoolmaster no end.

In Oliver's opinion, a love for the sea was something a man must have coursing through his veins from an early age for it could not be acquired or taught no matter how many classes and examinations were attended.

The sea, despite all its fickle faces, was part of him. Even now, the call of *full and by* sent a tingle running down his spine. The wind was his companion. The thrum of the rigging his music. The thud of a wave on the bow – his pulse. The aqua-marine of a tropical atoll, the gold-dusted spindrift in the setting sun, even the star-speckled black sky at night were all part of the rich palette which coloured his world. If only he could paint in the fashion of artists who captured such images on canvas. He envied them.

From the ship's rail, the Atacama coastline dissolved in a haze of mauve against a violet sky. Here the land encompassed a totally different world – harsh, dry, extreme and uninviting. For Oliver Quintrell, the sea was his comfort and companion and, when licking her salt from his lips, he had no doubt she was his mistress. Despite her foibles and fickleness, moods and mysteries, she was soft and sensuous, beguiling in her calms and tantalizing in her tantrums. She was the force which heaved beneath him everyday and cradled him to sleep every night. By constantly challenging him, it was the sea who made him fearless (not reckless), and eventually it was the sea who would receive him into her arms on the final day of reckoning.

Chapter 17

The Challenge

Having followed a northerly course as far as the Tropic of Capricorn, assisted in part along the Chilean coast by the cold north-flowing Humboldt Current, the frigate turned seaward and headed in a north-westerly direction to 15° south latitude. Not far from here, *Perpetual* again regained sight of the coast at it neared its destination.

It had been five weeks since he had left Valdivia and Oliver trusted that when the frigate arrived in Callao he would find *Compendium* anchored in the roadstead. He was eager to meet with the naval officer dubbed *Boris the Florist* and wondered if Captain Crabthorne would live up to the preconceived image he had formed in his mind.

From the freezing waters of the straits navigated by Magellan, the crew was now confronted with tropical heat and often unsympathetic winds. As they neared the Peruvian port, the crystal clear morning air of the far south was replaced by the same misty miasma they had encountered off the Atacama coast – a fog that often failed to clear by midday. This strange sea fret provided a palpable dampness that made visibility difficult. As such, because Lima's port was a busy mercantile harbour, with ships arriving from North America and from across the Pacific, with a veil of mist enveloping everything, a cautious approach was essential.

Another concern Oliver shared with his sailing master was the nature of the coast. From both memory and the chart, it was littered with rocky islands, a few large and many small ones, all pitted with caves and caverns that provided ideal breeding grounds for hundreds of seals, sea lions and penguins, and the thousands of seabirds whose dropping coated the rocks in a thick carpet of white.

The largest island, San Lorenzo, was rocky, barren and inhospitable. It was a long slender piece of land resting on a north-west to south-east axis. Sitting two miles from the mainland, it offered natural protection to the port of Callao and the city of Lima less than ten miles ride inland. But, together with a peninsula jutting out from the land leaving only a narrow channel between the two, it also contributed to the conflicting currents flowing around the island.

Despite that, after weeks of battling the prevailing winds of the Pacific Ocean, Oliver looked forward to whatever protection the island could offer. But always at the back of his mind were the memories he held.

As a boy, he had shivered to the island's name and had never forgotten the stories he had heard. That it was inhabited by ghosts, and its steep sides, which rose almost 1,000 feet into the clouds, were a stairway to the afterlife. But whether it was haunted or cursed had never deterred the English and Dutch pirates who, for more than two centuries, had landed there, perished there and been buried there. Suffice to say, such rumours and a total lack of fresh water meant the island was uninhabited and therefore was no threat to passing ships.

But it was not the island's history that currently bothered Oliver. His present concern was the currents which ran around it.

After charting a course for San Lorenzo Island, *Perpetual* cleared the island and approached Callao from the north-west. Once in the roadstead, the captain was delighted to learn from the lookout that a British frigate was in the harbour. It could only be *Compendium*. Shortly after, following an exchange of signals, a boat headed towards them.

When the visiting captain was piped aboard and stepped onto *Perpetual*'s deck, a few eyebrows were raised together with a few sly grins exchanged between the junior officers. But, apart from a brief greeting by Captain Quintrell and an introduction to Mr Parry, there were no other formalities and within minutes of arriving, Captain Crabthorne was conducted below to the great cabin where the captain's steward was waiting with a tray of refreshments.

'We meet at last,' Oliver said, after inviting his visitor to be seated.

'Entirely my pleasure,' Boris Crabthorne said, dabbing the sweat from his brow. 'However, I presume this is not a chance meeting?

Would I be correct in assuming that you arrived in this harbour under Admiralty orders to locate me and my ship?'

'You are correct, sir.'

'Then I must apologize for having led you on a merry chase. The voyage here took much longer than anticipated.'

'But, despite the time taken, the fact that you have arrived safely and with a sound ship is surely something worthy of celebrating.'

'Indeed,' Crabthorne said, pausing to collect his thoughts, then waiting until Casson had left and the cabin door was firmly closed. 'Worthy indeed,' he continued, 'and I thank the Lord that I have arrived intact. However, I find myself in an embarrassing and awkward situation because I have been unable to complete my mission. My purpose, in speaking with you so presumptuously, is to beg your assistance to help me rectify that problem.'

'*Perpetual* is at your disposal, sir.'

'Thank you, Captain, I felt sure, when I saw you sail into Callao Bay, that I would be able to rely on you.'

'Of that, you can be assured.'

'In that case,' Crabthorne said, rising to his feet, 'I will take up no more of your time but invite you and your lieutenant to join me for dinner in order that I can explain the situation in more detail.'

'I will look forward to it,' Oliver said.

The most striking feature of Captain Crabthorne's cabin, in comparison with his own, was the strong odour. Oliver's cabin in *Perpetual* smelled of dusty charts, papers, books, sweat, a salt-hardened boat cloak and the lingering aroma of his last pot of coffee. Boris Crabthorne's cabin, however, was scented with seedpods, dried bulbs, tubers, and freshly cut local flowers. The smell reminded him of his wife's linen store.

While savouring a glass of wine, Oliver leaned back in his chair and mentally mused over the naval officer seated opposite him. The appearance of a well-groomed young gentleman of pleasant appearance wearing the dress uniform of a post captain was not what he had originally visualized. It brought a spontaneous curl to his lips.

Boris Crabthorne was conscious of his gaze. 'I believe you were expecting an older man.'

Oliver could not deny the fact. 'From the information I had received—'

'My nickname,' he said. '*Boris the Florist*. It has a certain flare, don't you agree?'

'It does, indeed,' Oliver conceded, accepting that his preconception had been flawed. 'I have an adage,' he admitted, 'that one should never form opinions of people until one has met them. However, I fail to follow my own advice and fall into a trap occasionally.'

'Then, you will be relieved to know that you are not alone. The nickname always precedes me, but I have learned to take a certain delight in observing the receptions I receive. I feel sure I would be met without a passing glance if I wore a wig, powdered my hair, dressed in a peasant's smock and carried a pitchfork over my shoulder.'

The captain laughed. 'Exactly the image I had envisaged. However, I had been misled by a rumour that your interest in plants reached back twenty years or more therefore I had expected you to be a man of considerably more mature years.'

'Your information was correct. My botanical tutelage began when I was six years of age. That was the time that my widowed aunt began paying frequent visits to Sir Joseph Banks at the Botanical Gardens at Kew. Of course, I was too young at the time to realize that the excursions were not for my health and edification. I was later informed that I filled the role as chaperone more than adequately.'

'Sir Joseph had quite a reputation with the ladies, I hear,' Simon quipped.

'And still does today, despite his advancing years.'

Oliver liked Captain Crabthorne and it was obvious from the relaxed expressions of the officers around the table, his view was shared.

'Despite whatever my aunt's intentions were, my interest, even at that tender age, was in the extensive collection of plants Sir Joseph had amassed and the propagation methods that he enthused about so passionately. The number of specimens, which he and Dr Solander collected during their exploration of New Holland, is truly remarkable. I believe the good doctor identified and named over one thousand new species. But I digress. Surprisingly Sir Joseph spoke little of his voyages, either to the Antipodes or the Arctic but being in his presence was enough to implant in me the desire to sail to distant lands. Unfortunately, being neither a scientist nor born into the gentry, entering the navy via the hawse-hole was the only avenue available to me. However, as you will see from my flower boxes, my passion for botany, acquired courtesy of Sir Joseph, still remains with me to this day. And, so it seems, does the nickname – *Boris the Florist*, which I am quite proud to wear. Needless to say, I hope in the long term, it will be my naval career that will be remembered by future generations and not my collection of flowering plants.'

'Amen to that,' Oliver said, raising his glass.

The assembled company seconded the sentiment.

'If I might enquire, what part of your mission remains to be accomplished? Do your orders carry you north from here?'

'No, Callao is the limit of my cruise,' Crabthorne said hesitantly, casting a questioning glance towards Oliver's first lieutenant.

'If you are at liberty to share your information, sir, I can vouch for my first lieutenant. Simon Parry is a man of great integrity and is familiar with the responsibility of command. Any information you divulge will go no further than these wooden walls.'

Satisfied, Captain Crabthorne acknowledged Mr Parry, removed a bowl of seed pods from the centre of the table and replaced it with an Admiralty chart. Once unrolled, the officers re-examined the local coastline including the offshore islands and the long narrow peninsula pointing directly to the island of San Lorenzo. While there were few specific features marked on the island, apart from lines indicating the gradient of its precipitous sides, and a large pentagonal fortress, situated on the top of the peninsula, clearly delineated in red ink.

'This,' he said, pointing to the site, 'is Royal Phillip's Castle or *Castillo del Real Felipe* – a fortress constructed fifty years ago to protect the city from pirates and corsairs. It is the largest single fortification built outside Spain. As you may have noticed, it was built high on the promontory. That position was, no doubt, chosen as a fine vantage point, but also to safeguard it from a tidal flood that might sweep in and devastate the town.'

'A formidable stronghold.'

'It is indeed. But *El Callao* was once the main port for all of Spain's South American colonies. And it was through this port that all the country's gold, silver and precious gemstones were shipped north to Panama, where they were transported by llama and mule trains along *El Camino Real* – the Royal Road – a grand name for nothing more than a donkey track, and when they reached the Caribbean Sea they were put on ships destined for the Crown of Spain. For centuries those Spanish galleons attracted pirates and corsairs, not least Francis Drake, who attacked this coast and plundered its riches in the name of Queen Elizabeth.'

'An act the Spanish do not forget.'

'Yet, despite that fact, your ship received a gun salute from the battlements when you entered the roadstead.'

Oliver nodded. 'That welcoming fire may not be so congenial in the future.'

'That is true. And even now, I fear we must be on our guard. From their vantage point at the fort there is little that transpires on the surrounding waters which the Spanish lookouts are not aware of.'

He turned to Oliver. 'Let me explain my situation. This much I can tell you. I sailed here from England under Admiralty orders carrying a vellum pouch containing dispatches and items of extreme value. I had promised faithfully that I would not allow this item to fall into enemy hands, and despite the various disasters, that befell my ship along the way, I arrived here with it in one piece. However, in order to avoid the heavy seas breaking on the western side of San Lorenzo, I dropped anchor in the lee of the island.

From there, it was my intention to send a boat into the port to disembark the passenger I was carrying, request a pilot and ask permission to take on wood and water. But, before that could be done, a pair of Spanish ships approached to within speaking distance. From their rather aloof and dictatorial attitudes, I felt certain they had prior knowledge that I was carrying something of vital significance – arms or money perhaps. They wasted no time in making it clear they intended to board and conduct a thorough search.'

'Was the Ambassador sailing with you?'

'Fortunately, yes. He was the passenger I was referring to and his presence satisfied the Spaniards to a certain extent – but not enough.' He paused. 'My orders from the Admiralty were explicit. Were I to be boarded, the valuable item I was carrying must be destroyed. Though the Spanish Crown was not an enemy of war, I was bound by that pledge and could not let the pouch fall into foreign hands, therefore, I dispatched it to the seabed.'

'So all is lost?'

'I pray that is not so, and with your help, I am hoping it can be recovered.'

Oliver frowned. 'Is that possible? You talk of a vellum pouch. Surely, if it was consigned to the sea, its contents would have met with irreparable damage. But that will only be ascertained if and when the item is located.'

'Please go on,' Crabthorne said.

'I see several problems,' Oliver said. 'The pouch could easily have been washed away by the fickle currents or become buried in the sand, or even swallowed by a large fish. Even knowing the exact position on the chart will not guarantee finding it. The Admiralty's charts of this region are not always accurate. They may have been incorrectly drawn or the depths incorrectly recorded due to the steep declines and vagaries of the undulating seabed. I am already aware the currents around the island can, at times, be quite confused. All in all, I feel any chance of locating it unlikely.'

Boris Crabthorne raised his eyebrows. 'Your estimation of a successful recovery does not inspire confidence, Captain, though I must admit that my own thoughts initially followed on a similar vein. However,' he said with a hint of satisfaction, 'having travelled almost halfway around the world at considerable cost to my ship and the loss of four good men to the Southern Ocean, before parting with my precious cargo, I made certain provisions with a view to recovering it.'

'I am intrigued,' Oliver said. 'Pray continue.'

'In the limited time I had, before the Spanish officer and his men boarded *Compendium*, I had the pouch wrapped in several layers of tarpaulin, bound firmly and dipped in pitch in order to render it waterproof. Then, after securing a rope around it, the package was looped around the anchor cable and allowed to slide down the length of the cable to the ocean floor.'

'And what depth you were in?'

'Nine fathoms.'

'Too deep for a man to dive to, I fear.'

'For an English sailor, I agree, but I have onboard a pair of Lascars who, though they speak little English, assure me that they can dive to one-hundred feet on a single breath. Diving for pearls was once their occupation.'

'But you are now anchored at the port across the bay. Surely when you weighed and hauled your cable, the package would have come up with it.'

Captain Crabthorne rubbed his freshly shaved jaw. 'That was another problem I anticipated and had to resolve it hastily. After thoroughly searching the ship, including my cabin, and appearing satisfied, the Spanish officer invited me to weigh and accompany his ships to the harbour.'

'An invitation or an order?' Oliver smiled.

Boris Crabthorne shrugged. 'An instruction, I believe. I had no alternative and agreed to proceed to the port with them. However, as I knew I was being closely observed from the decks of both ships, and probably from Fort Royal on the peninsula, I chose to act with discretion. Rather than raising the anchor to retrieve the package and chancing the possibility that it might fall into the wrong hands, I had the anchor cable cut. Therefore, gentlemen, the prize for this mission now rests on the bottom of the channel. It is attached to a bower anchor bearing fifty feet of hempen tail that is currently swaying in the sea like a giant kelp plant.'

A patter of applause rattled around the table.

'I commend your ingenuity, Captain, and I sincerely trust this item can now be recovered. But, tell me how can *Perpetual* be of assistance?'

'Because of the suspicion which greeted my arrival, and because the Spaniards are still keeping a close eye on both me and my ship, I fear I cannot return to the place where I originally anchored without alerting their attention to that bay. If, however, you are prepared to sail to that location, I can provide you with two Lascars who have volunteered to dive, search for the cable and retrieve the package attached to it. If you agree to attempt this recovery, I would suggest all activity takes place on the far side of the frigate, so that it cannot be observed from the fort.'

Oliver and Simon exchanged glances.

'If I am permitted to make an observation,' Simon Parry said.

'Please feel free.'

'Much will depend on the currents and, from what we have learnt, the full force of the Pacific Ocean arrives first on the west side of San Lorenzo. From there the current is divided and flows around both the northern and southern tips of the island, meeting itself head-on on the eastern side, between the island and the narrow peninsula which points like an arrow from the land. Isn't it possible, therefore, that as a result of these confused currents, even a ship's bower anchor, weighing over a ton, could have been dislodged or been buried beneath swirling sand?'

All eyes turned to *Compendium*'s captain for an answer.

'Then there are the big tides to take into account,' Oliver added.

'I cannot disagree,' Captain Crabthorne said, 'and your arguments are commendable.'

'However,' Oliver said. 'While there is the slightest chance of retrieval and the means of doing so, I must accept the challenge. My hope is that the divers will succeed, but if they fail, I am certain there are other ways and means.'

'I am in your debt,' Boris Crabthorne said, glancing at the dwindling daylight through the stern gallery windows. 'Gentlemen, before we eat, you must allow me to introduce you to some of my specimens. I made several valuable additions to my personal catalogue in Valdivia for which I am very excited.'

'Delighted,' Oliver said, 'however, there is just one other matter that I must broach. I have, aboard *Perpetual*, a midshipman who, I understand, is from your ship. I encountered him in Valdivia.'

'You are referring to Mr Atherstone, if I am not mistaken.'

'I understand he is a relative of yours.'

'A distant cousin, very distant – but not distant enough for me not to be pressured into accepting him aboard my ship. How does he fare?'

'Quite well. In fact, surprisingly well considering the history of his earlier illness.'

Boris Crabthorne sighed. 'I had hoped he would remain in Valdivia at least until my business here was completed.'

'Might I enquire as to what ailed him?'

'That is hard to know,' Captain Crabthorne said. 'It puzzled the ship's surgeon. His bodily health appeared good, but his demeanour was troubled. For much of the voyage his behaviour was most acceptable, he performed his duties without question and I was pleased to have him aboard. Then for no apparent reason he became prone to bouts of temper, yet I could find nothing which provoked these outbursts, and, by the time we reached the west coast of Chile, his conduct on deck was, at times, totally inappropriate. When questioned, he appeared to have little control of his responses, and the following morning would have no memory of the events of the previous day. Because of this and because of *Compendium*'s mission and dire condition at the time, I had him removed to the sick berth, and shortly after entering the river at Valdivia, I made arrangements for him to be removed to private care until we returned.'

He turned to his guest. 'You say he is well at the present time. Did you notice anything unusual in his behaviour?'

'Not categorically,' Oliver said. 'Mr Atherstone performed his duties efficiently and with enthusiasm. Perhaps with a slight misguided overabundance of enthusiasm at times. But for a nineteen-year-old midshipman that is to be expected.'

The expression of joy, which *Compendium*'s captain had shown when discussing his plants, was replaced with a visage of concern.

'Is it your wish that I return him to your command, or shall I retain him on my books until we have cleared Callao and are returning to Valdivia?'

Boris Crabthorne was instantly relieved. 'The latter arrangement would be preferable. Thank you, Captain Quintrell. I find myself doubly in your debt.'

After spending an acceptable amount of time viewing Captain Crabthorne's specimens – some flowering, others seeding, some drying, others in the process of being pressed or preserved by other means, Oliver and his first lieutenant shared a fine meal with the captain and officers of *Compendium*. Freshly cooked crab, lobster and scallops were served with locally grown vegetables, accompanied by a pleasantly palatable glass of wine from an aged cask (courtesy of the captain of the Spanish ship of the line). The conversation over dinner veered from plants and official pouches to the discomfort experienced by ships and men during their various navigations around the Island of Tierra del Fuego. Remarkably, acute memories of the perils had already mellowed, which was as it should be, as ahead of both ships was the return journey around Cape Horn.

On hearing of the wrecked slave ship, Captain Crabthorne reported that two other Portuguese slavers were presently in Callao harbour and preparing to leave. They had discharged their cargo before he arrived. Also in the harbour was a Spanish man-of-war, and an assortment of trading vessels, one having arrived from San

Francisco, another from the East Indies and one having sailed from India.

With the meal completed and the table cleared, the chart they had examined earlier was again rolled out. This time, in order to prevent the corners from curling, four containers of strangely-shaped seedpods – the likes of which the visitors had never seen before, were used as paperweights.

'This is the only chart I have,' Captain Crabthorne said. 'And, no doubt, the Admiralty supplied you with an identical copy. Fortunately, it reveals all that is pertinent. As Mr Parry pointed out, the sea current running between the island of San Lorenzo and the point of the peninsula can be deceptively strong. This large island measures approximately eight miles long and two miles in width from west to east, but because it has no natural water, it is uninhabited.'

'Apart from its ghosts!'

Boris Crabthorne did not join in the midshipmen's laughter. 'Indeed,' he explained to his guests, 'for centuries the Inca Indians, who were the original inhabitants of this region, used the island as a sacred burial ground. And it is still used for that purpose today.'

Oliver retained a straight face. 'Which means we will not be observed from that direction.'

Pointing to a slight curve in the coastline near the island's north-eastern tip, Captain Crabthorne explained, 'There are a few bays along this stretch of the coast, though in some places the perpendicular cliffs rise straight from the sea. This one,' he said, marking it with a cross, 'is not a true bay, but it is partially sheltered. Like the rest of the island, it is barren apart from three petrified tree trunks that lean on each other like a trio of peg-legged sailors waiting on the beach for a ship that will never come.' He turned his attention back to the chart. 'I anchored in nine fathoms, a cable's length from the shore directly in line with these contorted specimens. And it was here that my package was dispatched to the deep.'

The ticking of the clock over the empty fire hearth was the only sound.

'My greatest fear is that the current has carried both cable and anchor into water which is too deep for the divers to descend to. However, as the name *El Callao* signifies, the beaches in this region are pebbled, therefore it is unlikely it has been swallowed by sand an disappeared from view. At best, I hope that the cable is floating just below the surface like a length of kelp waiting to snag a rudder.'

'And at worst?'

'I fear it could be lying on the bottom like an enormous sea-snake.'

'And if the package is retrieved,' Oliver ventured, 'will that allow you to depart from Callao immediately?'

'Once the pouch is in the hands of its intended recipient, I will have fulfilled my Admiralty orders and I will not linger in this port any longer than necessary.'

'Then I see no reason to delay, either. If you will kindly have your divers put aboard my boat, I shall attend to the recovery of this package as soon as *Perpetual* can make sail for the island.'

Chapter 18

The Barrel Bell

At the conclusion of his meeting with Boris Crabthorne, Captain Quintrell returned to *Perpetual* and, despite the hour being late, requested all officers present themselves in his cabin. Having pledged to Captain Crabthorne that he would recover the lost pouch, Oliver was intent on fulfilling his promise. For the present, however, he was not sure how best to proceed. The wine over dinner followed by several glasses of fine French brandy had not helped his dilemma. Perhaps his officers could conjure up some imaginative ideas.

Having received word that the state of their dress would not come under scrutiny, the midshipmen, who had retired to their hammocks for the night, arrived in the Captain's cabin in various states of undress, most without coats or neckerchiefs and one, despite the moist warmth of the Peruvian coast, with a blanket wrapped around his shoulders. When they were all gathered, Oliver proceeded to outline the content of the meeting he had attended on *Compendium*, however, he did not reveal all that had been discussed. While initially a few pairs of bleary eyes were in danger of closing, utterance of the three words *valuable sunken package* elicited a buzz of excitement and provided the captain with his officers' full attention. To young midshipmen with vivid imaginations, that could only translate to one thing – sunken treasure – Spanish gold, silver doubloons, precious stones. But their expectations quickly fizzled when Captain Quintrell explained there was neither treasure nor prize money to be had.

'Gentlemen, I need to recover an item from the seabed. It is sitting in approximately nine fathoms of water.'

Mr Nightingale cleared his throat. 'Are we permitted to know what this item is?'

'A small package,' Oliver said. 'And what it contains is immaterial. What I can say, however, is that it is of considerable value and were it to fall into the wrong hands, the consequences would be dire not only here in South America but also in Europe. This item was consigned to Captain Crabthorne by the Lords Commissioners of the Admiralty and it is our duty to provide assistance by recovering it.'

'You said, "falling into the wrong hands",' Mr Nightingale repeated. 'Might I ask who the enemy is?'

'Time will tell,' Oliver replied, evading the issue. Since his visit to Señor McGinty in Valdivia, he was acutely aware of the political unrest in various quarters of the Spanish viceroyalty, though he thought it unlikely his junior officers were familiar with the internal tensions simmering in South America. For the present, he did not wish to embark on a long discussion about it, as it had no immediate bearing on the problem confronting them.

'Tell me, Gentlemen, how would you retrieve an article from the seabed that is sitting in nine fathoms of water?'

A few looked puzzled, while the youngest midshipmen looked uncomfortable, appearing guilty for not being able to offer an answer.

Mr Tully volunteered. 'We could drag the kedge anchor along the bottom and hope to rake it up.'

Oliver nodded.

'Or trawl for it with a net,' Mr Lazenby suggested.

The sailing master was cynical, 'The Pacific is a mighty sea and not as peaceful as its name suggests.'

'That is true, Mr Greenleaf.'

'What size is this thing we are seeking?' Mr Tully asked.

Oliver turned to his writing desk and opened the top drawer. From it he took an empty Admiralty pouch which had previously contained his orders. 'A little larger than this,' he said, 'wrapped in tarpaulin and coated in pitch.'

The sailing master laughed. 'You'll never find that in fifty-feet of water. A blind man seeking a needle in a hayrick would have more luck.'

Without changing his expression, Oliver replied curtly, 'I don't believe luck plays a part in this equation. However, to make the search a little easier, the package is attached to a bower anchor weighing one and a quarter tons with over fifty-feet of hempen cable trailing from it. A slightly larger target than a needle, if I am not mistaken.

'Gentlemen,' he continued, glancing around the motley group seated at the table, 'this is a serious matter. Those of you, who were on deck when I returned from *Compendium*, will be aware I was accompanied by two Lascars. These Indian sailors once dived for pearls and could sink to a depth of a hundred feet on a single breath. But diving for pearl mussels in a warm tropical sea is a different proposition to descending into the cold currents which flow all the way from the Antarctic. Though these remarkable divers can grease their bodies and carry rocks to speed their descent, the Humboldt Current may be too cold and the Pacific currents too strong even for them. Though eager to oblige and demonstrate their ability, the two sailors are no longer young men and I fear the task will be too great. Hence we need to consider possible alternatives.'

Oliver paused, waiting for more suggestions, but no others were forthcoming. 'The idea of dragging the kedge anchor is reasonable, but I fear that will create a disturbance on the sea bed and may damage or dislodge the article in question. I therefore, discount dragging or fishing for it.' He looked to the silent faces. 'Have any of you heard of a diving bell?'

'I saw drawings of a bell by Halley,' Mr Nightingale said, 'at the Royal Society rooms. It was fitted with a window so the passenger who sat inside could explore the seabed.'

The midshipmen found the idea amusing.

Oliver commended him. 'Gentlemen, let me educate you. Over one-hundred years ago, £200,000 was plucked from the sea off the Spanish Island of Hispaniola.'

With the mention of money, the captain again had the officers' full attention.

'From a sunken treasure ship?'

'Indeed it was, Mr Lazenby – the wreck of a Spanish Galleon. That contraption was built by Sir William Phipps.'

The sailing master was cynical. 'In one-hundred years, yarns tend to expand a little.'

'Then let me remind you of the *Sydney Cove* which ran aground only a dozen years ago – as a result of inadequate Admiralty charts – off the coast of New Holland. The ship's master, Captain Hamilton, built a barrel bell, or under-sea breathing machine that was used to recover most of the ship's cargo.'

'A cargo of rum, if I am not mistaken?' Mr Parry added.

'Indeed,' Oliver said.

'I bet the crew enjoyed that,' Mr Lazenby added, laughing.

'Not so. It was an arduous job undertaken in cold rough seas and the men found it both dangerous and disappointing for, in his wisdom, the captain had the barrels deposited on an adjacent island which the crew could not reach. Captain Hamilton was obviously a wise man and familiar with his sailors' liking for a drop of alcohol.'

'Shame on him,' Mr Lazenby mumbled.

'I admit the story of this bell amused me at the time, but now I find nothing humorous about it.'

The sailing master looked puzzled.

'If my memory serves me,' Oliver said, 'the design was quite simple. It consisted of a large barrel – a hogshead or leaguer – sealed at the top and open at the bottom. It was suspended from a cable and forced below the surface with heavy weights attached to it. Breathing tubes were inserted into its sides and a thwart was fitted inside for a person to sit on.'

'He would have to be a small man,' Mr Greenleaf suggested.

'And one who doesn't breathe a great deal of air!'

'And doesn't chatter unnecessarily,' Oliver added. 'Breathing only the air confined in the barrel, the bell's navigator could visually scour the sea bed while propelling himself along with his feet.'

'Walking across the bottom?' Mr Tully asked.

'In a rather unusual manner, yes.'

'I doubt anyone on board would want to be dropped in the ocean in such a contraption,' Mr Tully said. 'Most of the crew can't even swim.'

'The man inside doesn't need to swim.'

'Unless the barrel tips over and he's tossed out. Then he'd have to swim back up to the surface,' the sailing master added.

'Could such a barrel bell be built on board? One that is big enough to accommodate a seaman and still be completely watertight?' Mr Nightingale asked.

'I see no reason why not,' Oliver replied. 'If the *Sydney Cove* could do it, then *Perpetual* can also. I will speak with the cooper and the carpenter and, I am sure that between them they will make a diving bell. The Lascars will help, but because of their age and the temperature of the water, I will not expect them to dive to the bottom.' With that, Oliver had resolved in his mind what had to be done. 'Thank you for you attendance, gentlemen. Sleep well, but first thing in the morning I require you to speak with your divisions. I need one man to dive in the bell, and a few sailors who are able to assist the Lascars on the surface.'

The chatter in the mess mellowed to a whispered hum when Mr Atherstone descended the ladder near the fire hearth and eyed the men. Most stopped talking and returned to eating their breakfast.

'Which of you lubbers can swim?' Atherstone demanded, knowing the sailors would be reluctant to admit to anything until they knew the reason for the enquiry. As a rule, questions were never asked out of passing interest and when put by a midshipman or lieutenant they always carried an ulterior motive which usually entailed extra duties.

'I can,' piped Tommy innocently. 'Who wants to know?'

Bungs kicked him, under the table – a warning to hold his tongue.

'As a matter of fact, the captain does,' Mr Atherstone replied. 'He needs a man who is small, agile and fairly bright, and one who won't drown in the water.'

'And what if he does drown?' one of the sailors called.

Mr Atherstone ignored the question. 'He also wants a couple of men who are not shy of the water.'

'I won't drown,' Tommy said to his mate, as the midshipman moved further along the deck.

Eku tapped Tommy on the elbow. 'If you volunteer, it'll get you out of the scraping shot for a while.'

Tommy thought about it. 'Can you swim?' he said to his friend.

'Of course. Everyone swims where I come from.'

Atherstone had overheard their conversation.

'All right you two, enough talk. I will take the pair of you. Go see Mr Parry. He'll tell you what you have to do.'

The task of converting a large barrel into a diving bell was fraught with difficulty, not for its construction, but for the tension it created between the ship's carpenter and Bungs, the cooper.

Being in charge of all the barrels on the ship, Bungs insisted the job was his responsibility and said he would tolerate no interference. He was confident he could make an airtight bell, capable of withstanding the deep water. He even swore he'd forfeit a week's rum ration, if a drop of water leaked into it.

To complicate matters, the captain requested a glass bull's eyes or prism be inserted in the top of the barrel to allow light to pass into it. He also wanted a thwart fixed across the inside near the bottom. For these jobs, Oliver designated the carpenter to do the work but insisted the two men work together.

Construction was further aggravated when the bosun was appointed to rig secure lines around the diving bell for lowering it into the water and returning it to the surface. He also had to attach a mesh bag, similar to the ones used daily for boiling the six pieces of meat for each mess table. However, this bag would have to be sufficiently large to hold three or four twelve-pound balls, or whatever weight was required to sink the barrel to the sea floor.

Preparing the barrel bell on deck created a considerable amount of interest from the crew and guaranteed the three tradesmen a regular audience.

'But if it's full of air, it's going to bob on the surface like a big cork?' Smithers sneered. 'It'll never go down.'

'It'll sink with a man in it and weights hanging from it,' Mr Tully explained. 'It'll drop to the bottom so Tommy can walk along the seabed or paddle his legs and move along while he searches.'

'Searches for what?' Muffin asked

'A bower anchor and fifty-feet of cable thicker than a man's forearm.'

'And all the while, the lad inside breathes the air in the barrel?'

'That is how it will work.'

'Sounds easy,' Tommy said. 'And if the air runs out, I'll just climb out and swim up to the surface.'

The midshipman quelled his enthusiasm. 'The captain said you mustn't do that. You won't know how far you've dropped and the water might be too deep and the current too strong for you to swim back up on the breath you have in your chest. Remember, if you want to come up, you must tug on the line that runs up to the boat. And you must do that before your air runs out, so the men can haul you up.'

'You'll be all right,' Smithers called. 'There's plenty of big jellyfish but not too many sharks in these waters! Though if you smear yourself with plenty of pork fat, you could attract a few.'

'We can do without your observations, Smithers,' Mr Tully said. 'One more word and you'll be on my list in the morning.'

'Only passing a hobservation,'

'Well I suggest you keep your *hobservations* to yourself,' the midshipman warned. Then he glanced at Tommy. 'Good,' he said. 'Once the bell is finished, I'll tell the captain you're ready.'

The following morning before breakfast, *Perpetual* sailed from its anchorage outside Callao's harbour to the north-east coast of San Lorenzo, only a few miles away. Though a veil of mist would have offered some protection from prying eyes, this morning the ever-present coastal fog was contrary and had dispersed, and the light breeze blowing off the land was welcome and necessary for the frigate to proceed.

Once the rugged northern tip of the island was reached, *Perpetual* followed the barren coastline in a south-easterly direction, carefully observing its cliffs and ledges habited only by sea lions, seals and flocks of noisy seabirds. It was not long before the specific bay was identified. The petrified trunks appeared just as Captain Crabthorne had described them. With two men on the lead, Oliver took his ship to within a cable's length of the shore. Nine fathoms of water beneath the hull was confirmed, as was the fact that the decline of the sea floor was an extension of the steeply sloping sides of the barren island.

No sooner had the anchor been dropped than two of the ship's boats were lowered on the frigate's starboard side, shielding any activity from the watchful gaze of *Fort Felipe* on the peninsula less than two miles away. The only other possible danger could come from the Spanish ships that had intercepted and searched *Compendium*, but having observed a convoy, including a Spanish man-of-war departing the harbour at first light, Oliver considered it unlikely they would be returning that day.

On deck, it being Thursday, the men were encouraged to perform their normal chores, scrubbing their spare hammocks and washing clothes. While extra lookouts were posted at the mastheads and every man was expected to be vigilant, for the present the strait between the island and the peninsula was quiet and the fortress on the headland appeared to be sleeping. Oliver hoped it would remain that way.

By nine o'clock, the wind had dropped and a malignant mist had swirled back in and settled over the sea. Resembling sunset rather than sunrise, the sun hung like a hazy ember over the port town, rising only slowly in the grey-orange morning sky. With the sand running quickly though the hour glass, the mercury rose delivering an uncomfortable sticky, tropical heat. Seals dived and fished from every visible outcrop of rock, some even ventured around the frigate to investigate. But by mid-morning the bulls and lumbering lions had dragged themselves from the water, noisily announced their presence then settled down to a day of idle relaxation. On the overhanging ledges, the cormorants stood in rows holding out their shabby wings in stony silence.

Once the men had finished their chores, the diving barrel attracted everyone's attention though no one was allowed near enough to touch it. With Bungs guarding one side and the carpenter patrolling the other, it amazed Mr Parry that the bell had been built at all as, throughout its construction, it was apparent the cooper and chippie did not have a civil word for each other.

The bosun was in charge of the tackle and of swaying out the barrel to the longboat. Froyle's job was to ensure the line from the barrel to the stern of the longboat was secure. Once the bell was submerged, he was to monitor its progress and have the boat crew follow the drift as it meandered around the sea bed. It was Foss's responsibility to hold the line running down to the boy in the barrel and if he felt a tug on it, he was to have it hauled to the surface immediately.'

The two Lascars, Ekundayo and two other sailors were already in the water holding onto the sides of the boat. Their task was to make sure the bell went straight down without tipping, and to assist when it came back up.

'Are you ready?' Oliver called from the ship's deck.

Several voices replied. 'Aye.'

When the captain gave the order, the yardarm groaned as the barrel was lowered to the boat where it balanced precariously on the gunnel. From there, the first attempt to launch failed. Losing his balance, one of the men in the boat splashed headfirst into the sea. The longboat swayed, the barrel wobbled and slapped into the water landing inches from the head of one of the Indians. The sea rushed in filling it within seconds, and with the weights dragging it down, it was in grave danger of sinking. The abortive performance raised a variety of responses from the observers both in the boat and on *Perpetual*'s deck.

'Silence,' Captain Quintrell ordered. Time was not on their side. They must achieve their goal while the sea was relatively calm and the tide was on the ebb. If the wind or waves picked up, and when the tide turned, the currents in the channel would be too dangerous to proceed with the dive.

Lifting the barrel bell back to its upright position proved exhausting for the swimmers and awkward for those in the longboat.

'It'll never work, you mark my works.'

'Shut it, Smithers or you'll be shark bait.'

With the call for more weights to carry it down, two additional twelve-pound balls were passed to the men in the boat.

'Hold it steady this time,' the coxswain yelled.

With five men in the sea and three leaning precariously over the side of the longboat, the barrel was manoeuvred carefully onto the water where it bobbed upright on the gentle surface.

Observing from *Perpetual*'s deck, the captain was satisfied all appeared well. 'Now,' he called, 'let the boy get in and take it down.'

Tommy was nervous, but ready. The sun was shining but the warm tropical air was melting the congealed pork fat smeared on his chest. Because of the rancid smell making his stomach churn, and having heard Smithers' warning about sharks, he had begged to go without it. But the Lascars had convinced the captain that is was essential to protect him from the cold water.

From the instructions, repeated to him several times, Tommy knew what to do. He must drop into the water, slide beneath the bottom rim of the barrel then squeeze himself up inside it and onto the thwart. If Bungs had done his job well, he would find himself in a chamber filled with fresh air. He was warned that when the barrel was lowered, the air inside the bell would shrink and the water level would slowly rise over his knees and up to his chest. He was told not to be alarmed. He was also reminded to hold tight to the loose line running up the coxswain and to tug on it firmly if he was in strife. But he was warned not to wait until the barrel was nearly empty of air before doing so, as the air that was left could be foul.

From the encouraging cries from the deck, Tommy felt excited.

'Silence, there,' Mr Parry called.

With a nod from the captain on *Perpetual*'s deck, Tommy kicked off his shoes and slid over the side of the longboat to where his friend was waiting. The shock of the cold water made him shiver.

'Take a big breath,' Eku said. 'I'll make sure you are all right.'

Tommy did as he was instructed, filled his cheeks with air and dropped to the bottom of the barrel. But squeezing through the narrow gap between the thwart and the rim was not as easy as he had expected.

In the boat and on deck, the observers fell silent as the barrel swayed back and forth and a rush of bubbles burst onto the surface.

Once inside, however, Tommy took his first breath – cautiously at first fearing there may be no air in the hollow space. But with his lungs refilled, he felt reassured and shuffled his bottom along the thwart and kicked his feet in the water. Then he remembered to knock on the side to indicate all was well. Eku replied with two knocks and instantly the barrel began its descent.

When the top of the diving bell disappeared from view, the atmosphere in the longboat changed to one of apprehension.

Sitting inside, Tommy's ears popped and he shivered as the currents of cold water swirled around his feet. But he didn't look down. At first, the light shining through the glass above his head was comforting, it quickly dimmed. He didn't know how deep he had sunk but noticed the level of water rising up to his belly. Perhaps he was swallowing too much air. He tried holding his breath for a while and then remembered the captain's instructions and returned to breathing normally.

He could feel his heart thumping and, though the prism provided a little light, he felt trapped. It was the same sudden overwhelming feeling that had taken hold of him when he was buried in the coal mine. Frantically, he pushed his elbows against the sides only to find that the staves of the barrel were as solid as the rock walls which had entombed him. Clenching his fingers around the rope, he was sorely tempted to tug on it.

Then he thought of his sister who had died that day and never been found. He thought of his mother who had wished him *God speed*, but in her heart had wanted him to stay home. He thought of his brother still toiling down the pit. And he thought of Captain Quintrell who had allowed him the opportunity to fulfill the promise he had made to himself. He owed all of those people a debt, and by succeeding, he felt he would be repaying a little of it.

Gulping air and watching the rocks, sand, clumps of seaweed and fish drift under his feet, he discovered that only his head and shoulders were clear of the water. A blue fish with yellow stripes swam into the barrel with him. It was like no fish he had ever seen before. He shook his head. He felt dizzy. The barrel smelled of vinegar. His skin smelled of salt pork. He thought of his mother's cooking, and realized he was not concentrating on the job he was supposed to be doing.

Having been warned of the danger of lingering too long, he stuck his face in the water, took a final glance at the sea bed, then gave two firm tugs on the hand-line and waited. When nothing happened he tugged again. The line was loose in his hands. Gripped with fear, he started hauling it in hand over hand. Had it come away from the boat? Had the barrel been cast free? He pulled again, taking in the slack till it was taut and he could pull no more. Then, with tension on it, he tugged two more times. Almost instantly the barrel juddered, swayed in the current and started to rise. With his head swimming, the return to the surface took longer than he had expected but when finally the barrel scraped against something solid, he knew the bell had reached the longboat.

The sound of knocking on the staves was reassuring. Tommy knocked back then tried to slide down in the water between the seat and the rim. But it wasn't as easy as he had imagined. Halfway out, he became stuck. He kicked. Thrashed his arms about. Wanted to scream. Unable to move either up or down, his head was beginning to spin. He had run out of air and his chest was about to burst. Then after a final weak kick, a pair of firm hands grabbed his ankles, yanked him downwards, out of the barrel and delivered him into the arms of the boat's crew.

It was over.

From *Perpetual*'s rail, a few cheered while others ogled the diver to see if he was cradling any sunken treasure.

'Did you see anything?' Froyle asked.

Tommy shook his head.

'Can you do it again?'

He couldn't speak. His lips were blue. He was trembling and still trying to catch his breath.

'Best rest for a spell.'

Tommy nodded.

From the quarterdeck, Oliver and Mr Parry watched in silence. The captain had mixed feeling. It was some consolation that the diving bell worked and the construction was sound, but searching the seabed was not going to be as easy as he had hoped. He was concerned for Tommy's safety descending into currents that could swirl or change suddenly, upend the barrel and throw the lad into the water. If that happened he could be carried for miles without ever reaching the surface. Nothing had been said about that. After only one dive, Oliver was sceptical. The boy was cold and exhausted, and hope of success was already fading. Could he make another dive?

By the time the diving barrel was ready to be lowered for the fourth time, Tommy was less fearful of the confined space and insisted he could tolerate one more dive. He had felt guilty because each time he surfaced, he was conscious of the disappointment registering on the sailors' faces and with little to entertain them, and nothing to celebrate, many chose to leave the deck and go below.

With each dive, the barrel was dropped to a slightly different location on the sea bed, but with the tide on the turn, the captain ordered this was definitely to be the final attempt. Despite his energy having been sapped and his enthusiasm dwindling, Tommy still wanted to succeed.

When something slithered over his ankles, Smithers' taunts leapt to his mind. Was it the fin of a shark or the wing of stingray, or a sea snake whose bite could kill a man in an instant? Keeping as still as he could, he allowed it to brush slowly across his legs. There was only one way to find out what it was, so taking a deep breath, he thrust his face into the water and opened his eyes. There in the dim light – sea-lion grey and measuring near twelve inches in circumference – was the anchor cable. Tommy was amazed. When flaked out on the ship's deck, it was a dead weight, yet in the water it appeared buoyant and swayed with the grace of a giant kelp plant. Reaching down, he slid his arms around it and pulled, but the cable had a mind of its own and didn't move.

Not knowing at which end the anchor was attached, he straddled the line and, by allowing it to run between his legs, pulled himself along, hand over hand, drawing the barrel with him.

'Avast rowing!' Froyle shouted, when he noticed the line from the barrel drawing away from the longboat in the opposite direction. 'Starboard oars! Go about!'

Inside the barrel, Tommy gasped. It was hard work. His head felt fuzzy and he didn't know how far he had to go. But he dare not stop, or release his grip for fear he may lose it and not be able to find it again. Suddenly, his hand touched a piece of rope looped around the cable. Attached to it was the package he was seeking. Feeling light-headed and unable to see what he was doing, he felt for the knot and untied it, making sure to hold onto it tightly. Once free of the anchor cable, he tucked it under one arm, squeezed it to his chest, let the cable fall from between his legs and, with his final effort, tugged hard on the line connecting him to the men above. And prayed.

When the barrel broke the surface, Eku was there to haul him out and push him head first into the longboat. Unable to stand or hear the men cheering for him, Tommy was swaddled in blankets before being hauled on board *Perpetual*.

'You have performed well, young man,' Captain Quintrell said, before ordering him to be taken below to the cockpit. Then he turned to Simon Parry. 'Sway the bell aboard as quickly as possible then prepare to make sail. Tell the master to head directly into Callao harbour. I wish to deliver this prize to Captain Crabthorne.'

Chapter 19

A Casualty of War

That evening, the mood in the mess was mixed. There was obvious pride from those responsible for building the diving barrel, satisfaction from some that *Perpetual*'s mission had been successful, and elation and relief from many that the ship was about to head home. Despite the obstacles ahead of them – thousands of miles of ocean, Cape Horn, the Doldrums, encounters with pirates or privateers, or French navy ships, and the fact it would take almost three months before they raised the Lizard, most of the men were optimistic.

It was something to look forward to, plus the thought of a share in the prize they had taken in the North Atlantic. Those proceeds would be dependent on Lieutenant Hazzlewood arriving safely in Kingston with Captain Liversedge and *Imperishable*, and on honest transactions conducted by the prize agents. At least they were heading in the right direction (albeit they must first sail over three-thousand miles to the south), with the anticipation of wages and prize money and family waiting for them in England.

But, as always, there was an undertone of disgruntlement by a small handful who felt hard done by. They resented not having been allowed time ashore either in Chile or Peru – time to spend money, to visit the bordellos, to taste the wine or sample the swarthy South American señoritas. And for a small number, having to remain aboard had deprived them of the opportunity to run – to escape from the life they had been pressed into – a life they had never wanted. For them this far flung foreign place had offered a faint chance of freedom – a place to hide – somewhere they would never be found. But they said nothing.

After spending two days in the sick berth, at the recommendation of the ship's surgeon, Tommy Wainwright was happy to return to the mess and thrilled to find himself the centre of attraction.

Because he had recovered the lost pouch and, because he had spent time talking with the captain, the men crowded around eager to hear his news. They were keen to learn what was in the package.

'I don't know,' Tommy said truthfully.

'You fished it up from the bottom. You must have some idea.'

'Did you feel anything in it? Gemstones, maybe? Diamonds?' Smithers asked.

'Has to be something of value for all the bother we was put to, making that diving barrel and all.'

'I didn't look heavy enough to have a gold bar or silver ingots in it,' Muffin said. 'Did the captain say aught?'

'Why would the captain tell me?' Tommy said.

'Piss off the lot of you,' Bungs yelled. 'Leave the lad alone. Like he says, if it's a secret why would the captain tell him?'

Though some thought to continue the questioning, when Bungs got to his feet with a sharpened piece of barrel iron in his hand, the nattering stopped and the sailors shuffled back to their own mess tables.

'You did well, Tommy,' Eku said, patting him on the back.

'Aye,' Bungs added, 'indeed you did, lad.'

'Thanks to you and Chippie.'

'The barrel bell worked all right, didn't it? But you'd not have got me in that device.'

Tommy laughed. 'Just as well,' he said, 'you'd never have squeezed in.'

With the initial excitement over, the shipmates waited for their daily ration of meat to be served onto their plates.

'Bloody salt pork, again. I hope we call into Valdivia and kill some more beasts. I fancy a piece of fresh beef.'

'We're not going there,' Tommy said. 'I heard the captain talking to the surgeon. He said we're heading to some islands where we'll meet up with Captain Crabthorne before doubling the Horn and heading north to Rio.'

'What islands? What else did you hear?' Bungs asked quietly.

Tommy shook his head.

'You did good to keep your ears open. And I'll tell you a bit of chit-chat I heard spoken between the officers.'

Five pairs of eyes were on Bungs waiting for his latest story.'

'Remember the ship in the strait?'

'The slaver?'

'Aye. Seems it was part of a convoy of three that had sailed from Africa bound for Callao. Two of them arrived a month before we did and off-loaded eight-hundred slaves.'

'Where did they take 'em?'

'Marched 'em south to the silver mines, I expect.'

'Marched? I doubt most of the poor sods could walk.'

'Poor devils, swapped the ship's hold for a black hole in the ground. Once there, they'll never get out.'

Tommy remembered the blackness. 'Just like pit ponies,' he sighed.

'It's said that ponies and mules don't last more than two months pushing the mills in the mint before they are done for. I heard that twenty slaves are cheaper than four mules. They reckon near thirty thousand African slaves have been sent to Potosí by the Spanish.'

'What about the women and children – Froyle said there were some on that death ship.'

'Sent to work in the fields, I expect.'

'Don't they let the families stay together,' Tommy asked.

Eku thumped the table, got up and left the mess.

'It ain't human what they do to them,' Muffin said. 'Chaining 'em like animals till there's no flesh on their bones. And trading 'em in the markets like cattle or sheep. It just ain't human.'

'No worse than the navy does when they send you aloft in a roaring gale and your fingers freeze to the yards. The only warmth you feel is when you piss down your leg.'

'Aye, and then your breeches freeze hard as wood and scrape your thighs red raw.'

'Aye, but that's only for a while, it's not everyday or forever.'

'Seems like forever when you're up there,' Muffin argued.

'Snuff that talk. You does your job and you gets paid for it,' Bungs said.

'Whose side are you on?'

'It's like the share of prize money we get. By the time the captain and officers have taken a big slice, we're left with nowt but crumbs – a pittance – hardly enough coins to rattle in your pocket.'

No one argued. Every foremast Jack knew it was the truth.

'So, what happens to these slave ships now they've collected their blood money?'

'Probably loaded up with rum or coffee or sugar, or chests full of money ready to head back to Europe to hand their profits to the rich merchants in Bristol or London or Lisbon. Then they'll be sailing back to Africa to pick up another load. It never stops, you know. It's a lucrative business.'

'Aye, if you've got the stomach for it.'

'And ain't got no conscience.'

'So why they got all these churches in every port,' Muffin asked. 'And the people pretending to be God-fearing. Ain't the Spanish the ones who break men's backs on the rack, burn out their eyes and cut out their tongues for not being good Catholics?'

'That's why the blacks on Hispaniola have had enough. They're turned on their masters and are doing unholy things to them in return for what they received. Ask Eku. He'll tell you some tales that'll make your hair curl.'

The men on the next mess table had turned around and were listening to the conversation.

'What's matter with you, Smithers?' Bungs said. 'It's not like you not to add your tuppence worth. Hatching some mischief are you?'

Smithers didn't answer. He was more interested in a large blister on his palm which he had just burst with the point of his knife. After watching the clear liquid run across his hand, he licked it off with his furry white tongue.

The Lord be praised,' Bungs announced. 'For once we are saved from the rantings of the ship's idiot.'

'Well, if I'm an idiot then so is every Jack Tar aboard.'

'How so?'

'We're dragged all this way to the far side of the globe. We near froze our balls off at the Horn. We chanced getting blown out of the water when we sailed under them guns in Valdivia. For why? To play lackey to some young cove, who's more interested in marigolds than men. Who just happens to drop this package overboard – *plop*! Then he expects us to wet our breeches and recover it for him.'

'I didn't see you volunteering to go down in the bell.'

Smithers stood up, 'I ain't stupid,' he said, 'And I wouldn't play lackey to no young upstart captain like Crabapple.'

'Watch your tongue, Smithers, you don't know whose listening.

The irascible topman was not to be daunted. 'Pardon me, Mr Crabapple. I think you dropped something, Mr Crabapple. Kiss my arse, Mr Crabapple. And what do we get for all this bowing and scraping – confined like rats in a stinking hot hold thousands of miles from home.'

'So what is it you want?'

'I want the chance of a decent prize not some worthless parcel, daubed in pitch, the size of a woman's purse. This place is so loaded with treasure you can almost smell it – gold, silver doubloon – and the whiff of Spanish beauties too. Not only don't we get no prize money, but we're not allowed women on board. It ain't natural not having women.'

'Is that why you've got blisters on your hands?'

Everyone, except Smithers, was amused.

'You might laugh. It's all right for them that's already rich, like Quintrell and Parry – aye, and that upstart, Atherstone. They don't need no extra.'

'And what do you need it for?' Bungs asked. 'I've been with you when we've sailed into port and the women and the Jews have been waiting on the wharf until the ship's been paid off. I've seen you spend half your money on gold baubles, that weren't gold at all, and the other half on women – and by morning you're looking for another ship to sign on because you're penniless.'

'How I spend my money is my business.'

'And how I spend this war is the Admiralty's business,' said Bungs. 'But if I can spend it cruising the blue waters of the Pacific Ocean and never see another Frenchy, that'll do fine for me.'

'It's a bloody waste of time, in my opinion,' Smithers whined.

'Suit yourself, because no one's interested in your opinion.'

At first the pattering on the door sounded like a rat in a cupboard, then the captain realized that someone was knocking very softly.

'Casson, is that you?' he called, despite the fact his steward was the one person not required to knock before entering.

The tapping returned.

Rubbing the sleep from his eyes, he glanced through the window. The sky was black as pitch. Swinging down from his cot, Oliver slipped on his shoes. 'What do you want?' he cried, flinging the cabin door open.

A figure was silhouetted against the dim light of the lantern which swung outside. 'It is I, Midshipman Atherstone.'

'Speak man. Am I required on deck?'

'I'll beg you not to raise your voice, Captain,' the midshipman whispered. 'They may hear you.'

'Who may hear me?'

'The enemy. The Frenchies. They're all around us.'

Oliver reached for his sword. 'Since when?'

'Shhh! If you come on deck, you'll hear them, but the night's too dark to see them.'

By now, Casson had roused himself and joined them.

'Pass the word to Mr Parry. Ask him to join me on deck immediately.'

'Did you report this to the officer-of-the-watch?' Oliver asked in a hushed tone.

'I am the officer-of-the-watch, that is why I came straight to you.'

Climbing the steps ahead of the midshipman, the captain was not surprised to see three sailors standing idly by the scuttlebutt and another snoozing by the main yard – all quite oblivious to the fact he had been called.

'On your feet you lubber,' Oliver yelled, almost tripping over a pair of feet protruding from under one of the boats. His cry prompted the other sailors to adjust their poses, dart to their stations and refrain from conversation.

'Aloft there!' the Captain called, rousing the lookout. 'What do you see?'

'Nothing to report, Capt'n.'

'Are you certain?'

'Not a speck on the sea.'

With the moon bright enough to cast wavering shadows back and forth across the deck, it provided the lookout with the ability to see for miles.

'You wanted me,' Simon said, fastening the buttons on his shirt.

'Mr Atherstone, please repeat the message you conveyed to me.'

Glancing from side to side, the young midshipman explained. 'I was on the quarterdeck when I heard voices off the starboard beam. I looked but I could see no one. Then I heard them on the larboard side. They were whispering, but undoubtedly the language they were speaking was French. I speak French quite fluently. I was tutored from a very young age.'

'And did the helmsman hear these voices?'

'Apparently not, or he was not willing to admit it.'

'And how many boats or ships did you see which conveyed these *Frenchmen*?'

'I saw neither ships nor boats, nor seamen, though I was certain there were shadowy figures climbing aboard from the larboard mizzen channel. I fear they have boarded already.'

'All hands on deck, Mr Parry. Instruct the marines to conduct a thorough search of the ship!'

Three hours later, with the first hint of morning mellowing the eastern horizon, Oliver emptied his cup.

'Did you expect to find anyone aboard?' Simon asked.

'No, I did not, but I couldn't take the chance that what the young man had heard was not real.'

In the captain's opinion, nothing has been lost by the exercise, save a few hours slumber which, under the present sailing conditions, the crew would soon recoup. However, what troubled him was that Captain's Crabthorne's young relative was again manifesting the effects of the brain fever he had suffered previously.

'Might I suggest that when Mr Atherstone is on watch at night, another midshipman is with him? I'm sorry, I realise we are short of officers, but I fear this may happen again.'

A week later, having crossed the Tropic of Capricorn, *Perpetual* was maintaining its southerly heading. The frigate was making nine knots on a westerly breeze and with no sightings of other sails, there was nothing remarkable for the captain to record in his log.

That night on deck, soon after three bells, Mr Tully lifted his head and sniffed. 'Can you smell something burning?'

At the helm, the quartermaster lifted his nose to the air. 'That's smoke, I reckon.'

The officer-of-the-watch strode briskly along the deck checking the sailors leaning against the gunnels to see if their pipes were lit, and after ordering them to stay alert, he instructed one man to accompany him. Once he was forward of the mainmast, the source of the smell was evident. Grey smoke was puffing from the galley chimney delivering small black flakes onto the breeze. Aware that the fire-hearth had been doused the previous evening and that cook would not rekindle it until seven o'clock in the morning, Mr Tully hurried below to investigate.

Situated near the bottom of the forward hatch, the galley was at the forward end of the mess deck where the sailors slung their hammocks. Descending the ladder, the first smells that confronted him were those of sleeping men – the foul farts resulting from eating a near indigestible diet, the stench of sweat and rotten teeth, and the rancid aroma of meat fat congealing in cold cooking pots. The smoke and smell of burning paper rising from the flames flickering in the fire-hearth was being carried up the chimney to the weather deck.

'What's going on 'ere?' Mr Tully demanded of the figure crouching down, feeding paper into the hearth.

Either not hearing or choosing to ignore the question, the man continued tearing pages from a leather-bound book and tossing them onto the flames.

'Belay that, I say. Stop now and step aside.'

'Stop your racket down there!' a voice yelled from one of the hammocks. Murmurs of similar, but less polite curses came from others woken from their sleep.

With no word of explanation, the man at the hearth stood up. In his hand was the leather binding of a book from which all the pages had been removed. Tossing the vellum into the fire, he bent down and picked up another volume from a collection of books piled neatly on the stone floor surrounding the hearth.

'Get Mr Parry and the cook. Tell 'em to come here immediately.'

A voice shouted from the swaying hammocks, 'Shut your yap else I'll shut if for you!' Mr Tully ignored it.

Mr Atherstone appeared oblivious to all that was going on around him and continued tearing pages from another volume and feeding them into the fire.

'Belay that, I said. Belay!' Mr Tully yelled.

As he snatched the book from the man's hand, the first lieutenant descended the companionway. He had made barely a sound, but the marines following him clattered noisily.

'Restrain that man and take him to the midshipman's berth,' Mr Tully ordered.

When a hand was laid on his arm, Mr Atherstone retaliated. 'I must destroy these. All of them,' he claimed, pulling free.

'Take him,' Mr Parry said, in a commanding voice. 'And make sure he remains under guard.'

'Aye aye, sir.'

When the nineteen-year-old took objection to being manhandled, his cries of indignation were accompanied by curses, rebukes and complaints from the sailors attempting to sleep. The cacophony rose when the marines forced their way between the rows of hammocks to deliver Mr Atherstone to the midshipmen's berth located aft on the same deck.

Once the noise had subsided and cook had damped the flames, Mr Parry examined the books on the stone floor beneath the hearth – a Book of Psalms, a Bible, The Arabian Nights, a midshipman's personal notebook and even a pair of nautical almanacs. 'Where on earth—?' he murmured.

'What on earth possessed him to do such a thing?' Mr Parry asked Oliver later. And where did all the books come from?'

'I believe you will have your answer when I ask the midshipmen to check their sea chests. I suggest Mr Atherstone collected all he could find in those quarters. I only hope he did not pilfer any books from the mess. The sailors have few possessions and though many cannot read their Bibles or prayer books, those are often the only items they have to remind them of loved ones back home.'

'But what of Mr Atherstone now? His crime is one of theft, destruction of property, and of putting the safely of the ship and its men in danger.'

'And I am sure there are other charges to add to that list.'

'I presume you are standing Mr Atherstone down,' Mr Parry said.

'Of course. I only wish I had been able to prevent this from happening. I feared something of this nature would transpire before too long. As Captain Crabthorne said, the man's mind is obviously deranged at times yet at others his behaviour is quite proper. But unfortunately this type of behaviour, which is both dangerous and criminal, will have an unnerving effect on the crew and some will be calling for immediate punishment.'

Simon Parry agreed.

'In which case, for his own safely and the safely of the ship, he must be kept under close guard. I suggest he is placed in the third lieutenant's cabin and a marine guard posted outside. I have asked the surgeon to administer some potion to sedate him. If all goes well, we should reach Juan Fernández in less than two weeks. Hopefully, we will meet *Compendium* there.'

The following evening, after the men had eaten supper and an hour after the hammocks had been piped down, four bells was sounded on the deck above. That was no reason to interrupt Oliver's conversation with Simon Parry or to stop the pair from sampling the goats' cheeses they had acquired in Callao, along with a fine wine grown on the foothills of the Andes that Oliver had purchased in Valdivia.

The sound of two musket shots, however, had a chilling effect.

Leaping to his feet, Oliver rushed from the table inadvertently dragging with him the hem of the linen table-cloth. Sliding easily across the polished table, it carried with it the platter of cheeses, a pair of Waterford glasses and the half-full decanter of wine. With the sound of glass crashing in their ears, and without glancing back, both men headed for the companion leading to the weather deck. Simon Parry allowed the captain to go first.

Standing by the helm, Mr Tully delivered a hushed warning. 'Watch your head, Captain. Sharpshooter in the futtock shrouds.'

'Anyone injured?'

'Jenks, one of the topmen. He was in the rigging and was hit on the arm. Fortunately he managed to climb down. I've sent him below to the surgeon.'

It was impossible to see who was aloft. The night was dark and, with the moon on the wane, the sky was black. But Oliver didn't need to ask who had fired the musket.

'Hell's teeth! How is this possible? Wasn't the man under guard?' Oliver cursed, as he stepped forward. 'I can accept a full broadside from an enemy's ship, but I will not condone a musket ball from one of my own officers on my own deck!'

'Be careful, Oliver,' Simon said, 'Mr Atherstone is a good marksman.'

'Bring me a lantern,' he demanded. 'I wish the man to see me.'

'You will make an easier target.'

'Do not question my order!'

Instantly, a lamp was handed forward. The seaman who delivered it quickly retreated to safety behind the mizzen mast.

Holding the lantern above his head, Captain Quintrell called out, 'Mr Atherstone, kindly refrain from firing and come down at once. I can assure you that there are no boarders on the ship.'

'But I saw them with my own eyes, sir. Must have been a dozen came swarming onto the deck. All in French uniforms.'

'Believe me, Mr Atherstone, the borders have been repelled and the deck is ours. It is quite safe for you to come down now. You have performed your duty most admirably.'

The whites of Ekundayo's eyes gleamed in the night light. 'Do you want me to go up and get him? He won't see my black skin in the rigging.'

'Thank you,' Oliver said, 'but I think not. He may mistake you for a runaway French slave or a Spanish rebel. Goodness knows what images his mind will conjure next.' He waited for a few moments but there was no response from the rigging.

'I shall go aloft. Mr Parry, attend to the men. I need silence and no sudden noises or disturbance on deck.'

Swinging up onto the cap-rail, he slipped his arm around the shroud and leaned back. 'Aloft there! This is Captain Quintrell. I am coming to join you and I assure you I am alone.'

As he climbed the ratlines, the standing rigging above his head dissolved into the darkness. On the deck below, a circle of light splayed around the lantern but nothing more was visible. The night air was warm with barely a breath of breeze. The sails flapped.

'A fine night,' the captain commented, in a casual tone, as he poked his head through the lubber's hole. Having resolved that the butt of a musket could easily send him crashing to the deck, it had seemed wiser to go that way than to climb out and around in the conventional fashion. 'Anything to report, Mr Atherstone?'

'All clear, Captain. Nothing on the horizon.'

'That is good, Mister. Then I will relieve you of your duty,' he said, slowly reaching out his hand and taking the musket from the midshipman. 'You may go down now.'

The young man's expression was one of confusion. His eyes glazed over, yet he acknowledged the order. 'Thank you, Captain. I bid you good night.'

'And to you,' Oliver said. Then, after waiting until the man had disappeared into the darkness, he hailed the deck. 'Mr Atherstone's watch is over. He is coming below.'

On deck, the sailors waited in silence and watched as the young middie clambered down the ratlines, stepped onto the rail and then dropped down to the deck. Mr Parry was waiting for him with a pair of marines ready to escort him below.

*

'This cannot be allowed to happen again,' Oliver said later. 'For the safely and peace of mind of the men, Mr Atherstone's cabin must not only be guarded at all times but a lock should be placed on the door. Believe me when I say, I do not enjoy taking these measures, but these are unusual circumstances and we must contend with them at least until we raise Juan Fernández one week from now.'

'And what then?' Mr Parry asked.

'A good question. While the officer is on my ship, he is my responsibility, and I cannot return him to Captain Crabthorne in his present state of health. Do I return him to England to face a court martial? What do I do?'

Simon was silent to the rhetorical question.

'If I charge him with all the offences he has committed according to the Articles of War he would be found guilty and likely be sentenced to being flogged around the fleet, if not hung.'

'Is there any alternative?'

Oliver thought for a moment. 'Captain Crabthorne or I could return him to his family in England with a report from the surgeon that he be committed to an asylum. There he will end his days clawing the stone walls till the nails are torn from his fingers and his mind has become so twisted his periods of lucidity will be gone forever. I have seen the inmates at Bedlam - St Bethlehem's in London.' He shook his head. 'So many hopeless cases.'

Simon Parry made no response. It was a problem he had never encountered before.

Three days later, and only three hundred miles from the Pacific Islands off the coast of central Chile, the body of the nineteen-year-old midshipman was delivered unceremoniously to the sea.

Because his final crime was not against the captain or crew, but against God, there could be no formal committal service. Yet, despite the lack of religious rites, most of the sailors gathered on deck, removed their hats and stood in silence as the hammock, enshrouding the body was heaved overboard.

The captain, in particular, had a heavy heart. He felt personally responsible. The young man had been under his care yet he had been unable to prevent the events of the past few weeks from happening.

In his estimation, most seamen coped with the fears and pressures they were subjected to on regular basis, but this young man's troubled mind had not been able to cope. For Captain Quintrell his death on board *Perpetual* confirmed one thing – that he was as much a casualty of sea war as men cut down in action.

His only hope was that Captain Crabthorne would understand and all that remained was to enter the event in his daily log:

Edward Sinclair Atherstone. Midshipman. Age 19 years. Died at his own hand. Buried at sea.

Chapter 20

Beat to Quarters

Apart from the death of Mr Atherstone, the voyage of 1,500 miles, sailing due south from Callao, had been unremarkable. Several sail of ships had been observed by the lookouts on both frigates but as they had never risen above the horizon it had been impossible to identify what they were, however, as they appeared to be heading south, it was considered likely they were bound for Europe. Oliver felt certain they included the two slave ships that had departed Callao harbour before them.

From the pristine sandy beach on the southern end of the largest of the Juan Fernández group of islands, the two captains gazed across the water to the pair of frigates anchored in one of the few sheltered bays. Behind them, the land rose steeply to a backbone of ragged peaks that stretched along the strip of land situated four-hundred miles west of the South American coast.

Oliver was pleased he had decided to *rendezvous* with Captain Crabthorne at this location. Though it was an undertaking he did not relish, it had given him the opportunity to convey, in person, the details of Mr Atherstone's unfortunate demise. The sight of the youth hanging from the overhead beam had disturbed him and would remain with him for a long time. Boris Crabthorne, however, appeared less concerned when he heard the news and spoke little about it.

Another more practical reason for breaking the long voyage south was to let the men expend some pent-up energy. They had not been permitted to do so in the other ports even though they had been at sea for many months. It was also an opportunity to replenish wood and water from the crystal clear streams tumbling down the forested hillsides.

Wandering back to the beach with their arms loaded with kindling, the men joked and laughed. The calls of others could be heard, as they scrambled through the bushes chasing goats that were as elusive as the ghosts that inhabited the island group. While their agile caprine prey had no intention of being captured, the men persisted, despite their obvious exhaustion.

Captain Quintrell's main concern, when sailing into the bay, was that Juan Fernández was renowned as a popular haunt for pirates and privateers and, reputedly, was still visited by French ships that patrolled the South American coast to monitor any activities going on there. But, whilst wandering around the bay, he found no evidence of recent visits.

Although in the same Ocean and on a similar degree of longitude, Oliver noted how very different this group of islands was to San Lorenzo. Unlike the barren outcrop off Callao, the towering peaks of Juan Fernández were draped with verdant forests, the trees alive with a great variety of birds. Similarly, the surrounding waters abounded with fish and shellfish, and the rocky bays and beaches provided an ideal habitat for seals and sea lions.

With their feet sinking into the damp sand, the two captains ambled slowly toward their waiting boats.

Anxious to learn the outcome of their recent activities off the coast of Peru, Oliver could not resist broaching the subject. 'I trust the contents of the package I delivered to you were intact.'

'Indeed. The pitch protected them well and I am in your debt. The pouch has been delivered to its rightful recipient and my mission is complete.'

'That is good,' Oliver said, and enquired, 'Are you at liberty to divulge the details? Obviously, I am intrigued to learn what you were carrying and why it was of such great importance. Being so far removed from the arena of war, I am surprised that what transpires here could impact greatly on Britain.'

'Because my mission has been completed, and we are now far from the Callao garrison, I can reveal this to you. That pouch contained several documents. Most important amongst them was a list of names, ranks and positions of certain people in Chile, Peru and the viceroyalty of the Río de la Plata – also of individuals in Spain and its colonies in the Caribbean, in England, Ireland and even France who secretly support the movement towards independence in South America. Imagine the financial hardship Spain would suffer if that came about. Imagine if the riches from the mines no longer sailed across the oceans but stayed here with the people under their own independent governments.'

'The consequences would be far reaching.'

'Not only for Spain, but reverberations would be felt in France and Britain. With no money to pay its guarantee to France, the Spanish Crown would be obliged to kowtow to Napoleon.'

'But how would this directly benefit Britain?'

'If Britain is seen to be instrumental in supporting the independence of these colonies by providing money, leadership and protection through naval support then a strong diplomatic relationship will develop between our country and the new South American nations. The resulting trade relations would provide vast opportunities for British investment.'

'Surely this is a dream that will take decades to come to fruition?'

'Perhaps and perhaps not. The list does not only include dedicated men, but prominent government officials, high ranking citizens, parliamentarians, members of the judiciary, relatives of the viceroy, even representatives of the clergy who are currently engineering the groundwork for—'

'Civil war?'

Captain Crabthorne shrugged. 'One way or another, independence will come to both Chile and Peru in the next ten or twenty years. However, had the list I was carrying fallen into the wrong hands, many heads would have toppled and the chance of the regions' independence from Spain's rule would have been lost forever.'

The two captains walked on in silence, occupied with their own private thoughts. Captain Crabthorne was satisfied he had fulfilled his mission. Captain Quintrell was satisfied his orders to find and assist Captain Crabthorne had been completed though he felt some disappointment that the whole affair had been rather underhanded in a diplomatic sense. In the navy (at least on the quarterdeck), one was in the habit of facing the enemy head on, though he didn't doubt that a similar type of secret subterfuge was commonplace in Whitehall.

One thing was certain in Oliver's mind, when his career at sea was over, he would never embark on a career in politics. It was a business awash with a maelstrom of deceit, intrigue, lies and falsehoods. It lacked both teeth and action and, for his own part, he preferred the exhilaration, excitement and challenge of a sea battle any day.

Over a final meal before the frigates weighed, Oliver suggested diverting to Valdivia to revisit the viceroyalty's Irish official, but Captain Crabthorne was anxious to proceed south. Autumn was approaching and in the higher latitudes its progress was more rapid than in more moderate climes. Though he did not express it in so many words, it was evident he wanted no repeat of the problems he had encountered on his outward voyage. If the Weather God's were in their favour, hopefully the prevailing westerlies would carry them round the Horn without incident, and very soon they would be heading north with England's green hills only two months' sailing away.

With that prospect in mind, the captains agreed, they would double the Horn together, but if separated by wind or storm or other eventuality, they would make their own passage home and meet in Portsmouth. Oliver promised that if the war with France had come to an end, he would visit Captain Crabthorne at his home in Hertfordshire. Likewise, Boris Crabthorne accepted an invitation to the Isle of Wight.

Heading south, both *Perpetual* and *Compendium* navigated a course to the west of the frozen Chilean fjords before clearing the tip of Tierra del Fuego and the scattered islands which made up the broken tail of the Andes Mountains including Cape Horn.

Fortunately on this occasion, the conflict, which usually raged at the confluence of the major oceans, had subsided to a relative accord and with a favourable wind to drive them around the Horn, the passage took less than a week, the two frigates maintaining visual contact throughout that time.

On leaving the Southern Ocean, the Furious Fifties slowly slid away to the south while the dependable winds of the Roaring Forties helped speed their passage north. During the next two weeks, it wasn't unusual for the men hauling the log to be asked to repeat their casts, as the speeds and distance the frigates achieved were remarkable. But the fickle winds and currents ahead of them would not always be so generous.

'Deck there! Sail on the starboard quarter.'

'What heading?'

There was no reply.

'What heading, I say?'

Everyone on deck craned their necks anxious to hear the answer.

'There could be two,' the lookout called.

'Get another man up there, Mr Parry. And a message to *Compendium*. Find out what he sees. And run up the colours, Mr Lazenby.'

While awaiting a reply, Oliver paced the quarterdeck considering the unremarkable sea ahead of them and the trim of *Compendium*'s sails some half-a-mile distant. As he watched, a series of flags were hoisted up the signal halyard. He needed no interpretation though the midshipman was quick to advise: 'Two sail of ships. Heading north.'

Mr Parry and the master were close by and, though they gazed in the direction indicated, from the deck and without a glass, they were unable to see any other vessels.'

'Coastal traders, perhaps?' Mr Greenleaf questioned.

'I think not. They are too far from the coast.'

'Or the Spanish man-of-war we saw leaving Callao heading home?'

'Or two slave ships carrying their tainted profits?' Mr Parry suggested.

Flags indicating a third ship were hoisted from *Compendium*'s signal halyard. At the same time, the master's mate stepped onto the ratlines and the cry came down from the lookout. 'Four ships. No colours. Sailing in convoy.'

'Goddamit, do we have the whole Spanish fleet in the Pacific?' Oliver muttered.

'Two corvettes and two ships,' Mr Tully called from the ratlines.

'The slave ships with a Spanish escort?' the master suggested.

'I think that is unlikely. The Spanish ship we saw was a seventy-four. But we will know soon enough. They will have seen us by now.

'Helmsman, maintain your present course.'

'They're tacking to starboard. Looks like they're making for the open sea.'

'If these were Spaniards with no quarrel with Britain, and being four in number to our two, they would have no reason to attempt to avoid us.' Jumping up onto the cap-rail and hooking his arm round the main shroud, the captain studied the small fleet.

'Privateers!' Oliver announced. 'If I am not mistaken – a pair of French privateers and before long we will see the *Tricolore* flying from their masts. The ships, however, are definitely the Portuguese slavers – no longer filled with human souls but certainly not sailing with empty hulls. In my estimations, they would be packed with produce and money and would have made easy pickings for the French pair, who were no doubt lying in wait for them.

'Will they be sailing them back to France?' Mr Lazenby asked.

Oliver doubted it. In his estimation the privateers would escort their prizes north to the nearest French colony in the Caribbean where, within hours of arrival, the vessels would be stripped, their cargoes removed and the hulls converted to floating magazines, or deliberately sunk in the entrance of the harbour to prevent British fighting ships from sailing in. Eventually, when they failed to return home, it would be assumed by the ships' owners that they had been lost around the Horn, and no trace of them would ever be found.

'I believe it is our duty to relieve those French pirates of their prizes. They will attempt to run but we will follow and, if they choose to fight, we will be ready.'

'Four against two. Hardly an even match.'

'Tosh, Mr Greenleaf. Be assured, the slavers will have few guns. And the handful of French sailors who have been put aboard will not be disciplined fighting men. I suggest they will try to outrun us until nightfall and lose us in the dark. But they will not succeed. Tonight, the moon will be almost full, and in the clear air of the open ocean, we will keep them in our sights until morning. He looked at his pocket watch. 'At our present speed, it will take several hours to close on this quarry. Let the men go to their supper. When they have eaten and are refreshed, we will beat to quarters.'

'Do you think we will reach them before nightfall?' Mr Parry asked.

'That will depend on this wind holding and the ships remaining in convoy. I would estimate those old merchantmen are struggling to make four knots against our six.

'Helmsman, north-east. Let us introduce ourselves to this motley fleet of Frenchies, if that is what they are, and drive them onto the coast.

The coloured flags fluttered as they hissed up the signal halyard requesting *Compendium* to follow.

With the convoy heading north and now sailing within sight of the coast, *Perpetual* and her consort closed on them from the sea.

'They will not escape me,' Oliver said.

'How far do we follow them?' the sailing master asked.

'All the way to France if necessary. But that is unlikely. They will not be welcomed in any port. Their destination can only be the French colonies in the Caribbean and that is many weeks of hard sailing ahead. I promise you, they are ours, but at what juncture, I cannot predict. For the present I shall go below. Tell me if the wind picks up or if they change their heading.'

The following day dawned to a flat calm with the six ships spread over a distance of fifteen sea miles. As the sand slid slowly through the hourglass, the sun sapped the men's energy resulting in little enthusiasm for the regular routine of the ship. Decks were swabbed haphazardly. Holystones scoured the planks without vigour. Brasses were polished half-heartedly but retained patches of green tarnish. At eight bells, the sailors ambled to the mess with little appetite for dinner, but grateful to go below.

No sooner were they seated than a south-westerly breeze sprung up, surprising the officers on watch. It reached the British frigates first, rattling the rigging and ironing the creases from their canvas. Minutes later the same wind breathed on the four ships lolling on the still water.

'Deck there,' the lookout cried.

'Report,' Mr Parry replied.

'One of the corvettes is wearing to port.' The sailor at the masthead watched for a few minutes. 'The other wearing to starboard. The two slavers are still heading north.'

'At last,' Oliver said, 'the privateers are preparing to stand and fight. Beat to quarters, Mr Parry, and clear for action. And relay our intentions to Captain Crabthorne.'

With the urgent *rat-a-tat* of wooden sticks drumming on taut goat skin, the sailors poured up from the mess and headed to their stations to prepare *Perpetual* for action. During the time it took to beat out his message, the twelve-year-old marine thrilled to his responsibility with a quiver of nervous exhilaration. Despite his badly fitting over-sized uniform, at no other time did men respect his call in such an unquestioning fashion. For the crew of His Majesty's frigate, the ritual was well-rehearsed. Every man knew his station and wasted not a second in arriving at it. No one needed prompting and no one spoke.

Emotions amongst the sailors varied considerably. Some welcomed the call. For them it provided a welcome break from daily chores and regular watches. It was perhaps the only chance to express emotion – anger, excitement, verve, enthusiasm, even grief, without suffering reprisals or ridicule from mates or officers. In action, there were no blows from the rope's end or threats of the lash or worse, unless, of course, orders were deliberately disobeyed. In addition, there was the added incentive of possible prize money. That was worth facing danger for.

Others despised the demands of the drum. These were the sailors who feared death, along with noise, smoke and the unnatural shudderings of the ship when a broadside thundered along its gun deck. The shock and horror of seeing an iron shot pierce two feet of solid timber on the starboard side, fly across the deck and exit through the larboard side without even slowing in its track. These sailors feared both the expected and the unexpected. The frightening reality that pike-sized splinters could impale a man, or heated-shot sizzle through his belly, cook his innards, and turn his wife into a widow in the blinking of an eye.

Within minutes of the drum's beat, the wooden and canvas walls, which provided privacy to the captain and his lieutenants, had been dismantled by the carpenter's mates and consigned to the hold, along with all other portable furnishings, leaving only the guns remaining. The captain's personal items, including charts and logs were gathered up by his steward and taken below or stowed in chests for safety.

While some men were designated to go below, others crowded the companionways heading on deck with spare hammocks to pack in the netting around the channels in order to protect the deadeyes and lanyards from being severed. If the shrouds or stays were damaged, the mast would topple, and if a ship lost its mast, the captain was likely to haul down his flag and all would be lost.

A few hammocks were hoisted aloft to provide some cover for the sharp shooters, and while their muskets were also hauled into the tops, the marines climbed the ratlines cautiously. For most of them, the fear of falling was far greater than the fear of the enemy. But they had their orders. They were to shoot down the opposing topmen. Without control of its canvas, the enemy was going nowhere and was doomed to defeat.

On the gun deck, every man in a crew of eight or ten, knew his post and the job it entailed. The cast iron cannon were released from their lashings. Gun ports opened and tied securely. Side tackles, preventer tackles and breeching ropes for each carriage were checked. From the cannon's breech, the leaden apron that prevented accidental fire was removed and the tampion unplugged from its cold muzzle. Handspikes, worms, and sponges were made ready, while cheeses of wads were brought up from the hold and piled close by. Spliced circular garlands were laid between the gun carriages to prevent the balls from rolling away on the heeling deck. From the beam above his head, the gun captain's powder horn swung pendulously from a hook, but he carried his priming iron in his belt.

Despite the sun shining in from the open port, a lantern was hung above it in case the action ran on into the night or the smoke was so thick the men couldn't see what they were doing.

'Light the glims?' Mr Parry shouted. 'And dowse the deck with sand. And you,' he said, turning to the black Jack, 'On deck to draw some water.'

Eku hurried up the ladder to the gunnel where a line of buckets was waiting to be filled from the sea. There was one for each gun and one to be hoisted to each of the mastheads. As every topman knew, a damp sail held more wind than a dry one, while a flaming sail would quickly drag a ship to a halt. The booms and boats also needed a dowsing, and water was required in the half-barrels on the gun deck for the gun-captains to hang their smouldering slow-matches over.

After making sure the fire hearth in the galley had been doused, cook hobbled to the powder magazine to assist the gunner and his mates filling cartridges ready for collection by the powder monkeys. In semi-darkness, sailors cleaned flinted gun-locks and prepared cartouche boxes of powder quills and tubes ready for the gun captains who came to collect them. They worked in silence, for although the gunner was stone-deaf, he wouldn't allow a word spoken in his magazine. The entrance to his domain was shielded by a frieze-screen, a woollen blanket wetted to prevent sparks shooting in and blowing him up and the rest of the ship with him. The curtain smelled of wet sheep.

Outside the magazine, a young marine stood guard preventing anyone, with no business there, from entering. Other members of the corps were posted at the hatchways to prevent cowards sneaking below to escape the action. Only the powder monkeys and officers were allowed to pass and, even then, the boys had to present their leather powder boxes and state their names to prove their intentions.

In his workshop, the carpenter prepared a spare sail for fothering any damage should the hull be holed below water level. He also selected several large wooden plugs, and an equally large wooden mallet for hammering them into position.

It was the bosun's job to check the pumps and hoses which would be needed to dampen sails or extinguish fires, and later to hose the decks clean of its slippery carpet of blood.

In the cockpit, the surgeon made preparations for the human cost, pushing sea chests together to make tables on which to operate on the wounded who needed stitches or amputations. He also dispatched a loblolly boy to deliver a tourniquet to each of the gun crews.

When Tommy was handed one, he turned it over in his hands, examining the short leather straps and turning the screw. 'What do I do with this?' he asked.

'You'll find out soon enough,' Eku answered. Then he thought better of his response. 'See here,' he said, laying it around the boy's arm. If a man's bleeding from his arm or leg, you fasten this on him, then turn the screw and squeeze it real tight. Squeezing it is the only thing that'll stop his blood from running out.'

'What if he's bleeding from his neck or his belly?'

'Then you step over him, or drag him out of the way and get on with your business.'

'Will he die?' Tommy asked.

'Likely he will, but that's not your concern.'

'Where is the bosun?' the captain asked of one of the mates on deck.

'Gone below for blocks and lines, Capt'n.'

Oliver nodded. They would be needed if the French fired grapeshot into *Perpetual*'s rigging. The sound of boys giggling made him turn around and glare at a young drummer and a pair of fifers sitting cross-legged on the deck joking while loading pistols and tossing cutlasses carelessly into the deck lockers.

'Corporal, give an eye to these men.'

With *Perpetual* and *Compendium* slowly gaining on the four vessels, Captain Quintrell completed a final inspection and was satisfied his ship was ready for action. The whole process had taken a little over ten minutes.

'It appears the corvettes are leaving the other two as bait and trying to make a run for it,' Mr Parry said.

'Then, it is time to teach these pirates a lesson,' Oliver said. 'We can mop up the slavers later.'

Carrying limited sail and manned by a small ill-disciplined French prize crew, the old Portuguese-built merchants would be an easy target.

'The hotter the fight the sooner it's over!'

'Or so they say!' Bungs said. 'But I've known fights drag on for days, ships crippled, men the same, and neither captain willing to haul down his flag.'

'Don't make much sense to me,' Muffin argued. 'Most of the men dead and the ships not even fit for kindling, and if a storm comes up, both sides will end up arguing over a patch of sand on the seabed.'

'It's honour. That's why they don't haul down,' Ekundayo said.

'Honour! My arse! Stubborn pride and greed – that's what I call it. Not a thought for the poor suckers on the guns especially those in the slaughterhouse.'

Tommy looked across to his black friend for an explanation. 'Where's the slaughterhouse?' he asked Eku sheepishly.

'The waist, that's what he means. It's the middle of the ship that takes most hits. It's not a good place to be.'

Tommy looked along the deck from where they were standing. The waist was only one gun's distance from them.

'Best get below to the magazine,' Eku said, 'or you'll be in trouble from the gunner.'

'Aye,' Tommy called. 'Good luck'.

While the sand oozed slowly through the narrow neck of the hourglass, waiting for the action to commence seemed to take forever. During that time, no man was allowed to leave his post and apart from swaying to the reel of the deck, no one moved, or said anything, or shifted a piece of equipment, or even took a drink from the water butt. Everyone waited, ears pricked for the order to be issued by the captain on deck, to be relayed by the lieutenant, to be shouted to the division officers and, finally, to be bellowed to the gun crews. But sometimes the roar of enemy thunder obliterated that sequence.

On deck the captain and master also waited. Aloft, the marines clung to the rigging as best they could, a few unable to control the flow of green bile that they projected onto the wind. Sitting almost directly beneath them, the youngest Royal Marine, barely eleven-years-of-age, stood ready to haul up mesh bags of musket balls when ordered.

Higher in the rigging, two of the topmen manned the swivel guns taken from the wreck in the Strait, hoping to pick off easy targets, or direct their aim at the enemy's helm, or capstan, or rudder, or the deadeyes and lanyards on the channels, depending on which target best presented itself.

Now an unspoken, but palpable feeling of euphoria, tempered with anticipation, radiated between the seamen. A quiver of positive excitement electrified the air dispelling any sense of fear or panic that had previously oppressed them. Struck with the stark reality that not every man aboard would see the day out, they accepted their fate; some even willing their belongings to their closest mates should they not survive the day.

Stripped to the waist, the sailors wound lengths of cloth around their heads to hold in place the rolled oakum which sprouted from their ears. A few wore knitted mittens or leather palms they had made to protect their hands against running ropes or red-hot iron. Occasionally, a man popped his head from an open port and related news to the rest of his crew – the number of enemy ships in view, their size and type, their flags, how far distant they were but, most importantly, how many guns they were carrying.

With *Perpetual* closing on one of the corvettes, *Compendium* headed after the other. One on one was a fair fight.

'Is everything ready, Mr Parry?'

'Aye, Captain.'

'Mr Greenleaf, kindly bring her up on the privateer's port side.'

'Aye, Captain.'

'Time to show these French sailors what we think of them.'

The fighting began with little warning. Balls hissed and screamed as they cut across the deck only a few feet above the officers' heads showering them with scraps of sailcloth, lengths of rope and twisted fittings. While spars and sails were captured in the protective netting, smaller fragments rained down and fell through the holes. A sailor was indeed unfortunate if he was standing below at the time. Most dangerous of all, however, was a loose block. Swinging like a huge wooden pendulum, it could slice through the netting like a hot knife through tallow and fell any man in its path without interrupting its rhythm.

For those below deck, able to hear, but unable to see what was happening, there was no knowing what course the action was taking or when it would end. The once orderly gun deck, where everything had its place and was in place, became a stage filled with smoke, smells and thunderous discharges rumbling one after the other. The planking bounced beneath the jumping guns and carriages, weighing two tons or more, searing flames spitting from both breech and muzzle. Splinters, from the size of toothpicks to the thickness of table legs, exploded around the deck impaling anything that got in their way.

Death on the gun deck was indiscriminate.

Just as Tommy was passing, the gun captain from one of the nearby crews was speared through the shoulder, the sharpened paling pinning him to the main mast – his feet full ten inches off the ground. The vibration of the next broadside set him dancing like a ragdoll, but he never released his grip on the length of slowmatch gripped in his hand till a member of his crew grabbed it from him.

After blowing across the ember till the core glowed red and fizzed, the sailor held it over the touch-hole and yelled, '*Fire!*' The powder exploded. The gun carriage recoiled. And while the rest of the gun crew prepared to worm and swab out the barrel, he called for help to lift his dead mate down. For those serving on the gun, even with the glimmer of the lantern, there was nothing to see until the smoke had cleared.

Ear-splitting explosions followed one after the other. And when temporarily deafened by the sound, it was only the look on the gun captain's face, or the movement of his hand over the breech that indicated he was ready to fire. Pity those who did not read the signs.

There were cries of relief, even elation, when an enemy shot failed to reach the frigate's side and splashed into the sea a few yards short. But what followed was the frisson of fear that the next ball would reach its target. Fear festered when the rope holding the port lid was severed and the lid slapped closed. Unable to see out, the crew feared another shot would follow on the same trajectory. Re-opening the port lid was imperative but often impossible, so the crew took cover while the gunner fired the next shot straight at it – blowing the wooden lid from its hinges and carrying it several hundred yards out to sea or transforming it into a shower of matchwood. Worst of all was when the call went out that a gun was about to blow. Immediately every man in the vicinity ran for cover or ducked and said a silent prayer.

When a sailor was down and done for, there were urgent calls for spare hands to replace him. There were calls, too, for powder when a boy failed to return. There were screams for help from the injured who'd been dragged clear of the gun carriages. But the moans of those dying went unheeded and, when a full broadside exploded, ears became deaf to any sound at all.

From the deck, around each gun, any trace of black powder was washed away, but nothing could shift the acrid smoke which hung beneath the deck beams and roiled with each new ignition. For the windward guns the smoke from the muzzle blew its vileness straight back through the port to the gun crew that had fired it. Cheeks ran wet with involuntary tears making it almost impossible to see.

And with no other means of escape than upwards, smoke drifted to the waist and billowed up in clouds worrying those on the quarterdeck that the belly of the ship was alight.

For the men who were designated to remain below decks, they could only imagine what was happening above them. When the ship heeled suddenly, they feared it had suffered a lethal hit. Was it taking water? Were they about to sink and drown? Or was the captain merely bringing his ship around to rake the enemy's stern? Then, as the ship continued to heel and waves poured through the gun ports, the deck was soon awash with a tide of frothy pink spume, while the smell of smoke, death and bilge water filled the sailors' nostrils.

Chapter 21

The Human Toll

Striding the full length of the gun deck, Lieutenant Parry stopped briefly at every gun, encouraging the crews and the junior officers, most of whom were much younger than the men in their divisions. If a flintlock had broken or a length of slowmatch was almost exhausted, he heeded the gun captain's needs. He covered his ears to the cry of *Fire*, and stepped aside when the boys ran by crying, *Make way for powder*! There were plenty of requests but, surprisingly, no complaints. The men had their designated jobs and were intent on doing them to the best of their ability.

Down in the hold, men who'd been loading round shot into baskets or passing them up by hand, where grateful to be relieved. With arm muscles worn to jelly they were hardly able to lift a six pound shot. Being sent on deck to fetch water was sweet relief. The idlers from the waist, whether they had the stomach for it or not, were sent to assist in the cockpit, to help with the injured, to move bodies aside or, in dire circumstances, to drag corpses to an open port and push them through.

In the magazine, the peg-legged cook seemed content to be with the gunner perched on a barrel of gun-powder filling quills and tubes. In his opinion scraping rust from shot was little different to peeling potatoes. Despite the gloom, he recognized every face that emerged from behind the damp blanket, saw tears glistening on the blackened cheeks of the powder monkeys – boys little older than nine or ten years – lads who should have been running errands for their mothers or improving their brains in the schoolroom with slate and chalk. Cook asked himself if the tears were stirred by emotion or the sting of acrid smoke. *A modicum of both*, he decided. Like the gunner, he said nothing but felt every vibration when *Perpetual*'s guns fired. He registered every *thwack* as a ball struck the hull, and he held his breath, waiting for the next, wondering where it would strike.

For the gun crews below deck, the only warning that the battle had reached its apex was the jolt as two hulls brushed together, or the appearance of the enemy's muzzle glaring directly at them, like a giant Cyclops, through their own gun port. Now urgency consumed them. A delay or misfire at this stage could mean instant death. But even a successful shot could deliver a shower of lethal splinters.

An ear-splitting *boom* shot flames and smoke through the open port and almost instantly the enemy returned fire.

When the forearm of one of his mates was severed, Tommy's face was splattered. He wiped the blood from his eyes onto his sleeve.

Without a cry or complaint, the sailor thrust his left hand over the stump but that didn't stop a fountain of blood spurting in the air. Pushing him to the deck, Hobbles grabbed the tourniquet, fixed it on the man's arm, tightening it around the mangled flesh that remained.

'You'll be all right,' he said. But the seaman seemed transfixed. He was puzzling over the sight of one of his fingers lodged in the deck beam over his head. That was all that had survived. The rest of his limb had been pulverized leaving blobs of blood and meat to drip down on the crew from the timbers above.

Young Francis, the powder monkey for gun Number 7 was not so lucky. Having caught a spark in his apron, the cartridge he was carrying had flared in a blinding flash, stripping his face clean off. Before he fell, his jaw dropped open, but not a sound came from it.

In the few moments of silence which ensued, the *pitter-patter* of dripping blood accompanied the stretcher bearers towards the companionway. As one man was carried by, Tommy noticed the tourniquet sitting uselessly on the sailor's chest. Wherever his wound was, it was obviously not possible to stop the blood from flowing.

Being deaf, Hobbles, was as oblivious to the silence as to the noise, but he felt every groan the ship made.

'God I hate it down here,' Muffin said. 'The waiting. The not knowing.'

No one saw the shot that caused the side of the gun port to explode, bombarding the crew with hundreds of tiny splinters. After taking the full force of the impact, the sailor who had been nearest to it was blown across the deck, his head quilled with lethal slivers of timber. Yet the second man, who had been standing next to him, was untouched. Eku was lucky too as, at the moment the shot hit, he had leaned down to retrieve a wad for the next firing.

Tommy didn't know what had hit him, but he felt the shock run though his every fibre. His legs collapsed from under him and instinctively he grasped his hands together and pressed them tightly against his chest. With blood running through his fingers, he could feel a warm wetness saturating his shirt. He tried to look down at it but the dizziness in his head stopped him – it was far worse than the giddy light-headedness he had experienced in the diving bell. He wanted air. He gulped like a fish. He wanted to get up. Wanted to move. But the narrow walls of his wooden world were closing in.

'Get him out of the way before someone trips over him,' Hobbles yelled. 'We need powder,' he cried, to the boy with a leathern case in his hands haring down to the magazine. The captain looked at Betsy. His gun had not been damaged. 'Re-load!' he yelled, to the men who remained.

'Let me take the lad to the cockpit,' Eku shouted.

Hobbles read his lips. 'Stand your ground. You can take him later. Run her out!'

The firing continued until the order to cease was relayed and the men, designated as boarders, were summoned to the deck. Those not chosen to go up would hear the sound of running feet above them, then a single cry would resound from the quarterdeck: *Boarders away*!

That order meant Captain Quintrell and his officers were heading into a fight – a scene which changed little, no matter where or when it happened. Men were hacked to pieces, as swords and cutlass blades clashed in the sunlight. Musket balls stopped men dead in their tracks. Those with deep wounds fought while they could then, if they were able, crawled into a corner or beneath a boat to wait for the end.

In the indescribable confusion, the sharp-shooters in the fighting tops had an impossible task. Who was friend and who was foe? Their best aim was at the soldiers in the opposing tops, or sailors descending the rigging. But not until one of the captains surrendered would the hand-to-hand fighting stop, and in the meantime scores of men would die.

216

On the gun deck, the men who remained below waited in fearful anticipation to hear the crack, the long creaking groan and finally the reverberating thud as a mast came down trailing miles of rigging behind it. That usually prompted colours being hauled down and heralded the end of the fighting. But without word of the fight's progress, the sailors could only guess if it was their ship or the enemy's that had suffered the damage.

Suddenly a flash of white light, brighter than any lightning bolt, along with an ear-splitting explosion resounded through the gun ports.

'What was that?' Muffin asked. No one answered.

From the weather deck, a cheer rang out. A British cheer.

'It's over!' Muffin yelled, jubilantly.

While a few shouted with him, others merely wiped their brows and eyes, or dropped to the deck, cradling their heads in their hands allowing the immense weariness they were suffering to overcome them.

'The captain must have taken her,' Muffin said. 'You mind my words. He'll soon have the Frenchies locked in their own hold. He'll have a prize crew aboard her and we'll sail her back to England. Easy peasy.'

But the resolution was not quite so simple. With its mainmast sheared in two and its helm shot away, the French ship was unseaworthy. And what the men below decks didn't know was that *Perpetual* had also suffered considerable damage.

As to the other privateer Captain Crabthorne had chased, it had caught fire and, despite frantic efforts by the crew to fight the blaze, the flames had reached the powder store. After the blinding explosion, some survivors had struggled in the water for a while but it wasn't possible for the Royal Navy frigate to get a boat off to rescue them. By the time the action was over, the flaming wreck had drifted some distance away leaving a trail of flotsam and floating bodies littering the sea. After burning for a while, the hull had succumbed. The burnt remains of the souls who had gone down with the hull would eventually wash up on the beaches of Patagonia, where sea lions and voracious leopard seals would quickly remove every trace of their existence.

On *Perpetual's* gun deck, the cannon were still hot and all that remained of the smoke was a fug hanging beneath the deck beams, lacing the air with the smell of spent powder. The rest had drifted out through the waist or the gun ports or the holes in the hull where the enemy's shot had penetrated,

'You can take him now,' Hobbles said, nodding to the Negro.

Throughout the fighting, Tommy hadn't moved an inch. His hands were still clasped tightly against his chest but the blood was no longer oozing between his fingers. Picking him up, the towering seaman cradled him in his arms and carried him from the gun deck as gently as a father would carry a newborn son. Tommy's head lolled onto the black chest now speckled white with ash, streaked grey with smoke and splattered with blood.

Though the deck heaved beneath his feet, Eku picked his steps carefully, avoiding the splinters and debris as he headed to the cockpit. Ahead, the sounds that greeted him were disturbing. Like the cries from St Bethlehem's Hospital – the wailing of lost souls waiting for the gates of Hell to be flung open. With little light to see by and his eyes still smarting from the smoke, the streaks of blood daubed along the bulwarks sign-posted the direction.

'Halt there. You can't go any further.' The marine's order was half-hearted and barely disguised the hint of fear in the fifteen-year-old's soft voice. For two hours, he'd been subjected to a cacophony of horrendous sounds coming at him from all directions. Through his feet, he had felt the reverberation that thundered through the ship. He'd had no warning when the guns would roar, or the enemy's broadsides would find their target. All he saw was a flow of broken men and dripping bodies being dragged or carried into the cockpit. He'd been subjected to the pitiful cries – the screams – the prayers, and been ordered not to leave his post.

'Is it nearly over?' he asked, timidly.

'Almost,' Eku answered, not knowing if he was right or wrong.

'Who's that?' the marine asked, trying to see the face curled in the Negro's arms.

'Young Tom. What do I do with him?'

'I'll take him now,' the surgeon's mate answered, appearing from behind the blanket pinned across the entranceway.

Eku held the boy close to his chest and was loathe to let him go.

'Give him to me,' the loblolly said, firmly. 'The surgeon'll look at him. But he'll have to wait his turn. Go back to your division. You're in the way here.'

Reluctantly, Eku gave his young friend to the mate and turned.

'Hey, wait. I need you,' he called, lifting the curtain. 'Take this one up,' he said, pointing a blood-stained fist at a sailor huddled against the hull – his arms wrapped tightly around his belly.

Eku recognized Old Silas. He was a quiet but nimble fellow who he had worked alongside in the mizzen top. Curled on his side, almost in a ball, the man's face bore not a single mark, merely an expression of slight surprise with his mouth half-open. In the flickering light of the lantern's glim, his eyes still glistened.

'What do I do with him?' Eku asked, unsure if he was to drop him over the side, as he had seen done on other ships.

'Place him with the others near the windlass. He'll have to stay there until the deck's been cleared and swabbed. Then get one of his mates to find a hammock and bag him up. The captain will read over him with the rest and that will be the end of him.'

When Eku lifted him, the old tar's arms fell from the gash across his belly and his innards slithered to the ground in a gush of yellow fluid. Without a word, the mate gathered up the intestines and tried thrusting them back where they belonged. But, with the body curled and the wet coils sliding through his hands, it was impossible.

'Hold him still,' the mate called, pulling out a knife and slicing through the loops that were getting tangled under his feet.

Eku had only one thought. The man's inside were no different to that of a goat.

'More sand!' the mate yelled to the marine. 'Don't just stand there, do something useful.'

Eku looked at the glistening loops of pink flesh. 'What will you do with that?'

'Do you want it?' the man in the bloodied apron joked, tossing the lengths into a waiting bucket. 'It's not much good to Silas now.'

The groans of another man being lowered through the hatch interrupted them.

'Back to your station. You're in the way.'

While the loblolly boy held the cockpit curtain open for the next patient to be delivered to the surgeon, Eku glanced into the darkness. Silhouetted by a single light, in the centre of the cabin, was the surgeon. He was leaning over a table, a saw poised in his hand. Above his head, the lantern was swinging rhythmically to the pulse of the ocean's swell. Everything else in the cockpit melded into the grey haze.

Chapter 22

Tommy Wainwright

By five o'clock that afternoon, Captain Quintrell was anxious to attend to the dead. Once the burial service was over and the bodies removed from the deck, the crew could then concentrate on their duties without having to constantly step over or around the mates they had lost. With most of the corpses collected from the gun deck or delivered from the cockpit, the bodies were lined up near the entry port from which they would make their final departure from the ship. All that remained was for them to be sewn into a hammock, but the sailors doing the stitching were not to be hurried.

'Where's Tommy Wainwright?' Eku asked.

'He ain't been brought up yet. Go ask the surgeon.'

Eku shook his head. 'The guard won't let me pass. Says the surgeon's too busy.'

The sailors' eyes never lifted from their work. The stitches they were weaving were neat, yet the hammocks themselves were far from pretty. Having been taken down from the netting along the rails, most were riddled with holes from grape and musket balls. The worst were in tatters and fit only to be tossed overboard. The least damaged were saved and put aside to be repaired later. Small holes from pistol shots or small rips from flying chain could be mended. Damaged ropes could be replaced, and tiny pock-holes would be ignored by weary sailors. But, as often happened, some hammocks used as burial shrouds were less than adequate. At times, a hand would poke out of a hole and appear to wave as the corpse was slid from the ship's side. But no one ever complained, not even the sailor whose name was on it, even though, because of the shortage of decent hammocks to go around, it was likely he would be sleeping on the mess-deck floor for the remainder of the voyage. At least he wasn't being heaved over the side inside it.

Emerging on deck for the umpteenth time, having just helped carry another victim up the ladder, the loblolly boy stretched his aching back and yawned. 'You looking for Tommy, the powder monkey?' he asked.

'Aye,' Eku answered, nodding.

'He's behind the curtain in the cockpit where Silas was. You can go get him – and mind you find a decent hammock for him.'

Eku didn't ask permission to be excused, but headed down the companionway into the gloom at the forward end of the ship.

Ahead of him, the woollen blanket was still draped across the entrance, but now, though smeared with bloodied handprints, it was bone-dry. But the young marine was no longer at his post. The only evidence he had been there was a wet stain on the spot where he had been standing.

Lifting the curtain aside, Eku blinked at the blackness. Ahead, in the gloom, the dimly lit lantern still swayed over the table, but there was little movement from within, and the shrieks and moans he had heard earlier had subsided. In the reflected light from the purser's glim, the whites of the Negro's eyes glistened with moisture.

'Are you all right?' a voice whispered.

'Tommy! God be praised! You're not dead!'

'Course I'm not dead! I've been waiting for you to come get me.'

Eku leaned down and touched the boy's head and ruffled his hair. 'Can you walk?' he asked.

'I think so.'

Despite that, he slid his arm around Tommy's back and hoisted him to his feet.

'The loblolly boy said I should find you a hammock!' he laughed. 'Whatever happened?'

'This' said Tom, as they moved from the gloom to the light of the companionway. Holding out his left arm, he revealed his hand, cocooned in a ball of linen bandages. 'I only lost a finger,' he said. 'The surgeon said it was likely a splinter sliced it clean off. I never felt no pain, honest, I didn't, but when I saw the blood coming, I remembered what you'd told me, and I squeezed my finger as tight as I could and stopped the blood from running out. The surgeon said it was the right thing, I did. And the surgeon said I was lucky in one way, I only lost a finger not the whole hand. But he said it'll prove I'm a real sailor. But he also said if I'd have lost the whole arm, I might have got a pension for the rest of my days. And he said that those who lose both legs—'

The white teeth flashed across Eku's ebony face, 'Seems like you lost a finger and found your tongue. Come on, young Tom, the mate says I've to find you a hammock, and I'll make sure you stay there until your hand is better.'

After the captain had read the burial service, and before the real job of cleaning began, the men lined up on deck. Suddenly the atmosphere was noticeably different. Sailors chatted and joked with each other. The fighting was over and there was no urgency for anything except to join the line for the gill of rum which was issued to every man and every boy.

It was questionable whether the navy's purpose was to reward the men or merely to blank their minds to the task ahead. But after having swallowed only a few sups of water throughout the day and having eaten only a biscuit, if they were lucky, the effect of the rum was instant and obvious. Men tripped over ropes, sang or made lewd remarks, even joked inappropriately about the dead. It was remarkable that no one fell from the yards. But the numbing effect was essential, and it worked.

The tasks before them were often distasteful and it would take several days for the job to be completed. Without a belly full of rum, there was only gloom and doleful faces. With it, the sky appeared clearer, the sun brighter and the sailors didn't appear to have a care in the world.

From the fire hearth in the galley, large pots, usually used for breakfast burgoo, were filled with vinegar, which was warmed, then ladled into pails and distributed to the hands who splashed it liberally on the hull, the beams and across the decks. Though it didn't get rid of the deeper stains, it proved effective in disguising the smell of blood. Thick pools of congealed blood had to be scraped with a shovel. The longer it remained in place the harder it was to remove. The smell of brimstone now pervaded the air.

In the rigging, above the deck where the bodies had been lined-up, the bosun and his mates were busy splicing lines, reeving new ones, replacing eyes and repairing ratlines. Topmen hanging over the yard arms hacked at the ragged remnants of canvas, tossing the shredded sails to the sea before bending new ones.

Whether drunk or sober, the thought of prize money, from sale of the French corvette, was now foremost in the sailors' minds. But, at least eight weeks and ten-thousand miles of sea lay ahead of them. *Perpetual* must sail almost the entire length and breadth of the Atlantic Ocean during which time the ships and crews had to survive the Doldrums and contend with opposing trade winds. Plus, before they raised the English coastline, they had to by-pass the French navy who, at any time, could break through the British blockade and gain the upper hand in the Channel.

Besides all that, they had to pray that the shots they had thrown so decisively at the enemy had not hit or damaged the vessel below the waterline, if it was going to be of any value as a prize of war. They needed it to be sold quickly and by an honest agent. And finally, they had to ensure they lived long enough to sign their names, or make their marks, when the frigate paid off in Portsmouth.

Little more than a gun crew could be spared from *Perpetual* to help repair the prize vessel and make it ready to sail. However, because *Compendium*'s fight had been shorter and Captain Crabthorne had suffered less damage and less casualties, he was able to supply more men and time to the task. While it was necessary to make the prize seaworthy, superficial repairs could be still done when they were sailing again. One early job was to remove the weapons – French pistols, swords, cutlasses, clubs, pikes and muskets, along with ball and powder from the corvette. Should the prisoners locked in the hold manage to escape, both captains needed to be assured that they did not have the weapons or firepower to retaliate.

For cook and his assistants, the need to prepare food for an additional hundred mouths meant extra labour, until the French cook with two of his mates were allowed up from the hold and ordered to labour in their own galley. Six marines from each frigate were rowed across to the prize to ensure no prisoners escaped, while the master of the privateer and his mates were transferred to *Compendium* and placed under lock and key in the second and third lieutenants' cabins.

Once the French ship was deemed seaworthy, Captain Quintrell saw no point in all three vessels wallowing on the water. Instead he insisted Captain Crabthorne and *Compendium* head north, with the prize vessel, without delay. He was confident he had sufficient skilled men aboard to attend to his own repairs and he promised he would be but a couple of days' sailing behind them.

Chapter 23

The Tears of the Moon

It was three days before the jury rig was hoisted and the standing and running rigging met with the satisfaction of both the bosun and Captain Quintrell. By then, the carpenter and his mates had completed the repairs to *Perpetual*'s damaged hull including plugging the holes closest to the waterline. Finally, the hold was pumped dry and everything battened down. Fortunately, the sea had remained relatively calm during that time but the wind had forced the frigate to drift a considerable distance to the south. During that time, they had seen no other sail, their only visitors being the petrels, snowbirds and albatross who swooped and dived but made no effort to settle in the rigging.

Though there was no urgency to proceed, Oliver had no desire to be sucked deep into the band of the Roaring Forties, or to allow Captain Crabthorne to extend the distance between them by too great a margin.

With the carpenter's confirmation that repairs to the deck timbers, gunnels and ship's boats could be attended to during the voyage, *Perpetual* was able to sail the following morning. With a favourable wind from the south-west, the naval frigate began the long voyage to England heading north and following the coast of Patagonia. Oliver hoped to encounter *Compendium* before they reached the Equator.

'Sail on the horizon. Dead ahead!'

'How many sail?' Oliver called.

'Only one.'

'British frigate?'

'No, sir. Not *Compendium*.

'You think it is one of the slave ships?' Simon asked.

Oliver didn't answer still hoping for the lookout to announce another sail. But the call didn't come.

'What is she?'

'Ship-rigged.'

One of the slave ships, Oliver thought. He was disappointed. He had hoped to see *Compendium* and the captured privateer.

'But why only one? And why is she sailing alone? Was the sister ship lost around the Horn?' He was thinking out loud and not demanding an answer.

'It will be interesting to see what flag she is flying,' Mr Parry said.

'Indeed. When they were in Callao, the slave ships flew Portuguese colours, that was until the French privateers took them. But with the French ships gone, where do her allegiances lie now? Does she have a French crew aboard her or are her original Portuguese crew sailing her?'

Oliver mused over it for a minute. 'It will be an interesting encounter,' he decided. 'More sail please, Mr Greenleaf. Let us introduce ourselves. Then we will have our answer. Beat to quarters, if you please, Mr Parry.'

As *Perpetual* closed on the aged Portuguese ship, she delivered a resounding introduction by means of a 32-pound shot fired directly across her bow from the forward carronade. The response was immediate, a white flag being run up on the signal halyard. From the deck, sailors hailed the approaching frigate with frantic cries and with the vessel sitting low in the water, it was evident the crew feared she was in danger of sinking.

'Bring me to within speaking distance, but not too close. Have the guns run out and the crews standing ready. Then lower a boat on the larboard side. I intend to board her.

The encounter was short and unremarkable. The acting master of the slaver was a young French sailor of little more than twenty-years of age who said he had been a mate onboard the privateer that Captain Crabthorne had sunk. He had been given command of the prize vessel and charged with sailing it to the French Caribbean. However, after sustaining damage to its hull, the vessel was taking water at a far greater rate than the handful of men onboard could handle. With the hold filling fast and fearing he was in danger of sinking, the young master seemed anxious to surrender to the naval frigate. Of the twenty hands aboard, most were French, with only two of the original Portuguese sailors who had been allowed to remain with her. But they too were grateful to depart the sinking vessel and to be transferred to *Perpetual*.

After a quick examination of the cabins, to ensure no one was hiding aboard, Oliver returned to the frigate to arrange for additional pumps and a crew of men to be ferried across to her. The carpenter was ordered to go with them. The captain wanted a thorough report on the condition of the hull, the extent of any damage and the possibility of adequately repairing the vessel in order for it to complete the voyage back to Europe. As soon as that was determined, work would begin immediately.

Later that day, with Ekundayo acting as interpreter, Oliver again questioned the slave ship's young acting-master and confirmed that he had been sailing in company with another ship and that they had been deceived by inaccurate charts. Oliver thought it more likely the inexperienced sailors had miscalculated their position as, for whatever reason, they had sailed too close to the coast and, during the night, the other ship had fallen foul of a rocky headland.

The young Frenchman insisted he had tried to give assistance, but said that getting a boat close enough to take off the men or cargo had been impossible. He was visibly upset when he explained, through the interpreter, that he had stood off in the lee of the headland for two days hoping for some sort of miracle, but that it never came.

'When the sun rose on the third morning, there was no trace of either ship or crew,' Eku translated.

'And you retrieved nothing from her?'

'It was impossible. When I tried to sail in closer, my ship hit the rocks and I feared we would founder also. Because we were taking water, I ordered the men to the pumps but there were not enough of them and they were soon too exhausted to keep going. With no carpenter or tools on board, it was impossible to repair the damage and with the water level in the hold rising, I ordered most of the cargo to be thrown overboard. Drifting seawards and in danger of losing sight of land, the men were on the brink of abandoning ship, taking to the boats and pulling for the coast.'

Eku continued. 'He said that was when he saw, *Perpetual*,'

'Thank you,' Oliver said. 'That is all I need to hear.'

Though Oliver commended his vain efforts, the young seaman and his mates were dispatched to the hold, under guard while the names of the two Portuguese sailors from the slave ship's original crew were added to the frigate's muster book.

Oliver now had two choices. He could haul his anchor and leave the slaver to sink, thereby forfeiting whatever prize money it might be worth. Or he could put men aboard her, attempt to pump out the water, assess the damage and have the vessel repaired so it was sound enough to make the long voyage back to England. Much would depend on the amount of damage and the time it would take to make her seaworthy. But despite her obvious age, her patched sails and stretched cordage, he leaned towards the latter.

Returning with Mr Parry to make a closer inspection, the carpenter, cooper and bosun, and another half-dozen hands accompanied them over the stretch of water which separated the two vessels. Sitting in the boat while being rowed across, Oliver was quietly pleased to see that subsequent to the construction of the diving barrel Bungs and the chippie had developed a tolerable working relationship and were at least able to communicate with each other.

For the next forty-eight hours, the pumps operated non-stop in the old ship, while the carpenter and his mates worked to make the vessel seaworthy.

Oliver regretted he had not encountered the ship earlier, as the cargo that had been thrown overboard would have been valuable and could have been transferred to *Perpetual*'s hold. Furthermore, had he and Captain Crabthorne been able to take both vessels before their unfortunate encounter with the headland, then the amount of prize money to be shared between the two commands would have been quite considerable.

But that was not to be. Suffice to say, if the slaver's leaking hull could be plugged and the ship sailed home, it would be worth something. In a time of war, spare masts, sails, cordage, blocks and other fittings were all saleable or re-useable items, even if the hull itself was worth nothing.

After three days of constant toil and despite the fact the vessels were drifting north on the cold current, Oliver was anxious to proceed under sail. The crew, also, were becoming frustrated at the delay, arguing that there was little to be gained from working on a rotten hull that was likely to end up in the wrecker's yard.

227

The following morning after breakfast, while walking *Perpetual*'s quarterdeck, Oliver gazed across the glassy water to the stricken slave ship only two cables' lengths away. It was the first time he had studied her beam-on but the flat calm, which was a source of frustration and inconvenience when under sail, provided a rare opportunity for such an observation. Tilting his head, he glanced first to the horizon, then to the ship and back again. She was certainly sitting higher in the water, but she was well down at the stern. Was it possible the French sailors had only jettisoned the cargo stored in the forward hold and left the largest and heaviest barrels in the after section? If that was the case, he needed Bungs to re-distribute the weight. Hopefully that would correct her line.

'Have you checked the hold since the water was pumped out?'

'Aye,' Bungs said. 'It's a stinking hell-hole, Capt'n, if you'll pardon the expression. It reeks worse than the wreck in the Strait.'

'But this one is empty,' the captain reminded him.

'True, but the smell's still there,' Bungs said. 'God's truth, it's the worst hold I've ever come across. It's not just the stench that fair takes your breath away, it's the mess them poor souls left behind. Blood and piss and spew and foulness like you can't imagine.'

'I think I can,' Oliver said.

'Well, all that vile matter has been washed down to the bottom and settled there, and now there's no way of swilling it out. And I reckon it's not just from the last voyage either. There's layers of it. I'd say she's never been scrubbed out since she first touched Africa. If it weren't that she might be worth something in prize money, I reckon she should be burnt like the other one.'

'That may well be her fate,' Oliver conceded. 'However, for the present, I intend to attempt to sail her home. What of the pumps? Should the men continue on them?'

'The bosun said if you go any lower, you'll only succeed in clogging them up. And I can't think of anything worse than having to clean out that muck. The problem is the stuff that's settled at the bottom. It's like cook's plum-duff – thick, suety and vile smelling. And you'll never get it out unless you dig up all the ballast.'

Oliver scratched his head. 'Thank you Bungs. I shall go back once again and re-assess the situation for myself. Casson,' he called, 'pass the word to Mr Parry. Tell him I shall require my boat and request him to accompany me.'

*

The cooper's description was not wrong, the stink was sickening. Not only was it repulsive to the nose, but it made the stomach heave involuntarily and no amount of vinegar or brimstone was going to disguise it.

With only a single lantern bracketed to the mizzen mast, it was impossible to see more than a few yards into the hold, but from the sound of scurrying feet and occasional splashes, it was evident the rats survived well in the near blackness.

Bungs descended the ladder ahead of the captain and, when he reached the bottom, another lamp was handed down to him.

'Interesting,' Oliver remarked, the light revealing that there were very few barrels or stores packed in any part of the hold either forward or aft.

Not knowing what the captain was referring to, neither man responded.

'It's almost empty,' he explained, 'apart from the ballast.'

'Indeed,' Mr Parry agreed, 'In that case, one would not expect her to be sitting the way she is.'

Stepping down onto the slimy surface, Oliver steadied himself before looking around. 'What do you make of the ballast, Bungs?'

The cooper wandered aft, swinging the light about and scraping his shoe through the fetid matter beneath is feet before answering. 'Blocks of pig-iron embedded in muck on a shingle base,'

'Apart from the odour, is there anything unusual about the ballast?'

'No, sir,' he said. 'I've seen blocks like this before. I was at the yard at Chatham when *Victory* was being built and I helped lay the ballast. Blocks of pig-iron just like these. Two-hundred-and-fifty tons were put in her hold. All laid out in neat rows. What a job that was!'

'I can imagine.'

'*Endeavour* also had pig-iron ballast when she sailed to New Holland,' Mr Parry added. 'When she grounded on a coral reef, James Cook had no choice but to lighten her. He jettisoned the cannon first but that wasn't enough, so he ordered the pig-iron to be hauled up from the hold and tossed over the side. Cook forfeited his guns and ballast, but *Endeavour* floated off when the tide was full.'

Bungs nodded. 'Pig-iron's heavy but the blocks are far easier to handle than sand or shingle.'

'Your handspike, if you please,' Oliver said.

Armed with the metal rod, he thrust the spike under one of the large rectangular blocks and tried to prize it from its base. But it was stuck firm in a mould of sticky dough.

'What weight are these things?' Oliver asked.

'Three of them together weigh a ton,' Bungs said. 'I should know, I've handled enough of them.' But on swinging the light over the rows of blocks, he was puzzled, 'It looks to me like they've been added fairly recently and mainly in the stern. That's what's thrown her out of trim, to my mind.'

Oliver examined one of the blocks again.

'Let me try, Capt'n,' the cooper said.

Oliver and Simon Parry stepped back cautiously, being careful not to slip or leave their shoes buried in the gluey substance.

Leaning his weight on the spike, the cooper heaved and slowly with a loud *slurp*, the block was freed from the suction.'

'Hold the lantern a little closer, Mr Parry. And I'll borrow your knife, Bungs, if I may.'

Trying not to inhale too deeply, Oliver wiped the sludge from the block. It was bluish-grey in colour. 'Thank you,' he said. 'Would you kindly go up on deck and ask for some water to be drawn. When I come up, I would like to wash my hands and shoes. Mr Parry and I will join you on deck in a moment.'

'Aye aye, sir.'

With the sound of the cooper's feet ascending the ladder, Oliver returned to one of the ballast blocks and gently scratched the surface with the point of the knife. There was no change in his expression, when he turned to his first officer.

'The Inca Indians had a name for it,' he said. 'They called it the *tears of the moon* because of its colour and sheen, but I think this ballast is tainted with the tears of the slaves whose lives it represents. Mr Parry, I will put you in charge of this vessel for I believe what we have is a fortune in Spanish silver sitting right here under our noses.'

Nothing was said by either Captain Quintrell or Lieutenant Parry when they returned to *Perpetual*, but that evening dining alone, they mused quietly about the consignment of Spanish treasure they had uncovered.

'How cleverly the bullion was being conveyed,' Oliver remarked, 'totally unconcealed – in an obvious location, yet no one would choose to enter that stinking hold and, if they did, they would not look twice at the ballast. Had the silver been minted into coins or moulded into bars and packed in cases, it would have been easily recognized.'

'Obviously, the Portuguese sailors didn't know what they were carrying,' Simon said.

'Nor did the French privateers who took her. But I wager there will be a small fleet of Spanish ships waiting off the Portuguese coast to intercept its consignment of treasure from the viceroyalty.'

'I fear their wait will be vain.'

Oliver agreed. 'Indeed. And no doubt the other ship which foundered spilled a similar cargo of *tears* into the ocean. And perhaps one day, a brave soul with a diving barrel will find the sunken treasure and bring it to the surface.'

'Perhaps.'

'Simon,' Oliver said, 'the ship is yours to command. Once she is seaworthy, I will make sure you are well supplied with stores and good men. Bring her home in one piece and we will all reap the rewards.'

Seven weeks later, *Perpetual* and the slave ship were securely moored alongside the quay in Portsmouth. With the ballast having been extracted from the hull, hosed clean, then loaded onto dray wagons and driven away under a marine guard, the empty slave ship was placed in the hands of the prize agent. And with news that *Compendium* and the other prize had arrived in Spithead, Captain Quintrell was at last able to breathe easy. His report was already in the hands of the Port Admiral and he had just received fresh orders.

On the dock, that morning, Mr Parry was supervising a line of men signing for the next voyage. Almost as quick as the semaphore could relay a message, word spread along the coast that two captains had returned to port with valuable prizes. As a result, there was no shortage of men willing to sign and the impress gangs were not required.

With a few hours to wait for a boat to take him across The Solent to his home on the Isle of Wight, Oliver wandered round the

Camber and headed to the saluting platform. Amongst the ships anchored in Spithead was His Majesty's Frigate *Compendium*. He was looking forward to renewing his acquaintance with Boris Crabthorne and revealing to him the unexpected outcome of his mission.

Heading back along High Street, the aroma of roast meat, issuing from the doorway of *The George*, was too appealing to ignore. A plate of roast mutton and fresh vegetables was a welcome change from his shipboard fare.

After enjoying a fine meal and feeling pleasantly satisfied, he stepped out onto the pavement where a young man, running full pelt, collided with him.

'Belay your hurry, boy' Oliver called.

'Captain,' Tommy cried, 'Sorry, sir. I didn't see you coming out.'

Oliver looked at the lad and immediately glanced down to his hand. The linen bandages had gone and the hand was completely healed – minus a little finger.

'I see you sport a hand almost like mine,' the captain said, holding out his clawed finger and thumb. 'Be careful. You now have the mark of a sailor who has seen action, and the colour of skin to boot. Beware if the Press is about.'

'I will, and thank you, sir. I'd never have sailed if it weren't for you.'

Oliver smiled. 'Have you signed again?'

'No, Captain. No disrespect, but I promised me ma that I'd find me a ship and I'd make me some money before I returned.'

'And is that where you are heading now? Home?'

'Aye, Capt'n. I'm not sure how I'll get there, but even if I have to walk, I'll manage it.'

'Did you know the mail coach leaves daily from this very spot? But I think you have not been allocated all your prize money yet.'

'Not yet, but I collected my wages from *Perpetual*, and I got fifteen shillings prize money from the ship Mr Hazzlewood delivered to Kingston. I reckon the navy will hold anything else that's due to me till later.'

'Indeed they will.'

'But I'll be back. I promise, and I'll bring my brother with me.'

'Then I wish you good luck, young man.'

'Thank you, Capt'n,' Tommy said. 'And the same to you.'

Printed in Great Britain
by Amazon.co.uk, Ltd.,
Marston Gate.